LONG TIME NO SEA

PORTIA MACINTOSH

Boldwood

First published in Great Britain in 2023 by Boldwood Books Ltd. This paperback edition published in 2024.

1

Cover Design by Leah Jacobs-Gordon

Cover Photography: Shutterstock

A CIP catalogue record for this book is available from the British Library.

Paperback ISBN 978-1-83617-896-5

Large Print ISBN 978-1-80426-669-4

Hardback ISBN 978-1-80426-671-7

Ebook ISBN 978-1-80426-667-0

Kindle ISBN 978-1-80426-668-7

Audio CD ISBN 978-1-80426-675-5

MP3 CD ISBN 978-1-80426-676-2

Digital audio download ISBN 978-1-80426-674-8

Boldwood Books Ltd
23 Bowerdean Street
London SW6 3TN
www.boldwoodbooks.com

For the unforgettable Betty Ellener

PROLOGUE
THEN – 14 AUGUST 2008

Today will not define you. That's what everyone has been telling us all day – our A-level results day – again and again, like a broken record, shaving our expectations down while simultaneously reassuring us that everything is going to be okay, no matter what happens.

'I said can you step back, please,' a firewoman demands, her cheeks bright red through a combination of having to scream her instructions at us *again* and the intense heat coming from the burning building in front of us.

A fireman runs back out from where the door used to be. He's wearing breathing apparatus, so he gestures to one of the other firefighters out here.

'No sign of him,' the second man shouts, confirming our worst fears.

I cough to clear my lungs as the smoke burns the back of my throat.

Today won't define us, today won't define us.

How could it not, though? And how can things ever be okay again?

1

NOW

'The last time we were at Saffie's house, her mummy made us special chips and they were all different colours, and she said they were healthy, not like *these*.'

Cecelia waves one of the French fries I just made around in the air, looking at it in disgust, like it's a stick she found in the park with a bit of shit on the end. Sierra chews her lip as she nods in agreement.

Wow, when I was eight, the same age as the twins, chips were chips. I didn't want them to be healthy and the only reason they would ever be a different colour was from me dousing them in ketchup.

'Well, I'm not Saffie's mummy,' I remind them. 'Saffie's mummy is a chef.'

And she isn't just any chef, she's a mumfluencer, with a YouTube cooking channel that boasts over a million subscribers.

'I don't like normal chips any more,' Cecelia persists as she drops the French fry back onto her plate, pushing it away, showing me she means business.

I pause for a moment. The basket of dirty washing I'm

carrying digs into my hands as I hover on the spot, staring at the kids, wondering how they got so spoilt.

Obviously, I would just love to make it my life's work to cook them multi-vegetable, multicoloured healthy root fries every night. Sadly, between driving them back and forth to school, doing the washing, tidying the house, and helping with their homework, I just don't have the time to get too creative in the kitchen.

'Well, I'm going to go and put these clothes in the washing machine,' I tell them. 'When I come back, I'm hoping you both will have eaten something – you only get dessert if you eat some dinner.'

'Dessert is probably just as unhealthy,' I hear Cecelia tell her sister as I walk away.

When I was eight, all I cared about was watching TV, dancing and I'm pretty sure that's when I went through my phase of my favourite foods being anything that was pink – pink wafers, ham, strawberry laces, fruit. Of course, I didn't refuse to eat other foods, and I certainly didn't sass my mum over anything she made for me. I feel a million years old for saying this but, honestly, kids today...

The twins are eating at the kitchen island, seeing as though it's just the two of them, and not a family meal night. They don't happen all that often these days, to be honest, with their dad working so much, but you don't get a big, beautiful house like this without someone putting in the hours.

I plonk the basket on the floor of the utility room. One machine is still washing a load, the other is almost done with a drying cycle. It never ends.

Sometimes it just feels like I move from one room to another, moving things from room to room, cleaning up after the kids, washing clothes, cleaning the kitchen, cleaning the bathrooms, cooking – and just when I think I'm finished, I have to start again.

The utility room is the size of a decent kitchen and, after a few rounds of washing, is in need of a tidy itself, so I make a start. I fold clothes, placing them in a neat pile on one of the worktops, then once the machine is done with the drying, I unload things into the basket for clean clothes and then reload the machine with Evan's work shirts.

'Jasmine?' I hear him call out.

Speak of the devil.

'Jasmine, are you there?' he calls again.

I sigh as I close the washing machine door and set it going again. Then I head for the kitchen.

'Daddy is eating my chips,' Cecelia informs me.

'Did you ever hear of kids being fussy about chips?' Evan asks me through a smile as he pops another into his mouth. He turns to his daughters. 'I would've eaten chips off the floor when I was your age.'

The girls laugh and I can't help but smile. They worship their dad and it beams out of them like sunshine.

'Have you got a minute?' he asks, nodding towards the hallway.

'Of course,' I reply.

Evan loosens his tie, in that way he always does soon after getting in from work, before he goes up to get changed – it's like he can't wait to get it off. He's tall, with short, neat greying hair – the kind society loves to see on a man because it makes him look dapper and distinguished. It certainly does suit him. Society has me suitably brainwashed too. I'm sure I'll be reaching for the dye when greys start sprouting in my long blonde locks – I don't know when they're supposed to start but I'm only thirty-two, so if they're not here yet, perhaps I've got more time.

The hallway is massive, with high ceilings and an ornate wooden banister, very much setting the tone for what you can expect from the rest of the property the second you walk through the front door – well, that is if you make it past the intercom, the electric gate, and up the long, winding driveway cloaked by rows of mature trees.

This room, like much of the rest of the house, is grey. Grey carpets, grey walls, grey furnishings – you know the kind, very modern, for now at least. I don't suppose it will be long before the next trend that is everywhere will slowly but surely take over the house. For now, though, it's fifty shades of grey, with the occasional pop of colour in the form of overpriced art or the green leaves of various houseplants – which reminds me, I need to water the plants.

Evan hands me a package.

'I collected this from the sorting office for you,' he tells me. 'I had a few to pick up, I'm not sure how long it had been there.'

'Oh,' I say curiously. 'I'm not sure what that could be.'

'Cerys orders things all the time and forgets,' he tells me, somewhat awkwardly. 'Perhaps you did that.'

I begin opening the box, picking at the tape, eager to see what's inside.

'Listen, Jasmine, we need to talk,' Evan says after taking and exhaling a deep breath.

Well, this can't be good.

'Is everything okay?' I can't help but ask, even though it's pretty obvious that I'm about to find out, and that it's not going to be good given the look on his face. I continue to pick at the tape on my package, more out of anxiety than curiosity now.

'We have a problem,' he continues, lowering his voice. 'Cerys thinks she caught me, erm, in the shower, with one of your... well, one of your bras.'

I feel my jaw part lightly.

'Why on earth would she think that?' I ask in overwhelming disbelief.

'Well... because she did,' he explains as his cheeks flush bright red.

Evan is clearly embarrassed to be telling me this – how could he not be? Getting caught by his wife, in the shower, with the au pair's underwear, doing God knows what.

Oh my gosh, I feel so creeped out and uncomfortable – and why is he telling me? I could have lived happily never knowing that happened.

Evan only makes the situation even more uncomfortable by, despite being mortified, maintaining an almost intense level of eye contact. There's something else in his eyes, something almost apologetic.

'Oh,' is about all I can say. I wonder whether he took the bra from my room, or whether he snuck into the utility room and lifted it from the washing. I wonder if it was a clean one or a worn one. I wonder why I'm wondering about any of this because none of the specifics are going to make it any less creepy. Not only is Evan my married boss but I'm really, really not paid enough for this shit. I'm not even supposed to be an au pair, I was hired as a live-in tutor, someone to help the twins with their schoolwork during their formative years, helping them to get the best start in life. Somehow I've wound up being a babysitter, a cook, a cleaner – none of the things I started out wanting to do, but just kind of ended up doing.

I don't really know what to say – what can you say, to such a revelation? I finally peel the long piece of tape from the top of my package, breaking the awkward silence. Somehow this encourages Evan to speak again.

'She says you can't work here any more,' he tells me plainly.

I mean, on the one hand, good. I don't want to keep working –
and living – somewhere with such a creep. On the other hand,
though, this is my job and my home we're talking about – and
they're both things I need, unfortunately.

'Oh, right,' I reply, bizarrely casual given the circumstances.

'We'll still pay you at the end of the month, for the full month,
obviously, but Cerys wants you gone before she gets home,' he
says. 'Sorry.'

'Wait a minute, you can't do that,' I insist quickly. 'Evan, I live
here, you can't just turf me out with nowhere to go, and no money.
I'm basically skint, what do you think I'm going to do?'

'I know it's not ideal,' he starts, making the understatement of
the century.

I lose my grip on the package and, as the box slips from my
hands, the contents fall out.

Evan, quick as a flash, reaches out and catches it for me. As he
hands me it, he pulls a face.

'A new Fujifilm camera?' he points out. 'Well, they're certainly
not cheap, are you sure you're as skint as you say?'

He raises an eyebrow suspiciously. Oh, this man is unreal.
Where does he get off, thinking he has the right to judge me? Oh,
now I remember, the shower. Grim.

'I didn't buy this,' I tell him honestly.

'It's addressed to you,' he reminds me.

My brain briefly wanders off, thinking about where this
camera came from, why it was sent to me…

'Look, I'll pay you early, but you've got to get out of here,' Evan
continues, snapping me back from my thoughts. 'I need to save
my marriage – think of my kids, Jasmine.'

If Evan thought more about his wife and kids, we wouldn't be
in this situation.

I puff air from my cheeks. Obviously, I don't want to lose my job, but I definitely don't want to keep working here now, so perhaps my best option is to take the money and run while I still can. My only option, really.

I take the camera (that I really didn't order, honest) and head upstairs to my room to gather my things. It's hard to think beyond the immediate, when I feel so uncomfortable, so bizarrely unsafe. It's not that I think Evan will do anything to me – just my clothes, apparently – but I want to get out of here, before Cerys gets home. Imagine if she thinks I've been doing anything to encourage what Evan did? Honestly, I couldn't think of anything further from my mind, take it from the woman who has to wash his socks and underpants.

I just need to get my things and get out of here, and fast.

'Obviously, I'll give you a glowing reference,' he calls after me as I head up the stairs. 'And don't worry, your missing, erm, item is back with you.'

Great, so that's a new job, a new place to live, and a whole new collection of bras I need then.

It looks like this really is going to be a fresh start – whether I want it to be or not.

2

Sitting on the train, sinking back into my seat, it has occurred to me that I have taken my swift sacking and eviction remarkably well but, other than the whole not-having-a-job-or-a-home thing (you know, those minor details), if I'm being honest, I'm sort of relieved.

Okay, it's not ideal to suddenly find myself in this position, and I know it's not a good look for someone in her early thirties, but I hated that job. I really, truly despised it. When I went to university to study English, I always imagined myself getting into publishing. When I wound up drifting into teaching, I didn't mind too much but, when my tutoring job wound up being a glorified cleaning and nannying gig, every now and then I would wonder where it all went wrong, and how I could get things back on track.

Today I am choosing to be an optimist, to take this as an opportunity to reroute my life, and to see the best in the situation – even if, right now, the only silver lining I can pinpoint is the free camera I seem to have acquired from somewhere.

As I root around in my bag to take a look at it, I feel my phone vibrating. I tap my AirPod to answer it.

'Hello?'

'Oh, Jas, I'm so excited,' Mum announces – sounding very much like she means it.

'Well, that's nice, at least,' I reply through a laugh.

'I know, I know, your life is falling apart, but I'm looking forward to you moving back in for a bit – your dad too, aren't you, Simon?' she says.

'Yes, yes,' my dad calls back, sounding less enthused. 'But she's going to need her own TV, I'm not watching any of that *Ex-Celebrity Big Island on the Beach* crap she watches.'

I know he's being sarcastic, but I would absolutely watch that.

'Oh, it's going to be so, so nice,' I say with my own playful sarcasm.

'Your dad is just worried about being outnumbered by women again,' she laughs. 'We're both so excited you're moving back home, honestly.'

Moving back home is, hopefully, not quite what I'm doing. I'm just going to be staying there, temporarily, until I find somewhere new.

'Your old room is ready for you,' Mum adds. 'I've even put your favourite duvet cover on.'

I smile to myself.

'Would that be the *Raggy Dolls* one?' I confirm.

'The one and only,' Mum replies.

It was my favourite when I was a kid, for sure. Now that I'm in my early thirties... No, you know what, it probably still is my favourite, just for the nostalgia hit. I'm just thankful Mum doesn't line up my *Raggy Dolls* dolls along the top of the duvet any more. No, no. They're on the shelf, because I'm a grown-up.

'I'm surprised the pattern hasn't completely faded away,' Dad chimes in.

'It's reached that sweet spot where the Calpol stains are long gone but the print is still perfect,' Mum replies with a laugh. 'I'm just trying to cheer her up, Simon, give it a rest.'

Mum says this second part under her breath, but I still hear every word.

I mess with my new camera, the *Raggy Dolls* theme tune firmly stuck in my head now, while Mum and Dad bicker between themselves about what is deemed an appropriate welcome for their adult daughter moving back in *temporarily* – I can't stress the word temporarily enough.

I'm pleasantly surprised when the camera springs to life – I'm even more shocked when I realise there's already something on there.

I cock my head curiously, realising I recognise the person in the thumbnail as my friend Maxi.

'Mum, I'll call you back,' I say, loud enough for her to hear over my dad's sarcasm.

It's so like Maxi to send such a seemingly random, elaborate gift. It's even more like her to put a little bit of herself in there.

I press play.

'Ciao, amici!' she announces brightly.

Maxi looks tanned and she's wearing one of those enormous sun hats – the kind that means no one can come within a metre of you from any angle – which would tip me off to the fact that she's on holiday were it not for the fact that she is always on holiday.

Maxi and I were best friends all through school. Growing up in the same small North Yorkshire village, our school years didn't have many students in them, so when it came to moving on to high school, we were the only two to do so. We would have to get a bus every day, and it was on this bus where we met the rest of our friendship group. There were the boys, Mikey, Cam and DJ, who were in our year, and then Clarky, who we met when he moved to our village from Liverpool, so that he could go to our sixth form. I can't imagine the six of us becoming friends under any other circumstances – it wasn't like we all had everything in common, it's more to do with the fact we were forced into close proximity on the bus each day – but we were tight until we all went our separate ways to different universities. We've all swapped messages here and there over the years, in evolving group chats that rarely see little more than typical seasons' greetings on varying occasions. Maxi and I still swap gifts on birthdays, and every now and then we'll have a bit of a natter over Instagram DMs, but we're not exactly what you would call close any more, and while a fancy camera does seem like an incredibly generous gift (and I'm not saying it isn't *but*), Maxi's husband is some tech entrepreneur (I say 'some' like lots of people haven't heard of him) and her bank balance is clearly endless, so gifts from Maxi are always elaborate. I always appreciate them, of course I do, but don't let the generous nature of her gifts fool you into thinking we're still besties. Gifting, for Maxi, is like an extreme sport.

'So, here I am, on a small private island off the southern coast of Italia, staying in this humongo villa, very kindly lent to me by someone you absolutely will have heard of, but whose name I couldn't possibly drop,' she explains. 'Have a look.'

Maxi removes her big hat. As she spins around, her long, wavy honey-blonde locks swish around, but remain absolutely perfect. Her waves are so neat, so perfectly formed, like the pattern the tide leaves on the sand as it dances in and out.

Behind her there's a large arched floor-to-ceiling window revealing an inviting-looking infinity pool outside.

'This is the pool,' she explains. 'That, there, next to it, is the Jacuzzi.'

The pool looks so inviting. I can't help but feel a twinge of jealousy that this is how she is spending her days when my own are going to be spent watching *The Chase* with my parents while I job-hunt.

The villa is a truly stunning building with arched doorways and a red-tiled roof. The gardens surrounding it are perfectly manicured, with colourful flowers and lush greenery.

'And let's not forget the view,' Maxi continues as she pans the camera.

The view of the sparkling blue sea is nothing short of breath-taking. I didn't think I could feel more envious of Maxi's current surroundings, but here we are. I always try to tell myself, when looking at her posts on Insta, that what I'm seeing is what she is showing me, a carefully curated selection of pictures and videos, and not necessarily a reflection of reality.

But this video isn't for Insta, it's her *Rope*, a seemingly one-shot video of her floating around the villa, unedited, showing us what a masterpiece it is.

Maxi approaches an outdoor dining area where an empty glass of wine and clear plates are laid out.

'This is where I could've shown you all the delicious seafood I've been eating, and the incredible pasta I had to start, but I couldn't resist polishing them off before I started making the videos,' she informs me.

Videos? Wow, I don't think I can stomach more of them. I'm already sick with jealousy.

I can tell from the excitement in her voice that she's loving every moment of it. As jealous as I am, I'm happy for her. She looks really, genuinely happy. What more can you ask for?

'The sun is shining, the sky is blue, and there's a gentle breeze blowing through the trees. It's the perfect weather for lounging by the pool or taking a dip in the sea,' she continues as she heads back inside, plonking herself down on a large, inviting-looking sofa in a room with an impossibly high ceiling. 'Jas...'

Maxi saying my name makes me jump. It freaks me out, like she's breaking the fourth wall, looking into my eyes somehow, a look on her face as though she knows I'm looking back at her. Although, I suppose she does know, because if I can see her, it's obviously because I'm watching the video.

'...it's over to you,' she says. She's really got my attention now – I feel myself literally shift to the edge of my seat. 'To all of you, my oldest friends. Remember how we always said we'd take a summer holiday like this together when we grew up?'

I find myself nodding, even though she can't see me.

'Well, here's what I'm proposing: why don't you all come and join me here? All expenses paid, of course. We can finally have that holiday we never had – when did we say we'd do it? After the first year of uni? I hate to break it to you, I don't want to send anyone existential, but it's been fifteen years since we were all together last – that's almost the age we were when we decided to take the trip in the first place. I've got this villa all to myself – it's like it's meant to be. We have to fix this. So, here's the details.'

Maxi holds up a piece of paper – the first thing that grabs me is the date. It's next week!

'If you want to come, you have my number, if you can't come because you're all old, boring adults then I'll be disappointed, but I promise I won't say another word about it. I would love to see you all, though. Let's get the gang back together!'

I can't help but smile, even though my jaw is still hanging at the shock, at Maxi's invitation. It's so like her, to spontaneously invite all of us to come join her on a luxurious Italian holiday. I know it's last-minute but I'm seriously considering it. Who wouldn't want to spend a week in such a gorgeous place with their closest friends?

I mean, it's not like I have anything else going on at the moment, is it? Is there ever going to be a better time for me to just take off on holiday? I doubt it. Well, I don't plan on losing my next job out of the blue.

I should do it. I should go.

My jealousy morphs into excitement. I start to imagine us lounging by the pool, sipping delicious drinks and enjoying the beautiful sunshine. We could take long walks along the beach, we could go for a swim in the sea – I'll bet there's so much to explore on an island like that. I'm imagining the breakfasts, the leisurely dinners, reconnecting around the table with...

I wonder who else will come? It's not like we ever fell out, but I wouldn't say we all drifted apart on the best of terms. We all planned to go to university together – all of us, to the same uni – but through things out of our control, that never happened. It's the reason why we all grew apart.

I'll worry about that later because all that matters right now is that I'm in, I'm coming, I'm going to call Maxi and RSVP ASAP.

It's funny how things work out for the best sometimes. This has certainly turned my bad day around.

3

I'm standing outside my parents' house with my two suitcases by my side. Funnily enough, when I took the live-in job with Evan and Cerys, I had to leave most of my things here in my old room, so it's like I never moved out, rather than me moving back in.

I imagine I would feel more bothered by this apparent step backwards were it not for the spontaneous holiday I am soon to embark on. Which reminds me.

I take a seat on the front garden wall and take my phone from my bag to call Maxi. It goes straight to voicemail.

'Hello, you've reached Maxine Beaumont's phone,' she says in a voice that doesn't quite sound like hers. 'Leave a message and I'll get back to you when I can.'

I'm a millennial, so leaving a voicemail is up there with getting a root canal. I hang up but before I have a chance to put my phone back in my bag, Maxi calls me back.

'Hello?' I answer.

'Jas, lovely, hello, hello,' she says brightly. 'Sorry about that, Rupe has this new call-screening software, he put it on all our phones. It's divine, I don't have to talk to anyone. Of course, it's lovely to hear from you, though. I almost thought you weren't going to call...'

'I know, I'm sorry, my parcel got held at the post office,' I explain. 'I've only just opened it now.'

'Well, that's okay, so long as it's good news,' she replies.

Maxi sounds awfully well-to-do these days. Her North Yorkshire accent has been replaced by something sort of neutral, but something that suggests she's doing well. That's down to Rupert, her husband, the tech genius behind various communication software and hardware. I remember, not too long ago, there was a scandal around whether or not he was spying on people through the video-calling devices he sold millions of in 2020 – a scandal which just seemed to disappear. It's so strange how even people who work in tech or own businesses have this sort of celebrity status these days. Everyone loves to hate Rupert Beaumont.

Maxi and Rupert met the summer before Maxi was supposed to start uni in Manchester (we had planned to go to York St John together but she didn't get the grades she needed) and I guess they fell head over heels in love because she decided not to go to uni and instead support her man while he worked on his business – not something you would ever encourage a young woman to do but, in hindsight, a solid idea because they have the most amazing life together now.

'I would love to come,' I tell her excitedly, leaving no room for interpretation. 'So long as it's not too late.'

'Of course not,' Maxi replies. 'The villa is all ready and waiting for us and there's plenty of room on the private jet. Oh, and, of course, this whole trip is on me. I want to treat my oldest friends.'

My eyebrows raise at the words 'private' and 'jet' because I've never been on a private jet – *obviously* I've never been on a private jet, what am I saying?

'Oh, lovely,' I reply, trying not to show how out of my comfort zone and price range this is. 'Are you not already there?'

'I was there with Rupe, but we had some business in London we had to pop back and take care of, so I figured I may as well fly back with you guys next week.'

'Who else is coming?' I can't help but ask, wondering about everyone else, where they are now, what they're doing with their lives. Boys being boys, none of them are big on social media, whereas Maxi gives everyone a blow-by-blow of her day, no matter what she's doing – I once saw her live-stream a cold, but I think that was some kind of sponsored post for dodgy vitamin drinks, so potentially not genuine (like everything else online then).

'I think I'll leave that as a surprise,' she teases. 'But let's just say it's a good turnout.'

'Wow, Maxi, this is so generous of you,' I tell her sincerely.

'Well, we always said we'd do it,' she replies. 'And it's only gotten harder as time goes on so, if I can force it, then why not?'

She laughs. I don't remember her laugh sounding like that either; in fact, she used to snort. I wonder how she's managed to upgrade her laugh.

I hear a voice in the background – probably Rupert.

'Listen, I need to dash, but I'll buzz you the deets, yeah?' she says quickly. 'All you need to bring to the airport is your case and yourself.'

'That I can handle,' I joke. 'Okay, well, I'll see you next week.'

'See you next week, lovely,' she replies. 'Ciao.'

I smile to myself for a moment. An all-expenses-paid trip to a fancy villa, on a private island, via a private jet, with my oldest friends.

Dad knocks on the window, jolting me to my feet with a scare. He's mouthing something at me. I'm clearly no lip-reader because it looks like he's saying 'lasagne'.

'I'm coming,' I mouth back at him.

There's just something about visiting the house that you grew up in, something that hits you with a double dose of comfort and nostalgia. From the familiar surroundings to the trademark smell of my mum's cooking – everything here feels like home.

Something about being here just feels so... timeless, and it isn't just because this house seemingly defies the decades, instead presenting as a mishmash of different eras. Some of the furniture in the lounge – the 'formal' lounge that no one ever uses – has been here longer than I have. There's an old-fashioned (although potentially classic) velvet sofa that could do with reupholstering (if not replacing altogether) and clunky dark wooden furniture that could do with a glow-up too. Of course, my dad always tells me that I'm wrong, that I wouldn't know an antique table if one landed on me, but this isn't a stately home, it's one of several detached houses of this size in this village. Potentially, the most modern things in the lounge are some of the photos. The papered walls are adorned with family photos from over the years, chronologically hung, creating a strange, framed timeline of our family's life so far. There is a suspiciously large gap towards the end – Mum always reassures me that it's for their retirement photos, but I do wonder if she's optimistically saving space for the husband and kids that are sadly not on the agenda for me anytime soon. She might want to take a few holidays or buy some art to fill the space.

Mum is on me like a shot.

'Here she is,' she sings. 'Just in time for dinner.'

'Great, I am starving,' I reply as we hug. 'It smells amazing.'

'Lasagne,' Dad says in place of a 'hello'.

'We're not having lasagne tonight, Simon,' Mum corrects him as she messes with my hair, tucking my long blonde strands behind my ear on one side, probably so she can 'get a good look at my face' – one of those cute, mumsy things she has always done.

'What?' he asks, with all the shock and horror you would expect had she told him he wasn't my real dad. To be honest, I think he might find that slightly less upsetting.

'But... but I saw the mince,' he says.

I purse my lips, trying not to laugh.

'Well, when Jasmine said she was coming over, I thought I'd make her favourite instead, to cheer her up,' Mum explains, almost embarrassed at my dad's extreme response.

'But we always have lasagne on a...'

'Simon, bloody hell, you sound like Garfield,' my mum claps back. 'You can survive without lasagne this evening – we're having tacos, which is sort of like lasagne, in a way, just with different flavours and textures. Now can you please welcome your daughter home?'

Dad sighs heavily.

'Good to see you, love,' he says.

Just not as good as it would be to see a lasagne, hey? I can't help but laugh. Dad has always led with his stomach.

'I'll serve, if you want to take your cases up to your old room,' Mum says. 'Simon, give me a hand.'

My dad, a broken man, follows my mum back into the kitchen.

Sure enough, my *Raggy Dolls* duvet cover is on my bed and it does have the desired effect when I see it, I can't stop smiling. My walls are a soft shade of pink – I hate to be one of *those* girls, but I was obsessed with all things girly. I suppose I still am quite a girly girl, although I'm not sure I would paint my bedroom – if I had a bedroom – pink, it's a bit much. I actually, for a brief time (and, in my defence, when I was a single-digit age), wanted to be a Barbie. Of course, I grew out of it, either because I figured out I was never going to have the perfect hair, perfect proportions, perfect teeth...

or because wanting to be a Barbie is incredibly silly. It's definitely the second one.

I always wanted to be a smart Barbie, at least. I was a total bookworm when I was a kid, a teen, an adult – when you find a love of reading you never give it up, do you? My bedroom book-shelves are still stacked. From the set of classic fairy tales my mum bought me when I was a baby to the likes of *Funnybones*, *Thirteen O'Clock and Other Stories* by Enid Blyton, *Room 13* by Robert Swindells... You know, for a girly girl, I never realised how spooky I was – it looks like I had the full set of *Goosebumps* books too. But at some point, things shifted. I remember, around the time I was sitting my GCSEs, I started borrowing my mum's romance books to try to de-stress. I would grab one of the brightly coloured romcoms from her shelf, run myself a bath, and let myself get lost in heart-warming, life-affirming tales, one after the other. I always wonder if that's what made me so rubbish with boys when I was at school. I think it raised my expectations beyond what was reasonable to ask of a sixteen-year-old boy. I always hoped for something more special.

But while I might not be much better with boys, my love of romance has evolved, at least. I run a hand lovingly over the unfinished set of Betty Neels Mills & Boon collection my great-auntie left me in her will. You really can't put a price on good memories and nostalgia, can you? Any problems I may be having aside, it's so good to be home.

By the time I'm back downstairs, the dining table is laid with one of my favourite dinners – tacos. My mum would always do this for me, to cheer me up when I was little. I think half the fun was in putting together my own creations, so Mum would lay out the shells, and all sorts of wonderful things to layer inside, from mince to beans to peppers, guacamole, sour cream, salsa – and lots and lots of cheese. My hunger is well and truly awakened.

'Mum, this looks so, so good,' I tell her as I take a seat.

'Well, dig in,' she insists. 'Don't let it go cold. Your father certainly isn't wasting any time.'

We both glance over at Dad, who is snapping taco shells in half, layering ingredients on his plate, making himself a sort of Mexican lasagne. Why are dads always creatures of habit? You can set your watch by my dad. His life reminds me of *The Truman Show*, everything happening on cue, always the same jokes, the same rituals. That's Yorkshire men too. They know what they like and they like what they know.

'I was thinking, I know you're a bit down in the dumps, so for the next week's dinners I thought I would make you your favourite foods each night,' Mum very kindly suggests.

Dad inadvertently crushes a taco in his hands.

'Aw, Mum, that's so lovely of you,' I insist. 'But you're not going to believe this… I'm going on holiday in a few days.'

'What? Where?' Mum asks, surprised.

'You'd never last, packing a backpack, and going off on one of those random trips because your life has fallen apart and you need to find yourself again,' Dad says, with my best interests at heart for sure, but wow. You can always count on your dad for a crushing yet hilarious dose of realism.

'Cheers, Dad,' I say with a laugh. 'But, no, Maxi has actually invited me on holiday. She's got this villa booked somewhere off the coast of Italy, and she's invited the whole gang from school, to have that holiday we always said we'd take after our first year of uni, but never got around to.'

'Oh, how lovely,' Mum says. 'That's so thoughtful of her. The break will do you good – take it now, while you can.'

'That's what I was thinking,' I say with a smile.

I love my mum so much, for always being so supportive. I know how much she was looking forward to me staying for a while, I'm sure she's a little disappointed, but I will, of course, be living here when I get back.

'So, who else is going?' she asks.

'Well, I think she's invited everyone,' I say. 'But I'm not sure who has said yes.'

'Are you looking forward to running into your ex-boyfriend?' she asks through a cheeky smile. 'Or *not* your ex-boyfriend.'

'Mum,' I squeak.

'Sorry, sorry, you were all such a strange little group,' she replies. Then her smile falls. 'It's awful, though. What happened that night.'

'I know,' I say with a sigh. 'It was a horrible accident.'

'Is that night not the last time all of you were together?' Mum asks curiously. 'All of you, in the same place before—'

'Come on, Jill, that was years ago,' Dad interrupts. 'They've all moved on with their lives.'

'I know, I know, it was just... sorry, you're right, you're all adults now.' Mum visibly shakes the topic of conversation from her head. 'I'm sure everyone has forgotten about it.'

I think to myself as I assemble another taco. The past should stay in the past, and it's pointless to dwell on things – especially things you can't change – but I often think of back then, of that night especially. That was the night when everything went wrong. The night that set us all on the paths we ended up on – separate paths. It was never supposed to be that way. I always wonder where I would be now, if things had gone the way I wanted, if things had worked out for everyone. Maxi may have landed on her feet, but I wonder if the same can be said for the rest of us.

I suppose we'll find out. Depending on who turns up...

4

THEN – 29 SEPTEMBER 2004

As Maxi and I hustle on to the bus, we are greeted by the glare of an impatient driver who seems to be suffering from a severe case of road rage. Funny really, given that the vehicle hasn't moved an inch yet. He's gruff and tough-looking, like a drill sergeant who has escaped from a military boot camp – or been let go for being too stressed out. His eyes are a little bloodshot, his face scrunched up like he drank neat lemon juice with his breakfast. I don't think I've ever seen him before. I'm sure I'd remember a driver so intense.

As we link arms and hurry past him, he barks out an order that makes us halt in our tracks. 'Come on, hurry up, everyone on the bus!' he demands.

I wouldn't say we were in any sort of excitable hurry to get to school, but we're hardly dawdling.

'Woah, woah, woah,' I hear his voice behind us. We turn around, our arms still linked, like we're some sort of nosy two-headed monster, to see what the drama is.

The bus driver is holding out his arm, firmly, like a barrier, blocking our friend Clarky from boarding the bus.

'Where is your school uniform?' the driver demands, unable to hide the irritation in his voice.

Maxi and I glance at one another, then back at the drama unfolding in front of us, both in complete silence. Clarky is always ready with a snarky retort, though.

'I don't wear one,' he announces smugly, his hands shoved in his pockets.

'Give over,' the driver scoffs in disbelief, his strong Yorkshire accent so thick I can barely understand him – and I was born here. 'Everyone wears one.'

'Not me,' Clarky persists, offering no further explanation, his chin jutting out defiantly.

I stifle a laugh. Clarky is like a bull in a china shop, always causing chaos wherever he goes. However, we do still need this man to drive us to school, otherwise we'll be late, and you can guarantee we'll all be punished for not being on time, even if it is because the driver refuses to set off.

The driver stares at him blankly for a moment. Clarky tries to push past his arm but the driver blocks him.

'Oi, get off,' Clarky snaps, his Scouse accent shooting up in pitch, like I've noticed it does when he's scared or annoyed. I think he's a bit of both right now. 'I'm a sixth former, you dozy get. We don't have to wear a uniform.'

'Go on, hurry up,' the driver demands instead of apologising for his mistake. 'You look too small to be out of uniform already.'

Clarky lets that one go.

It isn't a big bus – well, there aren't many people taking the trip from our village to the nearest secondary school, just a handful of kids, and it's kind of pushed us all together. We always sit at the back of the bus, where there are two clusters of four seats, two facing forward and two facing backwards on each side, so we can sit and chat on our way to school.

Mark 'Clarky' Clarkson is the latest addition to our group. His family recently moved here, from somewhere in the Liverpool area – for his dad's job, I think. He's in sixth form, making him a little older than us, but the fact that he's not very tall coupled with his complete lack of maturity makes him look and seem younger. The rest of us are in the same year. There's Maxi, my best friend, and her boyfriend DJ. They've been together forever, and they're so well suited. Maxi is so pretty, with her long, poker-straight blonde hair always pulled into the perfect high pony – always with the coolest scrunchies (one in her hair and one on her wrist for emergencies) – and I'm so jealous of her naturally skinny eyebrows. I can't seem to make my big, chunky ones look cool, no matter how hard I try, and when I asked my mum if I could wax them, she threatened to ground me. I thought that was a bit extreme, but she's promised me that, when it comes to eyebrows, everyone has their day. She got rid of most of hers in the seventies and was apparently livid in the eighties when thick ones were back in and she couldn't grow them back. I guess I'll take her word for it.

Everyone has noticed how much DJ looks like the main boy in *A Cinderella Story*. So much so, I think he's starting to try to look more like him on purpose. Boys are funny like that, trying to model themselves on whomever they think is cool, but never wanting to admit it. We always joke that Clarky is basing his entire personality on characters he has seen on TV, changing all the time, never for the better – and we do not point this out as a compliment, but I think he takes it as one regardless. He just can't seem to figure out who he is.

'Did I see you arguing with the driver?' Mikey asks as he joins us.

'He was arguing with me,' Clarky corrects him.

'Wow, big man,' Mikey teases. 'He doesn't know who he's messing with, does he?'

He ruffles Clarky's hair, Clarky gives him a shove – and you can tell by the look on his face that he instantly regrets it – so Mike punches him in the arm.

'Tosser,' Clarky says under his breath as he rubs it better.

Mikey is the self-appointed leader of our group, and one of the coolest boys in our year – depending on which of the two social hierarchies you follow. He's the coolest boy of the nice kids. He's sporty, kind of cute, and his rich parents buy him all kinds of trendy, expensive gear which cements his spot at the top. He would never admit it, but you can tell he's trying to model himself on Luke Ward from *The O.C.* – only in looks, obviously. I think that might be his tactic for getting a girlfriend, to look like a guy lots of girls fancy, but still be a nice guy at the same time.

'Wait, wait, wait,' I hear a familiar voice call out. 'Let me on, sorry I'm late.'

Cameron jumps through the doors just before they close.

'Don't make a habit of it,' the driver ticks him off. 'And do up your tie properly.'

Cam rolls his eyes as he sits down with us, taking a seat opposite me.

'There's no way he can tell us what to do,' he says quietly – just in case, I imagine.

'He's just in a bad mood because he mistook Clarky for a Year 8,' Mikey jokes.

'Piss off,' Clarky claps back.

I smile at Cam. He looks so effortlessly cool with his loose tie and his leather jacket. I know his blazer will be stuffed into his sporty backpack – he only wears it when he absolutely has to. He's got that same gorgeous hairstyle as Orlando Bloom, longish and floppy with a messy fringe, the kind that makes him look so cute when he has to sweep it out from his eyes. When he does it, he sort of smiles and laughs it off, he looks down, almost like he's embarrassed but he isn't. He's so, so cool.

Maxi nudges me. Oops, I must have been staring at him.

'Come on then, show us what you've got today,' Mikey says to Clarky.

Clarky unzips his bag and holds it open for everyone to see.

'I've got dinner money off my dad, but I had my sister's nanny pack me a lunch too,' Clarky explains. 'So all of that is up for grabs.'

'What's a fiver going to cost me?' DJ asks.

'Can I hit you?' Clarky replies.

'No,' DJ says plainly but in an instant.

'What about a shove?' Clarky negotiates.

'Obviously I'm not going to let you hurt me for five pounds, mate,' DJ tells him.

'Okay, okay – how about I say you've got a pinner?' Clarky offers as a non-violent option.

Cam laughs. 'Clarky, think about it,' he chimes in. 'You're doing this to look cool in front of everyone at the smokers' tree. I'm not sure telling them you've seen DJ's knob is the way to do that.'

Clarky's eyes widen, as though he's just dodged a bullet.

'Good call,' he says. 'Okay, I'll call you a knobhead. For a fiver, come on, it's easy money. You can't say anything back, though, you have to look upset.'

'Deal,' DJ replies, taking the money.

'You boys are ridiculous,' Maxi tells them. 'Honestly, Clarky, paying people in dinner money and snacks so they'll let you bully them is pretty silly.'

'Shh,' DJ playfully ticks her off. 'I'm saving up for your birthday.'

'I haven't had any breakfast,' Cam says. 'Can I have your KitKat?'

'Can I tell people I shagged your girlfriend?' Clarky asks.

'For a KitKat?' Cam says, cracking up. 'Throw in your sandwich, at least.'

I laugh.

'He hasn't realised he can tell people whatever he wants for free,' Mikey adds through a chuckle as he messes with his fancy Blackberry phone. I cannot imagine carrying a phone so big, with a full keyboard – my own little Motorola flip phone fits neatly into any pocket or bag I have, and anyway it's not like my parents would buy me a Blackberry. If I want one, I'm going to have to start letting Clarky push me over by the smokers' tree.

The smokers' tree is exactly what it sounds like: a massive old thing – I have no idea what kind of tree it is, but it must be more than a metre wide – on the edge of the teachers' car park where all the bad kids hang out to smoke. For some reason, Clarky is desperate to get in with the bad kids – to him they're the true cool kids, and he's willing to do whatever it takes to impress them.

'Oh my God, Clarky, what is that?' Maxi squeaks disapprovingly.

We all stare into Clarky's bag again, noticing something before he has a chance to hide it.

'Mate, are you smoking?' Mikey asks him quietly. 'You're so desperate to be cool you're going to damage your lungs for it?'

'It's just a bag of baccy,' he says, and he couldn't sound less cool if he tried. 'And papers, and what I'm thinking is, I'll look so cool, like I'm such a smoker I roll my own, none of those crappy cigarettes for me. But by the time I've rolled it, there won't be time to smoke it before the bell, so I won't have to actually smoke.'

'That's so stupid,' I can't help but blurt. 'You have friends, right here, who don't care if you smoke.'

'Friends willing to let you bad-mouth them for a KitKat so you can feel cool,' Cam adds. 'You don't need that lot.'

'It's not easy, moving schools,' Clarky informs us. 'This is my chance to reinvent myself. The rest of my life is going to depend on what happens to me now. If I'm a loser, I'll grow up a loser.'

'You think we're losers?' Maxi replies, offended.

'Of course not,' Clarky says quickly. 'But you're all goody-goodies. I want to be a bit more edgy.'

'So we won't see you at break then, you'll be pretending to smoke at the tree?' Mikey asks.

'If all goes well,' he replies. 'But I'll see you in the library at lunch.'

We all hang out in the library, after we've had our lunch, but it's less about the books, more that it's just a great space. The mood in there is so relaxed, the librarian is cool (she doesn't mind if we're not reading, but I do tend to swap my books while I'm there), we can use the computers and hang out on the sofas. It's a good laugh in there – it's also the only place Clarky feels like he can safely hang out with us, because the bad kids never go in there.

'My older cousin is friends with Nate Mills's sister, she's in Year 13 too,' Cam informs us. 'And she says Nate and his sister are entering the talent show together this year. They're doing "The Grease Megamix" together.'

'No!' I blurt.

'That's social suicide,' Maxi adds.

'He doesn't exactly have many cool points to begin with,' DJ says.

'Cool points?' Clarky teases. 'Knobhead.'

'I thought you were going to wait for an audience to call me that,' DJ points out. 'Easiest fiver I've ever made.'

'Nah, come on, that one doesn't count,' Clarky whines.

'Nope, you've done it now, we all heard it,' Maxi adds. 'You've lost your chance.'

Clarky folds his arms and slumps down in his seat.

'Double science today,' Cam says to me with a smile.

'Yuck,' I reply. 'I hate it.'

That's not true at all, I love it. Well, I don't love the double science part, I'm not all that great at science, English is way more my thing, but the best thing about double science is that Cam and I sit together, and I love hanging out with him, even if it is over a Bunsen burner I'm too scared to touch.

'You two and your chemistry,' Maxi jokes – and I'm grateful it doesn't mean anything to anyone else. 'Hopeless, aren't you?'

'We're working on it, aren't we?' Cam says to me with a smile.

God, that smile. Why is he so perfect?

Clarky fidgets with his laminated sixth form pass. I notice he's Tipp-Exed over his name, leaving only the 'Clark' part of Clarkson visible. Then he's used a marker to write a little 'y' at the end. Honestly, it is so surprising to me, that this boy feels like he needs to pay people to help him look cool, not when he's doing *such* a good job.

I'm sure we're lucky, to have such a scenic bus journey through the green of North Yorkshire each day, but it's annoying having to get up early enough for the extra time it takes. Eventually, we arrive at school and the unfriendly bus driver turfs us out.

'See you later, Clarky,' Mikey shouts loudly after him as he runs away from us.

Clarky turns briefly to shoot him a look, as if to remind him that at school, outside the sanctuary of the library, we don't know each other – as if Mikey didn't know that.

'He's a bit much, that kid, isn't he?' he says when he's gone.

'Yeah, but we're stuck with him now,' DJ replies.

'Funnily enough, he's the least cool of all of us,' Maxi adds through a laugh.

'I feel a bit sorry for him,' I say, my moment of seriousness stopping everyone in their tracks. 'He's just moved here, he's got no friends, it doesn't sound like his parents spend much time with him. I know he's a handful, but I suppose we're all he's got.'

'Gutted for us,' Mikey jokes.

A football appears from nowhere – kicked by a kid not too far away who must have spotted Mikey. Mikey snaps into action, kicking the ball back before running after it. DJ is close behind him, even though he hates physical activity, I don't think he likes to feel left out.

'DJ, DJ, wait,' Maxi calls after him. 'You've got my PE kit in your bag.'

She runs off down the school drive, leaving me alone with Cam.

'That's really sweet of you, you know,' he tells me. 'Looking out for Clarky like that. I'm with you, I know he's a bit of a dork, and he annoys us, but we've got to look out of him. He's like our annoying little brother, just, you know, older than us.'

Clarky moved to the village after his parents' very messy divorce. The first day he arrived at the bus stop, his dad was with him and, after Clarky boarded, his dad flagged us down. He took a chance, telling us what Clarky was going through, and how he had been bullied at his last school to the point where he was briefly homeschooled, before he moved. He asked us to look out for him, so we have – and we continue to do so. I feel sorry for him because, as much as he can be a dickhead, I know he's been through a lot. It makes sense, if he was bullied before, that he would do anything to try to be cool, to make sure it doesn't happen again. Sure, it's sad, that he keeps feeling like he needs to make cool friends to be safe or whatever – when we're his friends, and we're here, and we're looking out for him – but I get it. Being a teenager in a school full of other teenagers is shit. We're all just trying to get through it. It's like the final boss in a video game, before you complete childhood, and finally get to live freely as an adult.

I laugh.

'We're more like his parents,' I reply.

'Well, you're a great mum,' he says with a smile. Then he realises what he's just said and laughs it off. 'Proper awkward, sorry.'

I laugh.

'That's okay, you're a decent dad,' I reply.

For a few seconds, we smile at each other. Then we hear the faint sound of the first bell ringing inside the building.

'We'd better hurry up,' he says. 'But we can talk about our son in science.'

'See you there,' I say through a giggle.

As Cam heads off to his form room, Maxi finds me again and links up with me.

'You two like each other so much, it would be embarrassing, if it weren't so cute,' she teases. 'When are you going to ask him out?'

'Oh, never ever ever,' I insist. 'Because even if I did like him, there is no way I would be brave enough to ask anyone out, never mind someone as cool as Cam, there's no way he's interested in me.'

'Well, I think you like him,' she says. 'Maybe you need a boyfriend, any boyfriend, to show you what they're like. Then maybe you'll realise Cam is the only one you want.'

'You think I should get a boyfriend to get a different boyfriend?' I reply, confused.

'Exactly,' she replies. 'Has anyone asked you out recently?'

'Not since Nate asked, at his weird house party, right before we ran away,' I confess.

God, that was a weird night. Nate invited a bunch of people to a party at his house over the summer. Maxi and I were the only two who showed up, joining Nate, his big sister and his mum to share an awkward bottle of Lambrini in his living room. We made a quick exit, but not before he asked me out. It's weird because I just panicked, gripped with this guilty feeling, like I couldn't say no, but I definitely didn't want to say yes. I somehow styled it out without answering – thankfully, he'd had too much Lambrini. He hasn't mentioned it since.

'I can't believe he's entering the talent show with his sister,' she says. 'I can't believe anyone enters the talent show.'

'That's a shame, I was going to ask if you wanted to be Aly & AJ and do "Potential Breakup Song",' I joke.

'Oh, imagine the horror,' she says with a shudder.

The second bell rings.

'Right, come on, we can't be late again,' she insists as she picks up the pace. 'Ms Crawley says I'll be late for my own funeral.'

'You'd be too cool to attend,' I reply. 'But at least you won't get detention for that.'

As kids clear from everywhere, we filter into the building and head for our classroom. Ugh, another school day, do they ever end? And even when they do, I'm planning on staying on in sixth form, so that's another two years of it. It's what I need to do, though, if I want to go to uni, and it's nice being around my friends all the time, like Maxi and Cam... Cam who I do fancy, but I can't say it out loud, not even to Maxi.

Maybe one day. But for now, we've got double science together at least.

5

NOW

'Any nice plans today?' I ask politely.

'Just a trip to the airport,' he replies.

'Going anywhere nice?' I ask.

'Erm, I'm driving you there,' the driver replies.

I cringe. I feel so awkward, having a driver taking me from the train station to the airport, that I've been working overtime to make conversation with him. It's a fancy black Mercedes minivan – although that makes it sound like way less than it is, it's so luxurious with big seats, armrests, a table – it even has a TV.

'Right, sorry,' I reply. 'Are we there yet?'

I sing my question like a child.

'Do you get that a lot?' I ask.

'No, you're the first,' he replies, and I'm not sure whether he's being sarcastic or if his usual clientele is more sophisticated than I am. 'We are here, though.'

It looks like we're taking a different route into the airport, not driving up to the front where the car parks and the drop-off area is, we're heading around the back.

My driver – oh, listen to me, 'my driver' – takes my cases for me and loads them onto a trolly manned by a sharply dressed man.

'Who do we have here?' he asks me. 'Might you be Ms Jasmine Bartlett?'

'I am,' I say with a smile.

'Hello, Ms Bartlett, my name is Orlando, I'll be escorting you this morning,' he explains. Well, sort of explains.

'Escorting?' I reply.

'Yes,' he says brightly. 'Getting you safely on the jet with the rest of your party. Please, step inside, I'll have someone take your bags and be right behind you.'

'Oh, okay,' I say. 'Through here?'

'Through there,' he replies with a smile. 'Right behind you.'

I head through the large glass double doors into... what am I in?

It's like an airport lounge, only way fancier. There is a table laid out with food – fruit, pastries, cakes and so on – a fridge packed with drinks and a coffee machine with a selection of pods in a large glass jar. There are plush-looking sofas everywhere and ambient music playing. There's even a wall covered with glass cabinets, filled with an array of luxury items for purchase.

The most notable thing, though, is the fact that I am the only person in here. It's like I'm in my own private airport.

'Okay, Ms Bartlett, it's just us for now, so why don't you let me get you a drink and something to eat,' Orlando suggests.

Orlando is probably in his fifties. He has perfectly white hair and he's about as English as you can possibly be. He's very smart, seriously well spoken – I've hardly said a word and I already feel like a farmer. He seems lovely, though, and I suppose working in an airport, you meet people from all over the world.

'That would be great, thank you,' I reply. 'Is Maxine not here yet?'

'Mrs Beaumont is running late,' he informs me – wow, some things never change.

'So I'm the first one here,' I say pointlessly.

'Which means you get first pick of the pastries,' he points out. 'Although there's plenty more where that came from, and there's always a healthy amount to eat on the plane – not that it's a long flight you're taking today but, hey, if you can't overdo it when you're on holiday, when can you?'

'I can get on board with that,' I say with a smile. 'A coffee would be...'

My voice trails off.

'Ms Bartlett?' Orlando prompts me. 'Ms Bartlett, is everything okay?'

'Sorry,' I whisper. 'It's just... that's my ex-boyfriend outside.'

'Ooh,' he replies excitedly, turning around to have a peep. Of course, then he realises that this is the next person for him to greet so he excuses himself.

I watch as Orlando welcomes him. Of course people are going to look different when you haven't seen them since they were a teenager, it would be very weird if they didn't, but I almost don't recognise him. I mean, it's unmistakeably him, but the tall, skinny boy I knew at school is nowhere to be seen. In fact, he might well be inside one of this guy's legs. He's still tall – obviously, there's no changing that – but he's big, broad, and with one of the manliest beards I've ever seen. The kind men dream of growing. Short but thick. Neat. The darkness of it brings out the blue in his eyes.

He's wearing a white vest with an open plaid shirt over the top along with a pair of jeans and trainers. He looks so relaxed, like he's in holiday mode already. I knew I was going to have to face him if he came, of course I did, but I hadn't anticipated it being just the two of us, alone, in an empty mini-airport.

I watch as Orlando gives him the same instructions: head inside while I arrange for your bags to go where they need to go.

As he walks through the glass doors and his eyes adjust from the bright sunshine outside to ambient lighting in here, it takes him a second or two before his eyes focus on me. When they do, they sparkle and a grin spreads across his face. He looks pleased to see me – thank goodness, I can work with that. We didn't exactly end on great terms, and we haven't interacted beyond pleasantries in the group chat since the last time we saw one another, so I wasn't sure what to expect, really.

'Wow, Jas, look at you,' he says as he pulls me in for a hug. 'Look at you! Wow.'

I smile as he repeats himself.

'Hello,' I say with a smile. 'How are you?'

'I'm good, yeah, great even,' he insists. 'This is mad, isn't it? Good old Maxi.'

'I know, I can't believe it,' I reply. 'I can't believe we're finally taking this holiday. I never thought it would happen.'

He takes my left hand in his and examines it.

'Not married?' he can't help but ask.

'Nope,' I say, shaking my head. 'You?'

'Never found the right one,' he says, showing me his vacant ring finger.

'Right-ho, let's sort some drinks,' Orlando says as he joins us again, thankfully moving the conversation along. 'It's a coffee for Ms Bartlett. Mr Hensley?'

'Oh, buddy, none of that Mr Hensley stuff.' He laughs. 'I know it's a cliché, but Mr Hensley is my dad. Call me Mike.'

'Mike, of course,' Orlando corrects himself.

'And you're welcome to call me Jasmine,' I insist with a smile.

'I'd love a coffee, buddy, cheers,' Mike tells him with a pat on the back.

'Back in a moment,' Orlando replies.

'Mike,' I say to him through an amused grin. 'I don't think I've ever heard anyone call you Mike.'

'Mikey is not the name of a serious grown man, is it?' he replies.

I shrug.

'One of the things I love about the men in this country is that they get some stupid nickname, usually based off their surname, when they're a kid and it's perfectly socially acceptable to take this with you into adulthood,' I point out.

'Yeah, like Clarky is still Clarky,' he replies. 'Funny that, isn't it?'

I laugh. Of course Clarky is still Clarky.

'It got to a point where Mikey started to feel quite juvenile,' he says. 'I started work, pretty much right after sixth form, working at my dad's company, so I needed to use my serious grown-up name.'

'Makes sense,' I say with a smile.

'You know DJ is still DJ, though,' he tells me.

'Oh, really?'

'Yeah, but wouldn't you be, if your name was Darren Junior?' he jokes.

I snort.

'Oh, speak of the devil,' I say.

'Is that my next guest?' Orlando asks us as he hands us our drinks. 'Everything you need is on the table, help yourselves, please.'

'I've stayed in touch with DJ the most, I'd say,' Mike tells me.

'Yeah, I'm the same with Maxi,' I reply.

'Mad the two of them never worked out,' he says. 'I always thought they'd get married.'

'We all did,' I reply.

DJ walks through the door and grabs Mike for one of those manly hugs.

'Mate,' he says.

'Mate,' Mike replies.

'This is unreal,' DJ says as he grabs me for a hug. 'Jas, bloody hell, this is so weird. How are you?'

'So weird,' I reply. 'I'm great, how are you?'

'I think I'm in a bit of shock,' he says through a smile. 'I can't believe we're doing this. It's been a hundred years.'

'We were just talking about how we're not married,' Mike tells him, almost as though he's trying to tell him something extra, between the lines. 'DJ isn't married either. Who would have guessed Clarky would get married before us?'

'Mate, didn't I tell you?' DJ replies. 'Clarky's divorced.'

'Really?' Mike replies. 'What happened?'

'I don't know, mate, I guess marrying someone the year after you meet them at a wedding isn't a strong foundation for a marriage,' he jokes. 'Or maybe I'm just bitter that he never invited me to the wedding.'

'He didn't invite me either,' I add. 'He must still think we're not cool enough for him.'

'I wonder if he's coming,' Mike thinks out loud. 'Did Maxi tell you two who else was coming?'

I shake my head.

'It's going to be so weird, seeing her again, after all this time, after our history,' DJ says. 'Sorry, I know you two were together as well.'

Mike laughs.

'Hey, no worries, we were together a matter of months, right, Jas?' Mike replies. 'You and Maxi were together for years.'

'And now she's married to a multimillionaire,' DJ points out. 'Or is he a billionaire now? I forget whether he is, or if his charitable work keeps him under the bill.'

I laugh. DJ is obviously having a bit of a joke about Maxi's husband being more impressive than him, although I can't help but notice, as DJ moves his hands around while he talks, that he's wearing an expensive-looking watch. Bloody hell, don't tell me everyone is going to be in the prime of their lives and here I am jobless, living with my parents, single, and skint.

'You're doing all right,' Mike reminds him.

I don't think I know what DJ does. I knew he was smart when we were at school, though, so I can't say I'm surprised to hear it's paid off for him. He had a really tough time, after everything that happened before uni, so I'm really happy to hear that it hasn't held him back. A stupid teenage mistake shouldn't define anyone.

'There's a lass outside wearing the biggest hat I've ever seen,' Mikey – I mean Mike – points out. 'Almost as big as the stretch limo she's getting out of.'

'Why, that's Mrs Beaumont,' Orlando announces, clearly pleased to see her. 'Mrs Beaumont loves a statement hat.'

'That hat isn't a statement, it's a satellite dish,' DJ jokes quietly once Orlando has left us to retrieve Maxi.

'Wow, look at her, she looks amazing,' I say to no one in particular – I'm certainly not trying to rub it in with DJ, given that she's his one that got away.

'She really does,' DJ replies with a sigh.

Maxi enters the room with what can only be described as a murder-mystery scream.

'Ciao, ciao, ciao,' she greets us one at a time, kissing each of us on the cheek twice. She gets to me last and pulls me in for a hug, shaking me from side to side as she squeezes me. 'We're going to Italy, guys, you'd better get used to kissing.'

'That's what he's hoping for,' DJ jokes, giving Mike a playful nudge.

'We were just all talking about how single we are,' I tell her, in an attempt to make things a bit less awkward.

'And how Clarky is divorced,' Mike adds. 'Did you know?'

'Ooh, no, I didn't,' she replies, clearly eager for any gossip she can get her hands on.

'Is he coming?' I ask her curiously.

'Now, now,' she replies. 'I told you, the guest list is a secret. Until it isn't.'

'Well, is everyone here who is coming?' DJ asks, trying to get it out of her a different way.

'We are waiting for just one more passenger,' she says cryptically.

'Well, that's interesting, Mrs Beaumont, because I have two more names on the itinerary,' Orlando adds.

'Oh, really?' she replies, raising an eyebrow. 'Curious.'

'You're not expecting two?' DJ asks curiously.

'I am not,' Maxi says through a smile. 'So this should be interesting.'

We all turn to look out of the glass-fronted building as a car pulls up. Another Mercedes minivan, which means another guest.

Clarky bounds out of the car like a golden retriever – his driver doesn't even make it around the car in time to open the door for him. But instead of heading to the boot to retrieve his baggage, he opens the door and reaches into the back of the car. We see a hand take his – a woman's hand.

'Who is that?' DJ asks.

'I have no idea,' Maxi replies. 'She didn't go to school with us.'

'Was she born when we were at school?' Mike adds.

Clarky snakes his arm around the bare waist of a tall, slim brunette in her early twenties, tops. She's at least ten years younger than him. Clarky still has that immature look about him, that chaotic air of something that makes me brace for a split second, like something bad might be about to happen. He's certainly aged, though. He looks tired, even. I think he needs this holiday as much as anyone.

'So he's handling his divorce well then,' I joke.

'It would seem,' Maxi replies. 'I sent you all the same video, I didn't mention plus-ones, did I?'

We all watch Clarky and what is now quite obviously his date for the trip, all over each other, kissing their way through the door. To start with, the rest of us may as well not be here. Eventually, they separate and make their way over to us.

'Now then,' Clarky says. 'How's it going?'

'Air stewards aren't wearing much these days, are they?' DJ says, trying to break the ice, nodding towards Clarky's guest.

'Oh, no, I'm not a flight attendant,' she replies. 'I'm Clark's date. I would love to be a flight attendant, though, I wish, such a glamorous job.'

'Clark?' DJ repeats back to her, before turning his attention to Clarky.

'Clark,' he replies, as if to confirm that we should call him that now, although I can't imagine the boys being happy to oblige – not unless Clarky pays them off, like he did in the old days. 'And this is Drea.'

'Hi, all,' she says, shifting her weight like a hyper child. 'Thanks so much for inviting me on vay-cay with you all.'

'You are welcome,' Maxi replies, her voice unable to hide that she had no idea about any of this. 'So, you're officially coming, Clarky-er-Clark didn't just invite you today or anything?'

'No, no, I sorted it with the person you told us to call, to make arrangements for the holiday,' Clarky says. 'She cleared it.'

'Well, so long as she cleared it,' Maxi replies through thinly disguised sarcasm. 'Okay, so...'

I don't think she quite knows what to say. This is such a Clarky thing to do, though, bringing a plus-one on a holiday that is supposed to be a reunion for old friends. But what can we say? She's here now. You'd have to be so cruel, to send poor Drea packing now.

'We've got a few boring bits and pieces to do, before we board, so let's get that out of the way and then our holiday can officially start,' Maxi says excitedly.

I feel butterflies in my stomach as we go through the usual airport motions. I'm always a little nervous when I fly but these are the good butterflies. I'm excited, not just for the holiday, but for the private jet. I cannot believe the next vehicle I get in will be a *private jet*.

'Right-ho, everyone, time to board the bus,' Orlando announces.

The bus?

'The minibus,' Orlando says. 'To take you to the jet.'

Maxi hooks her arm with mine, just like she used to, as we all make our way out to the bus.

'Aww, wow, it really is like old times – all of us on the bus together,' she sings excitedly.

Almost all of us.

'Wow,' I blurt as we step out onto the tarmac of the runway.

There it is, Maxi's private jet. I'm not sure if it seems bigger or smaller than I'm expecting it to be. I'm used to big planes, owned by budget airlines with brightly coloured logos, with a full flight of stairs leading up to them. This jet is much smaller, bright white with a subtle gold stripe running along each side. There are fewer than ten steps to climb, to get on board. Maxi leads the way – assuming her hat will fit through the door. Thankfully, it does. I'm next on board, right behind her.

Flight crew are on hand to greet us – an absolutely gorgeous man and woman. I wonder if that's a requirement of the job? Everything about this is so far, so perfect.

The wood is so polished you can see your reflection in it. The floor is covered with a plush wool carpet. The air smells like sandalwood and champagne. I feel like I've just walked into another world.

'Sky home sweet home,' Maxi says as she makes a play for one of the eight luxury reclining seats, each spaced out nicely with its own table – and on each table is a bottle of water, a glass of champagne, and a fruit platter.

There's also a sofa.

'That opens out into a bed,' Maxi tells me, catching me looking at it. 'Great for long-haul flights.'

'Bloody hell,' Clarky exclaims as he joins us.

'Fuck me,' Drea adds, her voice suddenly so deep she sounds possessed by the devil. 'This is leng.'

Maxi looks at me, as though I might have a clue what that means.

Finally, Mike and DJ join us.

'And the gang's all here,' Maxi says. 'Take your seats, guys.'

'Whew,' Mike says as he sits down on one of the seats.

'This is really something, Maxi,' DJ adds, impressed. 'I was really looking forward to meeting Rupert, will he be joining us?'

'Rupe is busy, unfortunately,' she replies. 'But I wanted this to be just for old friends anyway.'

We all involuntarily glance over at Clarky and Drea – it's hard to say who is more oblivious to this remark: Drea, who is tucking into her fruit platter already; or Clarky, who is chugging from his water bottle. All of a sudden, his eyes widen with horror and he sprays his drink from his mouth like a really naff version of a fire breather.

'Oh my God,' he shouts.

'Mate, are you okay?' Mike asks him, concerned.

'It's fizzy water,' he says, disgusted. 'You really should warn a fella.'

Maxi laughs and rolls her eyes.

'Sorry, I didn't think,' she replies. 'Anyway, I'm sure the Krug will help.'

'Who's he?' Drea asks.

'The champagne, darling,' Maxi informs her politely. 'I know it's early but, when in Rome – or flying over it, at least.'

'Ooh, are we allowed in the cockpit?' Clarky asks like an excitable child.

'Erm, yes,' Maxi replies. 'Once we're up in the air, I'm sure the pilot won't mind.'

'I always wanted to be a pilot, when I was young – younger,' he says, choosing his words carefully, obviously not wanting to seem old in front of Drea.

'He'll let you watch, he won't let you fly,' Maxi points out. 'Not even if you offer him your lunch.'

'Ah, the good old days,' Mike says with a sigh.

'I didn't need a summer job, thanks to Clarky either giving me his lunch money or his lunch, just for letting him pretend to bully me,' DJ tells Drea.

'Couldn't you have just bullied him for free?' Drea replies.

Yep, that's the takeaway.

'I felt sorry for him,' Clarky tells her. Then he turns to DJ. 'And it's Clark, not Clarky.'

I really can't see that catching on.

'Why not just go by Mark?' Maxi asks curiously.

Clarky widens his eyes and then narrows them quickly.

'Because my name is Clark, obviously,' he corrects her.

'Your first name?' I check.

'Obviously,' he says again.

'So your name is Clark Clarkson?' DJ asks.

'I'm named after my dad,' he says in an attempt to explain his repetitive name.

'Your dad Clark Clarkson Senior?' Mike joins in.

'You guys don't know much about him, considering you're friends,' Drea points out before instantly adding: 'Can I get another glass of Krud?'

That's not quite what it says on the champagne bottles.

'Of course,' Maxi says with a politely disguised chuckle, beckoning a flight attendant over to top up any glasses that might need it.

I take a sip. Mmm, it's delicious. It feels like heaven as it tickles my tongue. I don't know if it's just really good champagne or it's the atmosphere of the private jet, but I could really, seriously get used to this life of luxury.

'Let's get this show up in the air,' Maxi says. 'The sooner we take off, the sooner we land in paradise. And then the fun can really start.'

'Do these TVs work?' Clarky asks.

'Do they work?' she repeats back to him. 'Yes, they work.'

'Do you have an Xbox?' he asks.

'No,' Maxi informs him.

'Mate, come on,' Mike insists.

'There's a PlayStation, though,' Maxi adds.

'I suppose it will do,' Clarky says with a shrug.

Mike leans over to me.

'Is that for him or his young friend?' he jokes.

I smile back.

'Okay, come on everyone, time for take-off,' Maxi sings. 'The holiday starts... now.'

So, this must be it, the whole gang, everyone who is coming is here – plus an extra person none of us were expecting, but Drea seems fine, I do think she's going to make us all feel old, though. But not even feeling like a thirty-something granny is going to ruin this holiday – how could it? I'm on a private jet to a luxury villa.

I'm not even sure Clarky can ruin this one.

6

Maxi is keeping tight-lipped about whom this villa belongs to. She describes them as a friend who has kindly let her borrow it for a holiday with her friends. Whomever they are, they must have a lot of money, because imagine owning a mansion or a villa like this and letting your friends borrow it. Where is the owner, while we're here? Somewhere even better, I'd assume, but where could be better than this?

We touched down in Naples, full of champagne, all excited to see where we were going to be staying. It turns out that the private island we are staying on is so small it doesn't even have an airport.

Apparently, most of the island is occupied by a holiday resort for couples. The villa (that belongs to the owner of the island, it turns out) is on the other, private side of the island, with mountains and woodlands between the two, so the only way to get from one to the other is by boat – and obviously the only way to get on and off the island at all is by boat. Of course, Maxi had a luxury boat waiting for us, to take us from A to B, and, my gosh, B is really something.

I got a glimpse of the villa in Maxi's video, but nothing could prepare me for the size of the place. It has large arched windows and a flat roof which only seems to make it appear taller and wider. Balconies pop out on many of the upstairs levels, some with multiple doors, creating an upstairs terrace that serves multiple bedrooms – I have no idea how many bedrooms we have but there's enough for one each. Well, obviously Clarky and Drea are sharing – Drea who, it turns out, is twenty-two years old, so not exactly a child, but she certainly seems it in comparison to Clarky. He may not act his age, but he certainly looks like he's in his mid-thirties. I still wouldn't want to share a room with him – trying to share a tent with him when we were teens was bad enough – so I was grateful to find out there were enough bedrooms for us each to have our own.

The décor feels iconically Italian, the rustic shades of creams and light browns are exactly what you would expect to find in an Italian villa. With a place like this, and a big chunk of change burning a hole in your pocket, I suppose there could be the temptation to turn it into something ultra-modern with all the mod cons, but it's nice to see that this place has been kept as authentic as possible – and I doubt it's lacking in mod cons, they're just integrated in a way that suits.

My room is stunning – and boasts not one, but two super-king beds, which I can't exactly utilise on my own but it gives you a sense of the scale we're working with here. Double doors lead out on to the terrace, which looks over the pool area one way, and the ornamental garden if you look the other way. I have my own bathroom, which I'm very pleased to have – I actually think this villa might have more toilets than it does people currently staying in it.

Maxi shows us all to our rooms, tells us to unpack, relax a little, and then all gather by the pool to hang out and decide what to do with our time here. She said all of this in such a low-key way that I don't think she would mind if we didn't do anything apart from sunbathe. To be honest, a nice relaxing holiday is just what I need right now. This place couldn't be more perfect.

I'm in my bikini, I've slathered myself in sun cream, my sunglasses are on my head and my towel is under my arm. Time to head for the pool.

There's an enormous infinity pool and Jacuzzi – I saw those in the video, but what I didn't notice was all the different seating areas around the pool, sort of like a classy take on the outside space on *Love Island*. Maxi is under a wooden gazebo, with creamy white curtains that blow gently in the delicious breeze. She's sipping an incredible-looking cocktail I feel like I can smell just by admiring the pretty colours and fancy garnishes as I walk over. DJ and Mike are here too, sitting on the edge of the pool with their legs in the water. DJ is laid back whereas Mike is upright. He notices me walking over and gives me a smile. I can't help but self-consciously move my towel in front of my bare midriff – I don't know why.

'I've asked our in-house barman to bring us a few more of these,' Maxi says, carefully waving her drink at me.

'Our in-house barman,' I repeat back to her. 'My gosh, how the other half live.'

'We also have our own chef,' she tells me. 'And cleaning staff. We don't have to lift a finger this holiday. Well, only enough to sip our drinks.'

'Ugh, this sounds like the perfect break,' DJ says, still in his reclined position. 'I've been working so hard, the break will do me good.'

'I'm looking forward to finding out what everyone is up to these days, but let's save the catching up for dinner this evening,' Maxi suggests. 'Let's switch off from real life first, then we can reference it like it's a distant memory.'

'Sounds perfect,' I say. 'How's the pool?'

'Nice and cool,' Mike tells me. 'Fancy a dip?'

'Maybe not a dip,' I reply. 'I could go for a float, though.'

'Come on, I'll help you onto one of the giant rubber rings,' he offers.

'Thanks,' I reply. 'I don't fancy my chances, unsupervised.'

Mike hops down into the water and swims across to the other side, to grab one of the gigantic pink rubber rings. If I can wedge my butt into it – and someone can pass me my cocktail – I think I can make it work.

A blur of white, flamingo pink and limp green flashes in my vision. It takes me a second or two to realise that I'm not having an ocular migraine, it's Clarky, in his luminous swimming shorts, charging past me as he springs towards the pool, with zero control over his limbs until he launches himself into the water, pulling in his arms and legs at the last minute to make the ultimate splash.

'Wooo!' Drea calls out, not far behind him. She doesn't jump in the pool, though, she's carrying a mini fashion backpack on her back and slurping straight from an open bottle of champagne. As she turns around to place her things down next to a vacant sunlounger, she reveals that she's wearing one of those teeny-tiny bikinis that go so far up your bum you may as well not be wearing them. And there's me thinking the front of her bikini didn't cover or support much. Everyone is entitled to wear whatever they want – lord knows I've made my own fair share of potentially question-able fashion choices over the years – but when I see these bikinis, I can never wrap my head around how people wear them. Even if they were comfortable, which doesn't seem possible given how closely they fit, you need a really specific body to carry them – and, no, I don't mean you have to be slim to look good in one, I mean you need to have exactly the right bits and pieces to keep one on and in place without flashing anyone. If I went down a water slide in one of those, I would probably find parts of my body popping out that I didn't even realise could. I can't even sleep in a vest without waking up with at least one boob chilling on the wrong side of the strap.

Clarky emerges from the water with a roar.

'Mate, are you okay?' Mike asks him.

'Yeah, I do this all the time,' he replies.

'I don't mean from jumping in the pool, I'm asking more generally, you seem really hyper,' Mike points out.

Clarky moves in closer with an obvious shiftiness. Funny really, give that we're on a private island, with no one else around.

'I've got some edibles,' he tells us, his words squeaking out, as though he can't quite believe it himself.

'Did you bring drugs on my plane?' Maxi asks, suddenly serious, leaning forwards.

'No, no, of course not,' he replies. 'I bought them in Naples, at the airport.'

'What, like in a shop?' DJ asks, sitting up.

'Don't be stupid,' Clarky claps back. 'Just from a man.'

'Right, because that's not stupid,' DJ replies.

Drea looks in her bag before taking something out and carrying it over to Maxi.

'You're totally welcome to have some,' she tells her kindly.

Maxi takes them from her. At first she seems annoyed, but then she starts laughing.

'These aren't edibles,' she says confidently. 'Well, I mean, they're literally edible, but they're gelées.'

'Gelées?' Clarky replies. 'What's that?'

'Like... Italian Haribo,' she tells him. 'I eat them all the time when I holiday here. Their shape is so distinctive, I'd know them anywhere.'

To prove her point, Maxi takes one from the bag and pops into her mouth without hesitation. Then her face falls and she spits it out again.

'Actually, it might not be drugs, but you did get them from a random man in the airport, in an unsealed plastic bag,' she concludes.

Mike is creased.

'You've done it again,' he tells Clarky. 'I can't believe it's been fifteen years and you've done it again.'

'What do you mean?' Clarky asks.

As my memory kicks in, I feel certain that Clarky definitely remembers what we're talking about.

'It was the last time we were all together, at DJ's party, and you turned up with a bag of weed,' Mike reminds him.

'You're a bad boy,' Drea growls excitedly.

'No, he's a bad drug shopper,' Mike corrects her. 'It was oregano.'

'All right, all right, at least I tried to bring the goods to the party,' Clarky protests. 'Like I'm trying to bring the fun here now. This is supposed to be a wild holiday.'

'Here, let me help you onto your rubber ring,' Mike tells me as he rolls his eyes at Clarky.

I step towards the edge of the pool.

'Erm, no, when we were teenagers it was supposed to be a wild holiday,' Maxi corrects him. 'Now that most of us are in our thirties, it's supposed to be a nice, civilised, laid-back break.'

'You didn't tell me they were in their thirties,' Drea says, semi under her breath, to Clarky – this makes me think he hasn't told her that he's in his thirties as well.

'Yes, darling, we're all so terribly old, and we're only here to relax,' Maxi replies, with just a dash of sarcasm. 'The drinks will be flowing but there will be no drugs, no joining hands and plunging into the pool naked, no more screaming. Just calm, relaxing vibes only from here on out.'

'Come on, Mike, surely you'll have a laugh,' Clarky says.

As I make the move from the edge of the pool to the rubber ring, without thinking it through Clarky grabs Mike and pushes his head under the water for fun. As Mike goes under, the rubber ring moves and I find myself falling into the water too. It feels like it happens in slow motion, the world continues around me before turning on its side. Next thing, I'm under the water. Why am I not coming back up?

I widen my eyes as best I can underwater. All I can see is blue.

I gasp as air fills my lungs again. I can't have been under for more than a few seconds, but it takes someone else to pull me out. Someone who pulls my body before carrying me up the steps and laying me on the warm floor by the pool.

'Jas? Jas, are you okay?'

I glance up at the person leaning over me – the person who saved me. The sun is behind their head, lighting them from behind, creating this angelic glow around them.

Cameron? Is that really him? No. It can't be.

He smiles.

'Cam?' I blurt.

'Hey, trouble,' he replies with a smile.

I rub my stinging eyes and then look again. It *is* him.

'Oh my God, Cam,' I blurt as I pull myself up, wrapping my arms around him, hugging him tightly.

'Erm, now doesn't really feel like the time to do what I was going to do, but Jas is fine, so I'll do it anyway. Surprise,' Maxi sings after her awkward explanation. 'I bet you all thought it was just us but, nope, Cam is here too. The whole gang! He couldn't make the jet so I thought it would be a nice surprise.'

'You wanker,' Mike shouts.

Maxi flinches but then she realises he's talking to Clarky.

'What?' Clarky replies, as though he didn't just see what happened. What did happen?

'You could've killed her,' Mike persists.

I'm still in Cam's arms, just not quite as tightly, as I'm glancing back and forth between people, waiting for an explanation.

'I just couldn't come back up,' I reason, my voice a little panicked.

'I arrived right as you fell in – luckily I'd already taken my shirt off,' Cam says with a smile. My brain starts to catch up. His cases are behind him. His trousers are soaking, water is rolling down the contours of his muscles, muscles he didn't have when he was sixteen (obviously!), muscles that I'm staring at from inches away.

'You probably didn't even need my help,' Cam continues, as I force myself to look him in the eye again. 'As you came back up, you were under that rubber ring. I thought you might be disorientated so, better safe than sorry. But I was the number one lifeguard at Waves, summer 2008.'

He still has the same cheeky smile.

'Oh, you were the number one lifeguard, were you?' I reply, my heartbeat quickening.

'There's no shame in being number two,' he tells me. 'Also, did I say hello yet?'

I smile.

'Sorry, Jas,' Clarky calls out. 'I was just trying to have fun.'

'You need to stop trying,' DJ tells him.

'Like I said, this is going to be a relaxing holiday,' Maxi says again.

Clarky pouts. 'I'll get you all having fun, one way or another,' he murmurs under his breath.

I notice the black on my fingertips.

'Oh, it's just your eye make-up,' Cam explains.

'You look kind of like you did when we were at school,' Maxi says with a smile. 'God, remember our eyelashes?'

'I remember it took us four different mascaras to create that spider's-leg effect we loved so much,' I reply.

'Thickness, length, curl, thickness,' she says. 'Extra thickness, obviously.'

'Okay, well, I'm sure I look a mess,' I say, backing away from Cam, pulling myself to my feet. 'I'm going to go to my room, sort my face out.'

'Sure thing, darling,' Maxi replies. 'You take your time. In fact, why don't we all go have a lazy afternoon getting ready for dinner, and we can all meet up here later for our big catch-up, now everyone has arrived. I need to show Cam to his room anyway.'

'Okay, sure,' I say. 'See you all later.'

Cam briefly grabs my hand and gives it a reassuring squeeze, flashing me his smile before I get up to walk away. His eyes seem as though they can hold mine in place, like some sort of mind control. I'm amazed he still has such power over me, after all these years.

'See you later,' he says.

I puff air from my cheeks as I head up the large staircase. I'm sure that incident wasn't anywhere near as bad or as scary as it felt but my brain didn't get the memo until after it felt like I might never come back up.

In my room, I lay my towel on the spare bed before lying down on top of it. Breathe in, breathe out. Breathe in, breathe out. I'm fine, I know I am. My heart won't stop racing, though, and... is it because of Cam? I wasn't expecting to see him. I thought for sure that when he wasn't on the jet he wasn't coming, and I was too embarrassed to ask, lest Maxi start teasing me for still fancying him. That would've been silly, though, because I hadn't seen him in years.

Now I have, though, and I can confirm, just between us, that I do still fancy him. In, what, a matter of minutes, I've spotted everything about his face that attracted me to him in the first place, all the parts of his personality that I loved when we were teens. He still has them all, only now they're wrapped up in this big, strong, handsome man package (okay, that sounds dodgy, but you know what I mean – I don't think my brain has enough oxygen yet). I sigh. I'm so glad he's here.

Eventually, I get up and glance in the dressing-table mirror. Wow, my make-up really does look bad. I'll take it all off, have a shower, and then a bit of a snooze before I get ready for dinner. Honestly, I feel exhausted – I don't know if it's from getting up early for the flight or my underwater near-death experience, but I'm yawning just thinking about it.

If we're all catching up tonight then I need to think about what I'm going to say, when everyone asks me about my life. Now that Cam is here, I care even more about what I'll reply. I don't want to look chaotic and unimpressive. I want to look sexy, sophisticated, and like my life is fully together and on track. So basically I want to lie – except I don't, because when did that ever work out for the best? I'll come up with a plan in the shower.

I take my time to remove my make-up – and my wet bikini, that funnily enough did end up briefly wedged in my bum when Cam dragged me out of the pool and I can still safely say I'm not a fan. Then I wrap my towel around my body and head into my bathroom.

I love having my own bathroom. I had my own at Evan and Cerys's house, and thankfully I'll have my own at my parents' too (something I was grateful for as a teen who loved to read in the bath for hours). I like to think that, when I'm married, my husband and I can have separate bathrooms. It's just so much better, with no one shouting to ask if you're nearly done, no one liberally using your overpriced conditioner, no need to worry about that gross razor you left in the shower covered in chunks of leg hair killing the mood if you forget to move it. Of course, I don't have a man to marry, or the means to buy a house, so worrying about how many bathrooms we'll have is very much a non-issue at this stage.

I can't help but feel like royalty as I walk into my opulent en suite – this sure as hell beats any bathroom I've ever had at my parents' place or in Evan and Cerys's big house. I feel like a queen, one who doesn't need a throne because she has a toilet and a bidet. There is even a chaise longue – a chaise longue in the bathroom, imagine that. I don't know what I'm supposed to do with it, but it certainly makes me feel fancy. I suppose, when I've had my shower (or potentially my bath, now that I'm looking at it) I could lie there and eat grapes, or have someone feed me grapes, like I'm Cleopatra. I wonder if this island has enough milk for me to bathe in it? Then again, I'd probably rather save it for the cappuccinos.

I'm pretty sure you could put anything in this bath and it would be incredible. No disrespect to the shower, it's like something straight out of a spa brochure, with all these fancy knobs and buttons that I don't know how to use yet (hopefully it's obvious), but I'm excited to see what they do. And it's huge, more like a room than a shower cubicle! You could fit a football team in here for their post-match shower, if you fancied it, which doesn't sound like the worst idea I've ever had – even if it's just because one of them might know how to work it.

This bath, though – the pièce de résistance. A bath so grandiose it has steps to get in. You could fit a fair few footballers in here too or – perhaps if I turned the jets up high enough – I could try to have a swim, although that might be a slight exaggeration and, let's be honest, reading books and drinking wine, surrounded by delicious-smelling candles, is far more my style.

Okay, I've convinced myself, I'm having a bath. I lean forwards to turn on the water. My towel comes loose so I quickly grab it, as a reflex, and begin fumbling to fold it back over – how do people keep towels wrapped around their body? I find myself dropping them if I so much as breathe in too enthusiastically. Just as I cover the bits you tend to keep covered from the general public (thank goodness it wasn't a split second earlier), the bathroom door opens – well, not the one I came in, a different door, one that I assumed was a towel cupboard or something, and in walks Cam.

He's still shirtless and wearing his damp trousers but the sun has dried his short, textured brown hair, giving me more of a sense of what he looks like now when he isn't soaking wet.

Cam has a jawline so chiselled he could probably remove the bathroom tiles with it. He has a dimple on his chin – one that he's always had, but that has deepened over time – that I'd forgotten about. I would describe his figure as lean, athletic even, but with purposefully defined muscle. He's big in all the ways you would want him to be (get your mind out of the gutter) without looking intimidating or like he lives for the gym. Wherever he's come from, the sun must have been shining because he's already got a tan. And then there's his eyes, so green, so sparkly, so... covered by his hands.

Cam meaningfully places his hands over his eyes and averts his gaze. When he walked through the door, time slowed down, I imagined the wind blowing in his hair as Cutting Crew's '(I Just) Died in Your Arms' plays, Cam walking up to me in slow motion. The reality is that it all happened so fast, him walking in on me here, fumbling with my towel. Oh, and now Maxi is here too.

'Jas?' she says, confused. She thinks for a moment. 'Oh my God, sorry, I think this is a shared bathroom, for these two rooms.'

'Ah,' I reply. My towel is tightened but I'm holding it for good measure.

'Sorry,' Cam says, laughing away the awkwardness. 'I had no idea.'

'I'm decent,' I reassure him, laughing it off too. 'It's okay, I didn't know either. If I did, I would've locked the door.'

'I'll just go unpack, give you guys a minute,' he says politely, heading back into his room, closing the door behind him.

'Well, that could've been way, way more awkward,' Maxi says. 'Imagine if you were already in the bath.'

'A few minutes later and I might've been,' I reply.

'Gosh, imagine, though,' she says, chewing her lip for a second as she considers what could have happened. 'It might've been like a porno. Him walking in, shirtless, wet, brooding. You in the bath, vulnerable, rattled from seeing him after all this time, the two of you still pining for each other after all these years, the old feelings surging back, him dropping his trousers and slowly walking up the steps to the bath...'

'Oh my God, all right, all right, I get the picture,' I interrupt her with a laugh. 'Do you need to step into the shower and blast on cold for a few minutes?' I tease.

Maxi laughs.

'He is hot, though, isn't he?' she reasons through a grin. 'If you fancied him when you were a teenager, how could you not fancy him now?'

'I hardly know him, Max,' I insist. 'I'm not in a place where I'm thinking about how to get him in the bath with me.'

Just an entire football team, apparently. But seriously, I haven't seen him in years. Yes, the physical attraction that I've always refused to own up to out loud to *anyone* is still there but we're not teenagers any more.

'Hmm, well, you do have a point about the shower,' Maxi

replies. 'Perhaps it would make sense for me to swap rooms with Cam, so that you don't have to share a bathroom with him. Girls sharing a bathroom makes more sense. Plus, we can secretly meet up at night and bitch about everyone – there's even a sofa in here, that must be what it's for.'

I laugh.

'You don't have to swap rooms for me,' I insist. 'I'm a big girl, I can share a bathroom with a boy.'

'It's fine,' she replies. 'It might be fun. I'll go tell him and leave you to your bath. I'm so excited for dinner tonight.'

'Me too,' I tell her sincerely. 'Thanks.'

Maxi heads back into Cam's room.

'Wow, okay, you unpack really quickly,' she says. 'Wait until after dinner, but if you want to repack...'

Maxi's voice trails off as she closes the door. I lock it behind her so that I can wash without an audience.

Is it silly, that I'm a little sad that I'm not going to be sharing a bathroom with Cam? Not that I'm thinking anything like Maxi suggested – although I can't quite seem to get the thought out of my head now – but, I don't know, now that I think about it, I like the idea of the two of us having a space together. Then again, it's the only space we would never be using at the same time under any circumstances. It's not like I'd be nipping in for a wee while he shaved, is it? No, better to share with Maxi, and continue to maintain the illusion to all men that women only use the bathroom to lounge in the bath and do their hair and make-up, even though everyone knows that's not true.

Gosh, I still can't believe Cam is here. Everyone is here. And tonight, we're all catching up. I just hope I'm not the most unimpressive person at the table. Although I'm seriously starting to suspect I might be.

7

THEN – 1 NOVEMBER 2005

Imagine a seriously scaled-down version of the Globe, with a roof, and no windows, and that's our school drama studio. It makes me laugh, that someone clearly made an effort, only for it to be wasted on teenagers who for the most part don't know or care what the Globe looks like, and see drama lessons pretty much as a free period to just mess around and not have to do any real work. I appreciate the tribute, and love to look up at the wooden beams and velvet curtains. I actually quite like hanging out in here, even outside lessons like I am today.

It's lunchtime and rehearsals for the school talent show are in full swing. I'm so nervous, so excited, my heart is beating at a million miles an hour. Oh, not because I'm taking part in the school talent show – hell no, there is no greater social faux pas for a teenager – I'm nervous because I'm here with Cam. Just the two of us. I don't know how it's happened, really. One minute we're buying chips in the canteen, about to go find the rest of the gang, the next Cam is suggesting we go check out the rehearsals.

'This is so awkward,' Cam whispers to me through a laugh and a wince.

'I've never been so happy to be an only child,' I reply. 'Imagine having a sibling who wanted you to do stuff like this.'

'Do you think she's the ringleader?' Cam asks. 'And he just goes along with whatever his big sister tells him.'

'I don't know, look at them, they're clearly both having the time of their lives,' I point out.

Nate and his big sister Millie are rehearsing their all-singing, all-dancing take on Tony Christie's 'Amarillo' – heavily influenced by the Peter Kay music video, which somehow makes it worse than if they'd choreographed something original.

'I don't know whether to laugh or cry,' I add.

'I could probably do a bit of both,' he replies, gritting his teeth as Nate pretends to fall a la Ronnie Corbett.

'So cringe,' I point out. 'Honestly, I actually think I miss the two of them singing "You're the One That I Want" to each other, and that was so, so awkward.'

'Pretty odd for siblings,' Cam adds, pulling a face.

We fall silent for a moment. I need to say something – anything, even if it's boring.

'Science next. Did you finish the physics homework?' I ask Cam, trying to sound casual, but I'm so nervous. Although I often wish the two of us could hang out alone, it happens so rarely, I spend the whole time feeling anxious about it.

'Yeah, it wasn't too bad this week,' he replies. 'I think I've done a decent job.'

I smile.

'Of course you have,' I reply. 'You're so much better at science than I am – I'm amazed we're still in the same set.'

'Well, you can't leave me alone with Cockburn,' he says. 'So, if it comes down to it, I'll do your homework too.'

I laugh at the way he says Mr Cockburn's name. I mean, come on, we're teenagers, so obviously we're going to say it how it looks like it should be said, and not how it's actually pronounced.

'I'm surprised anyone is good at physics, given how boring Cockburn's lessons are,' I reply. 'And it's like he's speaking another language sometimes – one only he understands, and then he expects everyone to know what he's going on about.'

'I know exactly what you mean,' Cam replies with a laugh. 'Although I'm not even sure he understands it, I think he just reads it out of a textbook and hopes we're all too embarrassed or bored to ask any questions.'

'For me it's a bit of both,' I confess. 'I'd do anything to drop science.'

'Okay then, I have a question for you,' Cam starts. 'If someone said you could skip science for the rest of the year, but you had to join Nate and Millie on stage in the talent show, would you do it?'

'Would I still get a good science grade?' I ask, instantly followed by: 'I don't know why I'm asking. It's got to be a no, right? No one would ever talk to me again – even the teachers would snub me.'

'I saw the librarian hiding from Nate under a desk the other day,' Cam replies through a chuckle. 'So you might be right but, then again, you know I'd still talk to you.'

'Well, let's go further with it,' I suggest. 'If you could skip science for the rest of the year, would you perform "Amarillo" in the talent show with me?'

Cam recoils in horror. Then he smiles.

'If it would be fun to do it with anyone, it would be fun to do it with you,' he replies.

I feel myself blush, only slightly, at his choice of words. Obviously, he doesn't mean do *it* with me, but my God, I have such a crush on him, it's the first place my mind goes. Not that I've ever done it with anyone – I've never even kissed a boy, which I don't suppose is a very cool thing to admit but at this age I suspect most people are the same, then you've got those who have kissed, and then the smallest number of teens who have gone all the way. Honestly, there's no way I feel ready for that. I read *Cosmopolitan* magazine, marvel at the featured sex positions, cringe at the idea of trying to contort my body into them – one time, alone obviously, I even tried to roll back onto my shoulders, with my legs in the air, but I fell straight back down. It was always going to be ambitious, for the girl who doesn't have her gymnastics patch on her gym skirt because she can't do a forward roll without flailing off to the side (although I suspect it has less to do with my athletic ability – toddlers do forward rolls – and more to do with me worrying about everyone seeing my knickers, because a skirt is a dumb thing to do PE in and, if I ever have kids, I hope they grow up in a world where the girls can wear shorts like the boys do).

My cheeks still feel warm – I really caked on the foundation today, as I do every day, but I desperately hope Cam can't see me blushing. I dare to look at him. Does he look nervous too?

'Oh, here you are,' Mikey interrupts.

My attention suddenly shifts from Cam to everything else around me. It's like I was so deep in thought, so into him, that I forgot where I was, or what I was doing. I'd even managed to tune out from 'Amarillo', although now I'm back in the room I see they're taking it from the top again. Wonderful.

'Mikey, hi,' I blurt, unable to hide that little something in my voice that isn't usually there, but I feel like we've been caught.

'I've been looking everywhere for you,' he explains. 'I just spotted you, as I walked past – I couldn't help but look in and see what that horrible noise was, you know like when people stare at car accidents? This is the last place I expected to find you. I'll let the others know.'

Mikey takes his phone from his pocket and types as he talks. Then he suddenly raises his gaze and looks at us suspiciously.

'Are you hiding from us?' he asks.

I laugh – practically cackle – in a way I don't think I've ever done before.

'Ha, no,' I reply. 'We just wanted to get a sneak peek at... this.'

'And talking about our physics homework,' Cam adds.

I feel like we're on the same page.

'Couple of nerds, aren't you?' Mikey teases. 'I expect it of him but not you, Jas, I thought you were cool.'

Oof. There's nothing worse you can say to a teenager, is there?

Still, I'd rather be lumped in with Cam, even if it means being uncool.

'Hey,' Maxi squeaks as she and DJ approach us, hand in hand, as usual.

I notice Maxi give me a look, her eyes wide in a way that hopefully only I'm noticing, as she glances back and forth between me and Cam, silently telling me that she knows we were here together, alone – well, alone until this lot arrived.

DJ feeds her a chip, seemingly from nowhere, then he kisses her. I can't help but roll my eyes at their over-the-top affection for each other. They're so obsessed with each other, it's gross – well, it's gross or I'm jealous. Perhaps it's a bit of both.

DJ pulls out a carton of canteen chips from his pocket and eats a couple. Maxi leans in for another kiss, then DJ pops another French fry into his mouth, alternating between snogging and snacking. Maybe that is just gross.

Finally, we're joined by Clarky. If three is a crowd, then God knows what six is.

'Ay, are those chips?' he asks DJ. 'Give us one, I'm starving.'

'Did you give away your lunch money?' Maxi asks with a roll of her eyes.

'No, saving up for something, aren't I?' he replies. 'Come on, give us a few chips.'

'Go on then,' DJ gives in. 'We're all meeting up later – we thought we might go hang out at the playground, in the park. Are you coming?'

'I'll have to see what I'm doing,' Clarky replies, although we all know he's doing nothing.

'Yeah, check your busy social schedule,' Mikey replies sarcastically.

'Freaks,' a voice bellows in from the doorway.

Ergh, it's Spiller and Tommy, the Hardaker brothers – also known as Stuart and Thomas, if you've known them since nursery, although I suspect their real names don't sound 'hard' enough for them. They're the so-called cool kids, the ones Clarky is always trying to impress.

'Shit, they can't see me in here,' Clarky says.

'Well, you can't get out, without going past them,' DJ points out.

'Let me peanut you,' Clarky practically begs.

'Piss off,' DJ replies.

'Don't even ask me,' Mikey tells him.

'And I'm not letting you peanut me,' Cam adds.

For some reason, Clarky looks to me next.

'Oh, yeah, because yanking a girl's tie is going to make you look so cool,' I say sarcastically.

With no other option, Clarky does what any other self-respecting teenager would do. He drops to the floor and crawls under the piano.

'Can we leave him under there?' Mikey jokes.

I smile but secretly I'm gutted. It was so, so great when it was just me and Cam. Now the whole gang is here and, as much as I like them all, they're really starting to get in the way. Unless of course Cam doesn't like me too, and I'm deluding myself into thinking he does, but how am I ever going to find out?

Mikey interrupting when he did couldn't have happened at a worse time. Who knows when we'll get time alone together again?

8

NOW

If you had told me this time last week that I would find myself sitting at a table, with my oldest friends, outside a luxury Italian villa, on a private island, eating pasta and drinking wine – honestly, I would have laughed in your face and then probably gone to my room to cry at how unlikely the idea was. What a difference a week can make. Suddenly, I feel like I'm in a movie and, while I'm no Sophia Loren, I feel amazing in my long, floaty white sundress.

Obviously, I didn't overthink it when I put it on, because even though I *know* I'm in Italy now, I didn't think twice about wearing a white dress while I drink wine and eat pasta. I definitely have previous, when it comes to spilling on my clothes, in fact it's usually a sure thing. The worse it would be for me to spill on my clothes, the more likely it is to happen, and I have a cousin who gave me her wedding flowers to hold in front of my bridesmaid's dress in some of the wedding photos to prove it.

We're eating outside, at the dining area by the pool, just outside the villa. Large doors from the inside dining room open up, leaving us with access to the bar, and giving staff a way to pop in and out while they serve our food. It's a large wooden table – practically a work of art. Its size leaves lots of surface area but it's beautifully filled with fresh flowers, lit candles, and plate after plate of antipasti. We've got more Italian meats and cheeses than I can name, different types of bread, olive oil and balsamic dip, fennel-flavoured taralli which I am obsessed with – all a meal on their own, but then we have the pasta.

It must be because we're in Italy, that such a simple pasta dish can taste so phenomenal. It's penne in a rich tomato sauce with freshly grated parmesan cheese on top, which doesn't sound fancy, but the tomatoes taste so sweet and the basil so fresh. If pasta grew on trees (you know what I mean) then I'm eating it freshly picked. It's unreal.

And with great pasta comes great wine. Luca, our barman, has been serving us a red wine from a vineyard over on the mainland, where apparently most of the wines here come from. He says that we can take a tour around the vineyard, and taste the wines, if we fancy a day out, and that we should just let him know when to arrange it for us.

Of course, Clarky scoffed that he couldn't think of anything more boring than walking around some fields and then drinking wine that he would only have to spit out. Maxi once again reminded him that this is a civilised holiday for adults, not a drug-powered piss-up for horny teenagers – the look on his face suggested he would love that, but he's outvoted.

Honestly, this evening is perfect. Everything here, as expected, is perfect. The silverware, the plates are intimidatingly nice – I would be scared to touch them, were they not the only things standing between me and all this food and drink. The warm evening weather envelops us, with a cool, soothing breeze taking the edge off, and as we chat, between the natural pauses in our conversation all you can hear is the soft ambient music and the distant sound of the ocean. *Perfecto*, as the locals say.

'Maxi, this is incredible,' Cam says, dabbing his mouth with his napkin. 'You think you know good pasta but then you taste pasta in Italy.'

'Rupert once flew me all the way to Milan on the jet, just to get me my favourite carbonara for dinner, from a restaurant we visited years ago,' she replies. 'It wasn't even an expensive place. When we visited it originally, we weren't all that rich. That's what keeps us grounded, though. Romantic trips to our favourite place, even if it isn't the most expensive.'

I smile. Popping to Milan for pasta on a private jet isn't exactly keeping grounded but I take her point about the two of them treasuring their older memories together, and I think that's lovely. They're clearly really happy together. You wonder, don't you, when people suggest that money can't buy happiness, whether or not it's true. I'm hardly in a position to decide for myself but Maxi and Rupert do seem really, really happy, and it might not be because of the money but I'm sure it helps, even if it's only because having no money worries takes a certain amount of strain from a relationship, as far as finances are concerned.

'I was really looking forward to meeting Rupert,' DJ says again. 'I actually wanted to pick his brain about something.'

'Oh?' Maxi replies.

'Yeah, just a work thing,' DJ continues. 'Nothing interesting.'

'Well, I want to know what everyone has been doing since we all saw each other last,' Maxi insists. 'I'll get the ball rolling. So I married Rupe, I'm sort of his right-hand woman, we travel around a lot, go on lots of holidays. The urge to pop out some little Beaumonts hasn't come to me yet but you never know. For now, we're just enjoying ourselves, and he's doing so well, with the company. It's a really exciting time.'

'So you're the only one who is married,' Mike points out. 'Well, unless, Cam, are you married?'

It takes every muscle in my neck to carefully control the speed with which I look up from my food to watch him answer this question.

'No, not married,' he replies. 'Never been married, not currently in a relationship. I've been quite busy with work recently.'

'Just Maxi then,' Mike concludes. 'And Clarky, you were married—'

'Married to my job, yes,' Clarky quickly adds. 'Still working in social media, for Max G Protein, but now that things are running smoothly, I'm taking the time out I need. Life isn't about working.'

Clarky gives Mike a look. Okay, so we're all pretending Clarky hasn't just got divorced, got it. Drea, as always, is just too happy to be here, too busy tucking into her food, she's not even listening.

'What have you been busy with?' Maxi asks Cam. 'I was thrilled for you when I heard you got into Oxford to do your master's.'

'Ah, thanks,' he replies, toying with a piece of pasta with his fork, looking down at his plate. He always was shy about how smart he was. 'I started working on something, while I was studying. It's essentially a way to learn English, as a foreign language, quickly and efficiently. I started out trying to help out international students who didn't speak the language but wanted to study here. It was effective, though. I've just finished a bit of a world tour, travelling round, teaching people how to teach it.'

'That's incredible,' Maxi replies. 'We always knew you would do amazing things. Congratulations on your success.'

Cam smiles and shrugs.

'I just want to make a difference,' he says.

That's so like Cam, to wind up with a job that helps people. It's not exactly in the same category as taking a summer job as a life-guard but he's always wanted to help. It does sound like he works abroad, though – ha, I say 'though', as if the two of us would be married if it turned out we still lived in the same village.

'I'm still working for the family business,' Mike joins in. 'It's going well, though. All of Dad's dealerships are still open.'

'Still can't believe you're a used-car salesman,' Clarky says through a mouthful of bread.

'I wouldn't call myself a used-car salesman,' Mike insists, unable to hide that he's a little ticked off at Clarky's summary of his job. 'I'm the heir to a used-car empire.'

'Yeah, but for now you're selling used cars,' Clarky says. He doesn't mean anything by it, but Mike takes offence nonetheless.

'All right, says the lad who tweets for a living,' Mike claps back.

'I'm head of social media and marketing now,' Clarky informs him. 'I got promoted with perks and a big salary bump.'

'One of those perks isn't free protein, is it?' DJ jokes. 'You should give it a go, you might grow a bit.'

Clarky is still a little on the short side but people have been telling him this all his life, so he is completely unbothered by it.

'Go on then, big shot, what do you do?' Clarky asks.

'I build software,' DJ replies.

'You always were so intelligent and so brilliant with that stuff,' Maxi says with a smile. You can tell she still cares about him a lot, it shines out of her skin, but how could she not after being in a relationship with him for so many years when they were younger?

'Ha!' Clarky scoffs. 'Neeeerd.' He basically sings his insult.

'I do all right with it,' DJ says casually. 'Drea, can you pass me the green olives, please?'

'Uh, I can't really reach,' she says, even though she's the closest one to them.

'He does more than all right with it, he's being modest,' Mike adds, speaking up for his friend. 'He and one of his professors invented some kind of software for universities to use – sold it for an absolute packet, didn't you?'

'I did all right,' he says again, through a slight smile.

'Was it black or green olives you wanted?' Drea asks, all smiles, suddenly interested.

'Er, green,' DJ replies with a chuckle.

Clarky has a face like thunder now.

'Is that what you wanted to talk to Rupert about?' Maxi asks him.

'Yes, well, I won't bore everyone with it...'

'Good,' Clarky barks over him.

'But I'm developing something for remote teaching and learning and I think that with my software, and the right hardware, it could be something brilliant,' DJ explains. 'I think it would be right up Rupert's street.'

'I'll mention it to him, next time he calls,' she replies. 'Sounds interesting.'

'It sounds boring as hell,' Clarky insists. 'Come on, is this really how we're spending our holiday? Talking about who is doing what at work, what our pensions are shaping up like, where we see ourselves in the next twenty years...'

Clarky's voice trails off, as though he's just had a thought he doesn't like. A waiter comes to clear our plates, so Clarky waits until we're alone again before he continues.

'We've got to have some fun,' he eventually says.

'We will,' Maxi tells him. 'I promise. 'Just... age-appropriate fun.'

'You said there's a resort on the island?' Clarky enquires. 'It must have like a club or something?'

'I'm desperate to dance all night,' Drea says. 'Do you like to dance, DJ?'

DJ pulls a face, surprised that Drea is talking to him.

'I'm not much of a dancer,' he replies politely.

'It's a romantic resort for couples,' Maxi tells him. 'No night-clubs, it's not that kind of vibe. You can take the boat there but unless you're up for a hike or a couple's massage...'

'Not that sort of massage, sorry, mate,' Mike tells Clarky with a wink.

'We could get the boat to the mainland then,' Clarky practically pleads. 'Come on, DJ, big shot, you must want to go live it up?'

'Are we calling me big shot now, eh?' DJ says with a laugh.

'Sounds like you are one,' Clarky concludes. 'And to think, you didn't want to go to that uni. It turns out what happened was the best thing that ever happened to you.'

DJ's face falls.

'What did you say?' he asks seriously.

'Just that, you know, you're doing really well, and if it's because you built something with your professor then, well, you had to go to that uni to meet him, so all's well that ends well,' Clarky reasons, although he suddenly seems more unsure of his phrasing as he utters each word. We're all picking up on some intense body language from DJ.

'That night ruined my life,' DJ tells him. 'What are you talking about?'

'No, no, not that night,' Clarky quickly backtracks. 'I just mean not going to your first-choice uni.'

'Poor choice of words, perhaps,' Maxi says diplomatically. 'We know what you mean, Clarky.'

'I don't,' Drea pipes up. 'What happened that night?'

I purse my lips. Oh, God. I was wondering how long it would be before this came up – I was hoping it wouldn't come up at all, but I really wasn't expecting it on the first night.

'You've got to love the directness of Gen Z,' Mike jokes, trying to dispel the tension.

'Nothing worth talking about, darling,' Maxi tells her. 'It's nothing to talk about on holiday.'

'It sounds spicy,' Drea says, not reading the room at all.

'It's not a big deal,' Clarky tells her. 'Leave it, yeah?'

The silence spreads around the table until eventually...

'Tiramisu,' our waiter announces excitedly as he begins placing delicate little plates of it in front of each of us. He notices the mood. 'In England are you not excited for dessert?'

'We are, thank you, Sal,' Maxi assures him.

Silently, we all tuck into our dessert. Gosh, it's awkward, I just wish someone would say something, anything.

'Jas, you never told us what you're doing now,' Mike pipes up.

Oh, for God's sake, anything but that. I was starting to think I'd got away with it.

'I'm in teaching too,' I say. 'I've been working with a family, privately tutoring their kids, trying to give them the best start in life.'

'What an educational bunch we are,' Maxi concludes with a smile. 'You could be forgiven for thinking we liked school.'

I laugh.

As we eat our dessert, we manage to find our way back to polite chit-chat. I'm not surprised that night is still a tough spot for DJ, it really did pull the rug from under him. His relationship with his parents changed, his relationship with Maxi ended, he didn't get to go to the uni he wanted, he had to go where his parents told him to go, far away from all of us. Just because something has turned out well for him, it doesn't strike all that from the history books.

When dinner is over, Clarky and Drea grab a bottle of champagne, wish us all a good night and head up to their room –

confirming for all of us that we'll all avoid upstairs for fifteen minutes, tops.

Mike has gone to the bathroom and Maxi and DJ are talking about his idea. You can tell there's still a little something between them, it's in their eyes, their body language too. Do old feelings ever go away?

'Fancy a walk on the beach?' Cam asks me.

My heart skips a beat. I guess they don't go away.

'I'd love to,' I reply.

Cam and I walk away from the villa.

'This way,' he tells me. 'I found this pathway earlier, when I was looking around before dinner.'

I feel like I'm floating a little – probably down to all the drinks we had over dinner – but I manage to stay upright as I follow Cam down the winding, grassy pathway until we eventually get to where we're heading.

'Wow,' I blurt.

'Right?' Cam says with a smile.

I slip off my heels and carry them in my hand so I can feel the sand between my toes. As we stroll along the sand, I'm struck by the serenity that surrounds me. All I can hear is the gentle lapping of the waves against the shore and the occasional rustle of a sea breeze in the trees – oh, and the sound of my heartbeat thudding inside my chest, although perhaps I can only feel that.

Looking out to sea, all I see on the horizon is the moon's reflection. The water is calm and still, reflecting the moon's silvery light like a mirror. It's almost as though the sea is holding its breath, waiting for something to happen.

'I still can't believe we're here,' Cam says.

'I can't believe we're here but I definitely can't believe you're here,' I tell him. 'When you weren't on the jet, I assumed you weren't coming.'

'I have genuinely just finished my work tour,' he explains. 'So I flew in from the last stop. I was going home to see my family but – you know what my mum is like, when she heard Maxi was suggesting this trip, she insisted I had to come. She sends her love, by the way.'

I smile.

'I always liked your mum,' I tell him.

'Your parents are great too,' he replies. 'How are they doing?'

'Oh, on top form, as ever,' I reply with a chuckle. 'I went for dinner the other night. Mum made my favourite, instead of Dad's usual lasagne, and he banged on about it all night.'

'He sounds no different,' Cam says. 'So you still see them often?'

There is no way, after everyone was talking about how impressive they are over dinner, that I'm going to tell him that I'm living with my parents, or that I've lost my job.

'I try to,' I say. 'It's hard, with work, isn't it? I love my job, I love the family I work with – those kids may as well be my own.'

Well, they may as well be, given how much I had to do for them.

'There's talk about them moving abroad for a while,' I lie. 'So, naturally I would be travelling with them.'

The words leave my lips before I've had a chance to consider whether or not it's a good idea to say them. I just really, really don't want to look like a loser. It's like school again – the last thing I want is to look uncool.

'You sound very devoted,' he replies, giving me an encouraging nudge with his elbow. 'Travelling with them, to keep on top of their education, is admirable. I'm exhausted in a way that I can't quite explain after flying all over the place. But hopefully that part of the job is done now. Just between us, my grandma isn't doing so good. She's moved in with my parents, so I thought I'd move back home for a bit, while I work out what I'm going to do next, to help out. I think that's why Mum insisted I take this holiday first, to rest up after work, before I throw myself in at the deep end in the madhouse.'

Why, why, why did I just tell all those lies? I wanted to seem like I was professional and travelling and not still hanging around with my parents like a baby. I thought that's what Cam was like now, but I should have thought about what he was like before. He's a home bird. He loves his family. Of course he's happy to move back to live near them and of course he wouldn't have judged me. But I've done it now, I have to own it.

The sand is cool and smooth beneath my feet as we walk along the shoreline. I can feel the cool night air on my skin and smell the salty sea air mixed with the scent of the nearby trees that hide the villa from our sight. Right now, we could be anywhere.

Eventually, we reach an unlit firepit surrounded by seats. They look like the kind that usually have cushions on them so perhaps they're in the house somewhere. It would be nice to get the whole gang here, hanging out by the fire, drinking and chatting. But not right now, though. Right now, I'm happy it's just me and Cam.

Eventually, we sit down on the sand together. I bury my toes deep into it as I gaze up at the stars.

'Isn't it beautiful?' Cam says, reading my mind. 'I didn't realise how much I needed this right now.'

'Me too,' I say with a sigh. 'Adult life is... a lot, isn't it?'

'We should've just kept our summer job, kept things simple,' he jokes.

I smile as more memories of our days working at a swimming activity centre for kids comes flooding back – no pun intended.

'That was a fun summer,' I reply. 'Pretty much from the

moment we finished sixth form to the day we collected our results. That was one of my happiest times.'

'It all went a bit pear-shaped that day, didn't it?' he replies. 'Life was simpler when we were in the baby pool, pretending to be mermaids to make toddlers laugh.'

I snort.

'I'm not sure how many places expect you to be a lifeguard and a kids' entertainer,' I say. 'But I feel like we nailed it.'

'We were the king and queen of the pool,' he says with a laugh. 'All the kids thought we were married. I felt so grown-up – although even when you're a teen, it's easy to look grown-up in front of kids. To their parents, we probably looked like babies too.'

Cam smiles at me, and I feel a spark between us, the one I used to feel, the one that neither of us was ever willing to acknowledge until... ergh, that night. I wish we could all just forget about that bloody night.

'Do you remember that kid who kept jumping off the diving board even though he couldn't swim?' Cam asks – it's as though he knows my mind has wandered somewhere I'd rather it hadn't.

I laugh. 'Oh, yeah! And we had to keep rescuing him every time,' I reply.

'Only for him to jump in again,' Cam adds. 'His mum thought it was hilarious.'

'It sort of was,' I say. 'Although, in hindsight, incredibly stupid of him.'

'We had his back,' Cam concludes. 'And we made a good team.'

'We really did,' I reply. 'We were good together.'

'Jas...'

Before Cam gets the chance to say what he's going to say, we're interrupted by a voice behind us.

'Hey, what are you two doing down here?' Mike asks.

Either there is a vague accusatory tone to his voice or I'm just feeling guilty, like we've been caught doing something, even if we're only chatting.

'Oh, we're just taking in the night sky,' Cam says, standing up and brushing the sand off his shorts. He offers me a hand to help me up.

'Very romantic,' Mike teases. 'Shame it's wasted on a couple of old friends, eh? Anyway, me, Maxi and DJ are going to play cards. Come and make the numbers up.'

I feel my face flush with embarrassment as Cam and I exchange uneasy glances. We do as we're told, following Mike back up the path to the villa, to join the others.

Mike, ever the athlete, speeds his way to the top, like a regular Rocky. Cam takes it slowly with me – something I'm thankful for when I catch my toe on a rock or a tree root or something.

Cam reaches out, grabbing me, stopping me from falling flat on my face.

We both freeze for a second, our faces just inches apart. I can feel my heart pounding in my chest as Cam looks into my eyes.

'Are you okay?' he asks, his voice soft.

'Still clumsy as ever,' I tell him through a smile.

He smiles back.

'Come on, you two, hurry up,' we hear Mike call out from somewhere at the top of the path.

Eventually, we join him at the top and make our way back to the villa garden, where an incredibly awkward-looking Maxi and DJ are sitting. I'm surprised to see them looking so uncomfortable because things looked so easy between the two of them when we left.

I don't have to wonder what went wrong between the two of them for long and thankfully I don't need to ask. It's obvious, as soon as we're in earshot of the villa.

The door on the terrace above the firepit is open and... noises are drifting down. Is that...? Oh, God, it's Clarky and Drea.

Maxi pulls a face at me.

'Wow,' I mouth at her.

'Right, let's play cards,' DJ says loudly. 'And turn the music up, yeah?'

Ah well, if Clarky and Drea making a lot of noise gets him off our backs about having a wild holiday, then I'm all for it. Plus, from the sounds of it, there's no way this can go on for much longer.

Here's hoping, anyway.

9

I woke up this morning to the smell of fresh coffee drifting in through my open terrace door. There is nothing like sleeping with the door open on a warm night in a hot country, is there? Providing you keep the net curtains closed to keep the bugs out, of course.

Enticed by the smell of coffee and the idea of breakfast (I'm excited to find out what it might be), I rolled out of my bed, stretched my arms above my head as I took a deep breath of the smell drifting in from outside, and then got dressed with a real spring in my step. I put on a bikini – the only really acceptable holiday underwear for during the day – and slipped a sundress on. Then I grabbed my sunglasses and headed downstairs, ready to see what today has in store for me. This really is the life. I would say I could get used to this, but I'm not exactly going to get the chance to, am I? This is a holiday, an interlude from life, before it's back to reality. But that's a problem for Future Jasmine, not me.

I'm the last person to arrive at the table, where my friends are all gathered, sipping coffees and fresh fruit juices, in front of the breakfast buffet of my dreams.

'Good morning, darling,' Maxi calls out to me, her infectious smile taking over her face. 'Sleep well?'

'I don't know if it's the sea air, the massive bed, or just knowing that I didn't have to get up for work today, but I slept amazingly,' I reply as I take my seat.

'I was just saying what a good night's sleep I had,' Clarky adds. 'I went out like a light, I was knackered.'

Cam and I exchange a subtle, knowing glance, both recalling the horrors of being subjected to the sound effects coming from Clarky's room as he and Drea got it on.

There is a large platter of small pastries on the table so I grab a plate and take a few. Some are filled with chocolate, some cream – and I'm assuming the green ones are pistachio but I won't know unless I try one of each, will I?

'We were just talking about our room swap,' Maxi tells me, nodding towards Cam. 'We mostly moved everything last night, apart from a few bits, but Cam was just telling us all about his new room.'

Maxi smiles.

'Oh?' I say.

'I guess I'm in the master suite now,' Cam explains, mildly embarrassed. 'The bathroom is the size of a spa, the walk-in wardrobe is the size of a bedroom, the terrace is bigger than most gardens.'

'And you're in it all alone,' Mike teases him. It feels a little out of place.

'We're all single, apart from Maxi,' DJ chimes in, easing the tension.

Clarky opens his mouth to speak but then realises Drea – who is cramming the best part of a croissant into her mouth – takes no issue with this fact, so Clarky retreats. I would *love* to know what the deal is there, what they are to one another.

'Oh, Maxi, you've gone from that to sharing a bathroom with me,' I point out with a smile.

'I must really love you then,' she tells me.

'I'm just imagining the two of you fighting over the shower,' Clarky jokes. Ew. Classic Clarky, though.

'Rather she fights over the shower with me than with Cam,' Maxi tells him. 'All girls shower together.'

'Really?' he replies, his eyes wide with delight, his jaw hanging open – I'm amazed he isn't drooling.

'Of course not, you perv,' she ticks him off.

Clarky sulks, disappointed.

'Are you not eating, mate?' Mike prompts him.

'I'm not hungry,' he says, pouting.

Clarky is still like a little kid, very much wearing his heart on his sleeve. If he isn't eating, he's obviously in a mood about something.

'Come on, what are you being mardy for?' Mike persists.

Clarky lets out a deep sigh. 'I just don't understand why we travelled all the way to Italy to sit on our arses and do nothing. I came here to have an adventure! I want to have fun!'

This again.

'Come on, *Clark*,' DJ says, adding a dash of sarcasm as he uses Clarky's new cool-guy name. 'We've been over this. We're here to relax.'

'Relaxing isn't adventure,' Clarky insists. 'We can relax when we're old.'

I bite into a lobster tail pastry. The crisp pastry makes the most satisfying sound as all the different layers snap between my teeth. Then the delicious chocolate hazelnut filling hits my tongue. Wow. So long as I keep eating these, this lot can bicker all they want.

'Okay, well, I was thinking we could all go for a gentle hike today,' Maxi suggests. 'There's an entire wood to explore, not to mention the beaches and the hidden caves. How's that for adventure?'

'I didn't come on holiday to go for a walk,' Clarky moans. 'And that idea isn't exactly *Lord of the Rings*.'

'Then why did you come as a hobbit?' Mike jokes quietly, as though he knows it's going to piss Clarky off, but he can't quite resist cracking such an easy joke.

'You've all got your cameras,' Maxi reminds us. 'Perhaps we could make a bit of a competition out of it, to see who gets the best photo on our hike. And I could have the staff prepare us a picnic – we could eat on the beach.'

'That sounds amazing,' I reply genuinely.

'Are you taking the piss?' Clarky asks me directly. 'That sounds like the single most boring thing I have ever heard. Exercise? For fun?'

I can't help but roll my eyes at his dramatic over-exaggeration.

'Come on, bud, it's not like we're suggesting we all trek to the top of Mount Vesuvius,' Cam reasons.

'I would rather climb a volcano,' Clarky insists. 'I would rather throw myself into the volcano than endure this snoozefest.'

It's hard to recall if Clarky has always been this bad or if he's got worse over the years. People usually mature, Clarky only seems to have intensified.

'I'm up for anything,' Drea says with a shrug. 'I just need to go get ready.'

Sometimes I get the sense she isn't really listening. She's in a world of her own. Then I notice her tap her ear and I realise she's hiding a pair of AirPods under her glossy brown hair. Oh, that makes so much sense now – not just why she isn't always listening, but how she's able to put up with Clarky too.

Drea sucks the remains of her breakfast from each of her fingertips, gets up and walks off. Clarky glances at her, then back at us, then at Drea again. He stands up to follow her, his chair scraping loudly against the floor.

'Listen, I'm going to find a way for us all to have fun, even if it kills me,' he practically threatens before walking away.

DJ sighs playfully.

'Well, he never changes, does he?'

'I'm starting to wonder if any of us have changed,' I think out loud.

'I certainly have,' Maxi insists. 'We've all matured. We've all got fantastic lives. It's just Clarky who has never quite snapped out of it.'

'I can understand why his wife left him,' Mike says quietly.

'Harsh,' Maxi replies. She shifts in her seat. 'But so can I.'

'Well, we still wouldn't do this without him, would we?' Cam joins in. 'He's part of the gang.'

'That's true,' I say with a smile.

Cam is such a sweetheart.

'All this and you know he'll come for the hike with us anyway,' Mike points out. 'I wish we could cut out all the messing around, it's like having a teenager.'

'Hilariously, the only person here who knows what it's like to have a teenager is Clarky,' DJ jokes. 'It isn't that long since Drea was one.'

'Do you think she's just here for the free holiday?' Maxi asks quietly, almost as though she feels bad for even suggesting it.

'Of course,' Mike replies. 'Do you really think a young lass like that is going to be with a dramatic hobbit fast approaching middle age for any other reason?'

'That's a bit mean,' I can't help but point out.

'Look, I'm just joking, but you know what I mean, it's a bit suss,' Mike reasons, retreating a little.

'He's clearly going through a tough time with his divorce, and trying to find himself again,' Cam says.

'All right, Dr Cam, therapist,' Mike jokes.

'I think Cam is right,' I say. Mike's face falls. He looks almost angry. 'We need to look out for him, make sure he doesn't get hurt.'

'I'm sure once we start our hike he'll relax into it,' Maxi reasons as she drains the last of her coffee.

'Or he'll find a way to kill us all,' DJ jokes.

I grab another pastry – what? It's fuel for the hike – and pour myself a glass of peach juice. Ugh, it tastes like heaven. Why does everything taste so good here?

'Fancy finishing up here and chilling by the pool for bit?' Maxi suggests. 'Get a little relaxation in, while it's just us adults?'

'Sounds great,' DJ replies.

'We can hike later in the afternoon, when the sun has eased off a bit,' she says. 'Or we can do it tomorrow. That's the beauty of a chilled-out holiday.'

I let out a contented sigh as I sink back into my chair a little.

Clarky's immature dramatics aside, this trip couldn't be more perfect.

Well, not unless I can find a way to spend more time alone with Cam, but I'm working on it.

10

Now that my body has adjusted to the icy-cold pool water, being in the water feels amazing. You really can't beat a cool pool on a hot day when you're on holiday, can you?

I twirl around in the water playfully. With the exception of my accidental dip yesterday, I don't remember the last time I was in a swimming pool. I'm sure I have been, since Cam and I were lifeguards together that summer, but nothing can compete with this.

Cam is next to me, floating on his back.

'This is the life,' he says.

I glance over at our friends. Mike is lying on a sunlounger. He's wearing mirrored sunglasses so I can't tell if he's looking at us or if his eyes are even open. The look on his face is very serious, almost unhappy. Perhaps he has drifted off.

Maxi and DJ are sitting under the gazebo, drinking cocktails, looking like they're flirting up a storm. I'm not sure how DJ can forget that Maxi is married, given the way the sun keeps bouncing off the giant rock on her finger, but I suppose it's not that strange, with the history the two of them have. It's almost like muscle memory, flirting just comes naturally to the two of them.

It's been a little while since breakfast – enough time that I'm already starting to think about lunch, anyway. I'm already obsessed with the food here, fantasising about what's to come.

I allow the water to take my weight, letting my body rise to the surface so I can float along next to Cam. It feels so good, to feel so weightless, so unbothered by anything. I link my arm with Cam's, to keep the two of us tethered together.

'Is it sea otters that hold hands while they sleep, so they don't float away from each other?' I hear Cam say with a chuckle. 'Amazing that sea otters have such a level of intimacy but I'm still single.'

I laugh at his cute joke.

'I've seen videos of them, they're so adorable,' I reply. 'I'm doing it so we can chat, without accidentally floating off to different ends of the pool. Honestly, I could stay here all day.'

'This is just the break I needed from work,' he says. 'I'm trying to clear my head, before I think about what to do next, but my brain is racing. You said you were happy with your work, didn't you?'

'Oh, absolutely,' I say – doubling down with my lie.

'It's almost a shame,' Cam continues. 'I was thinking it might be good to open up some kind of creative hub, for teens, where we grew up. I never felt like our passion for English was nurtured at school – well, not beyond the point of simply passing our exams, at least. Just think of what creative kids could achieve if they had an outlet. We could get kids writing – imagine younger voices being published.'

Cam sighs.

'Just an idea that I'm letting my brain run away with,' he concludes, winding in his enthusiasm. 'I knew you would appreciate it.'

'Cam, that sounds incredible,' I tell him. 'You should absolutely do that.'

'We'll see,' he says. 'I'd need to find the right team, maybe some other investors to help get it up and running.'

And I need to find a way to backtrack how happy I am in my current job because, my gosh, if Cam gets this set up, it would be my dream job. I wish I'd had access to something like that when I was a teenager, who knows what I might be doing now? I might be rich, like everyone else here.

'Oh my God, guess what, guess what?'

I slip my body back down into the water, making myself upright again so I can see what's going on.

Clarky is bounding over to us like an excitable child.

'Guess what,' he says again.

'What? What? What?' Maxi replies unenthusiastically, sounding like his mum.

'You'll never guess,' he insists.

'What?' I ask, raising an eyebrow.

'I've booked us all on a trip this afternoon,' he says. 'A boat is going to come and pick us up and take us on a leisurely trip to – get this – an untouched island where we can relax, eat and enjoy a few drinks in the ultimate serene setting before the boat comes back to get us later.'

Clarky jigs on the spot, like a kid who needs a wee.

'Wait, what?' Maxi replies. 'Where and how have you done this?'

'Have you been talking to pirates?' Mike asks him. 'Have you been on your fake edibles again?'

'I took the boat to the resort,' Clarky explains, ignoring Mike's teasing. 'They had this place where you can book activities and trips and they all sounded dull as hell – apart from this.'

'Wait, so what are we doing?' I ask, confused.

'A boat is coming to pick us up,' he says, as though he were talking to an idiot, annoyed to be having to explain it again. 'It's going to take us a nearby private island. This island is untouched by man, as natural as they come, making it the perfect place to relax with that picnic Maxi was on about, but it's a good compromise because I get to feel like I'm going somewhere, seeing somewhere new. It's a win-win situation.'

I glance around at my friends' faces and they all seem pleasantly surprised by Clarky's effort to compromise with an activity that would please everyone. Well, who wouldn't want to spend an afternoon on a deserted island?

'I suppose a place like that would be the ultimate way to switch off from the real world for a bit,' I reason.

'Yeah, that actually sounds pretty cool, Clarky,' Cam adds.

'Nice one, mate,' Mike replies. 'Go on then, let's do it.'

'Okay, sick,' Clarky says. 'I'll go tell Drea it's on, but you all need to go get ready now. Grab your things, the boat will be here soon.'

I glance at Cam.

'We'd better get a move on then,' he says through a bemused laugh.

'Yeah, okay, this is exciting,' Maxi says.

DJ gets up and pats Clarky on the back.

'Good work, pal,' DJ tells him. 'You're a good kid really.'

'I'm older than you, big shot,' Clarky happily admits while Drea isn't around. 'Right, let's go go go.'

'I'll go tell the kitchen to knock us a picnic together,' Maxi says giddily. 'Jas, meet me in my room, I have an outfit for you that would be perfect for this.'

'Okay,' I say with a smile. That's incredibly sweet of her. I've missed having a female bestie for things like this. It's not that I don't have friends, but nothing compares to your teenage bestie, does it?

With everyone in agreement that the trip sounds like a fabulous idea, Clarky runs off to tell Drea that 'Mum and Dad said yes'. I can't help but smile at his intense level of excitement. He's like a little kid who's just been told he's going to Disneyland for the first time.

As I head upstairs, I find my imagination running away with me. A private island, untouched by man, nature at its most perfect. Just me and my friends – me and Cam. Perhaps the two of us can find a space alone to chat. My old feelings are creeping back, but I need to sound him out before I get carried away. A secluded island seems like the perfect place to talk – well, it doesn't sound like there will be much else to do there.

Clarky is right, this may not be all that wild, but it definitely feels like an adventure.

I arrive in Maxi's room and wait. I pop into the bathroom briefly, then back to her room, but as I'm about to sit down on the bed I notice one of those soft plastic folders full of papers, splayed out, partly sticking out from under the bed. It looks a little squashed, like it's been stepped on, so I reach down, pull it out, folding it closed, ready to place it on the bedside table but before I can let go of it a few keywords catch my eye. I gasp.

'Ooh, what's that?' Maxi asks excitedly. 'No one ever gasped like that at something that wasn't interesting.'

She skips over and takes it from me.

'It's divorce papers,' I tell her.

Maxi cocks her head.

'Jas, are you getting divorced?' she asks me, her eyes wide.

'No,' I quickly insist. 'I've never even been married.'

Maxi can't resist flicking through the pages, having a nosy at what's inside.

'Oh, my goodness,' she blurts. 'They're Cam's. He must've left them in here, before we swapped rooms. Where did you say you found them?'

'Sticking out from under the bed,' I tell her.

'Oh, the poor love,' she replies. 'He must be embarrassed. He hasn't said anything, so I don't think he's realised that he left them here yet. I can sneak into my old room, plant there somewhere – somewhere obvious, so that he doesn't realise he left them behind. Oh, poor Cam. He needn't feel so embarrassed, we're his oldest friends, if he can't tell us...'

I'm speechless but my thoughts are racing.

Maxi places the papers in a drawer.

'Maybe you can keep him talking, when we get back, while I sneak them into his room,' she suggests.

'Yeah, good thinking,' I reply, finding my voice again. 'I'll just go grab my sandals.'

I make my excuses to head into my own room, via our shared bathroom, to give myself a bit of space. I don't want Maxi to see that this has rattled me but of course it has. Look, I don't care if Cam is divorced or getting divorced or whatever – we're in our thirties, lots of people are married already, at this stage it's getting less and less likely that if I do ever marry someone they won't have at least been in one long-term relationship, who cares? What I care about is that he lied to me about it. He lied in front of the group, which I get, but then he lied again to my face. Maybe I'm a hypocrite, because I pretended I still had my job, but that's different. That doesn't affect him. Cam and I have history, we almost got together once, and he wasn't completely honest with me then either, something about him not being honest about his marriage makes me feel uncomfortable. I'm not dragging up those old memories today, though, I'm supposed to be on holiday.

I force myself to shake it off. Cam doesn't have to tell me

anything about his love life, he owes me nothing, but if I'm taking anything away from this it is that perhaps he and I have always had bad timing for a reason. He's still technically married and for some reason he's not being honest about it. Nothing is meant to happen between us. At least now I can let it go, before I ever really picked it up again.

It's just such a shame...

11

I'm not saying that I don't want to trust Clarky, it's just difficult to trust him, when I have so many negative experiences to draw on. He's always been a bit of a wild card, not really thinking things through, acting on impulse, getting us into all kinds of difficult situations. Whether it's accidentally letting Mike's first car drive itself into a lake or that disastrous summer camping trip he arranged for us all. Even with the best intentions, Clarky rarely gets it right.

But today, dare I say it, I am pleasantly surprised.

As I approached the island dock, I would be lying if I said I wasn't shocked to see a real boat waiting for us. Well, it could've been anything from a dinghy to a bunch of logs tied together with vines, but it wasn't, it was a real boat – a big one, the kind that looked like it could survive any weather conditions Mother Nature threw at it.

We all took seats on the big, open deck, on delightfully comfortable sofas, popping the cork on one of the bottles of champagne Maxi had brought with our picnic.

The journey was lovely but this trip isn't about the journey, it's all about the destination, and – once again – I can't believe I'm saying this, but Clarky has delivered.

It's been heaven sitting on this deserted beach, the warm sun on my skin, making me feel alive. The sand beneath my feet feels so soft and powdery, shifting with each gentle breeze that blows across the shoreline. The soothing lullaby of the waves crashing against the shore echoes in my ears.

The water in front of me is a vivid blue-green. As I gaze out at the endless expanse of water, the horizon stretching out infinitely in front of me, I feel a sense of calm wash over me like a big wave.

The breeze picks up now and then, sending my hair flying in all directions. It feels cool against my skin, as if it's blasting away all my worries and stress. I close my eyes and inhale the salty air, enjoying the sun's warmth on my face.

We've felt like the only people in the world, let alone on this island, for the entire time we've been here, and it's a feeling I've been strangely enjoying. It's as if all of my problems have been left behind, allowing me to enjoy a day of peace and solitude.

'I've just realised what this place reminds me of,' DJ announces, briefly pausing to burp as the bubbles from his champagne catch up with him. '*Lost*.'

'*Lost*?' I reply. 'Wait, the TV show *Lost*?'

'That's the one,' he says with a laugh. 'I know it's not exactly the same – obviously the climate, the geography and so on are different.'

'Obviously,' Clarky teases, mocking his voice. 'Neeerd.'

'I know what you mean,' I say, coming to DJ's defence. 'I think it's because we're here on the beach, on the sand, a whole island behind us – containing God knows what.'

DJ makes a noise like the Smoke Monster, even if I'm the only person getting his references.

'What's *Lost*?' Drea asks.

'It's a bit like a dramatised *Naked and Afraid*,' Clarky tells her – I'm not sure that's right. 'You know *Naked and Afraid*, don't you?'

'Erm...'

'You saw me watching it once,' he continues. 'The one where there's a naked man and a naked woman...'

'So far that sounds like everything you watch,' Mike jokes.

'There's a naked man and a naked woman,' Clarky continues, ignoring him. 'And they drop them off in, like, Botswana, or somewhere like that, and they have to survive together with nothing but what they find wherever they are. But it's always people with, like, mad survival skills.'

'That sounds really hard,' Maxi joins in.

'It is,' Clarky replies, with a seriousness not usually afforded to what sounds like a reality TV show. 'People get dysentery. Basically, they determine your PSR score, when you start – your primitive survival rating – and then they reassess it after your time. I reckon my starting score is about an eight.'

'Out of a hundred?' Mike asks.

'Out of ten, obviously,' he corrects him. 'Big shot, go easy on the food.'

DJ freezes, a ham and mozzarella sandwich hovering in front of his face.

'I'm still hungry,' DJ tells him. 'If that's okay with you.'

Clarky frowns.

We're on a secluded beach, in a cove, on stunning sands with beautiful blue ocean out in front of us, and trees behind us that lead up to the rocky hills that surround us. Despite feeling like we're in our own little nook of beach, the sea breeze still finds a way to dance past us. It's perfection.

'I'm just saying, there's no toilet,' Clarky continues.

Okay, so it's not quite perfect, but it's close.

'I can wait for the boat back to the villa,' DJ tells him. 'Or to go in the sea.'

'Oh my gosh, shall we go in the sea?' Maxi suggests excitably.

'That's not what I meant,' DJ says with a laugh. 'But I could go for a dip.'

'Me too,' I reply.

'Let's do it,' Maxi says. 'All of us.'

Drea waves her hands and taps her ear, lying back on the sand to take in more sun.

'The rest of us then,' Maxi concludes.

Maxi lent me a long, floaty, see-through bodysuit to wear over my bikini. It's barely there, with splits up the side, but it looks so elegant. I take it off and fold it carefully, placing it on a rock to keep it clean and dry.

Maxi is the first one to charge off towards the water, running into it until it's up to her chest. Then she starts swimming.

'Wait for me,' DJ says, hot on her heels.

'I suppose I should keep an eye on you,' Cam says with a smile as he catches me up. 'You know, just in case you get into difficulty again, or float off.'

'I'm pretty sure I'll be fine in the shallow of the shore,' I say, rather flatly, but with a bit of a smile.

Cam picks up on my attitude right away.

'Oh, yeah, no, I was just joking,' he babbles.

I stare at him awkwardly for a second or two. To be honest, since I found his divorce papers earlier, I've been avoiding him all day. There's no way he hasn't noticed.

'Last one in the water is a loser,' Mike bellows.

Before I know it, he's grabbing me, wrapping his arms around my hips, lifting me high, charging into the water with me.

I can't help but scream with delight. He takes me by surprise, it's a real rush. Eventually, the two of us crash into the salty water.

'Oh my God, Mike,' I squeak.

He takes me by the hands and pulls me out into the water, away from everyone.

'You looked like you needed saving,' he tells me. 'Not from the water, from Cam.'

'Thanks,' I say with a smile. 'We were just having a bit of an awkward moment.'

'Well, at least you know things could never be awkward with me,' he points out. 'We've got too much history.'

He's right, you would think him being my ex would make things awkward, but I'm actually finding him really easy to be around. To be honest, I didn't really fancy him when I was at school. Don't get me wrong, he was cute, but I was young, I didn't really know what I wanted, the most popular boy in our group – if not the whole year – asked me out. Saying yes felt like the thing to say, but there was never any spark with him. He was definitely the kind of boy girls fancy, but he never really felt like my type. He's more my type now, to be honest – on paper, at least.

The water feels so cool and refreshing, and I can feel all my worries practically melting away.

'Do you reckon we could do the lift?' Mike asks me.

'The lift?' I repeat back to him.

'Come on, *the* lift,' he says again. 'From *Dirty Dancing*.'

I snort. 'Those biceps may be big, but I don't fancy my chances,' I tell him.

'You don't think I'm strong enough?' he asks playfully.

'Oh, no, you look plenty strong enough,' I reply. 'I don't think my core is strong enough, to hold myself that straight. I'd fold over you like... like a... trouser press.'

'Don't say things like that around Drea,' he whispers. 'You'll make yourself seem old.'

'I *am* old,' I reply. 'At least in her eyes.'

'It makes sense, though, that Clarky would go for someone with his mental age,' Mike says. 'Although I'm not sure what she's doing with him. Now, come on, let me lift you.'

'Are you serious?' I ask. 'Can I get you to sign some kind of disclaimer that says you won't sue me if I damage you?'

'You have my word,' he promises me. 'Come on.'

'On your head be it,' I reply.

'On my *hands*,' he corrects me jokily. 'Here we go...'

Mike lifts me up for and for a moment I feel like a ballerina. It is only a moment, though, because – while he can lift me – I can't quite hold the position for very long. I quite literally fold into his arms, but he catches me.

'Go on, Magic Mike,' Maxi calls out. 'You two are looking like the good old days.'

Mike pulls me in close, I wonder what he's doing, until he whispers in my ear.

'I could say the same about those two,' he says quietly. 'They're looking close, aren't they?'

'I've noticed that,' I reply.

Something else catches my eye. Cam, looking over, trying not to seem like he's looking, but the side-eye is definitely there. He's probably wondering what's going on between us, and why I've suddenly gone so quiet on him, but as annoyed as I am, the last thing I want to do is embarrass him by bringing it up. It's none of my business, is it? If he wanted to tell me, he would have.

I climb up on Mike's shoulders and Maxi gets on DJ's, then we wrestle, to see who can knock the other person off first. Mike must be a stronger base than DJ because we are victorious. Clarky asks to play the winner but Drea isn't interested and Cam refuses to let him on his shoulders, so Clarky gets out of the water and goes to hang out on the sand with Drea – not that she's much conversation. A few of us have brought our cameras with us – the ones

Maxi gave us as invitations to this holiday. I notice Cam taking photos of the scenery, capturing the memories. Once again, credit to Clarky, this really is a wonderful, beautiful, totally unique experience.

All at once, the weather turns much cooler and the sun seems to dim.

'Do you know what, I have no idea what time it is,' Maxi says. 'And do you know what else? I love it.'

'Yeah, it's oddly liberating, not knowing,' I add. 'It's getting chilly, though.'

Clarky, who reckons he has a PSR (or whatever it was called) of eight out of ten, starts a fire... with a lighter. He piles up sticks, surrounds them with stones, drops on some dry grass and then lights it. It's actually quite impressive that he gets it going – until he holds the lighter in place for too long, feels the heat on his skin, and drops the lighter into the flames.

'We should stand back for a moment,' Clarky tells us seriously. 'That thing is going to blow.'

'Your PSR is going down for that,' Mike teases him.

I glance across the fire – from a safe distance – to where Cam is sitting, and he gives me a half-smile. I smile back. I'm being a baby, I'm just hurt because I let myself get carried away and I started imagining this whole future for us, without stopping to consider the fact that I don't really know him, not any more. I think it's just seeing him after all these years, being around our old friends, old habits dying hard, my overactive imagination – I need to forget about all that. But we can be friends, though, just like we've always been. I'll grow up and start acting normally around him again.

Once the lighter has popped, we all take our seats around the fire.

'This really is unbelievably cool,' Cam says as he watches the fire crackle and pop – in the normal way. 'Thanks for setting this up, Clarky.'

'Yeah, this was seriously cool of you, bro,' DJ adds.

I can't help but feel grateful for this truly wonderful and unique moment as we sit around the fire, chatting and laughing together. There's no drama, fighting, or tension to worry about. Just a group of friends, on a beautiful beach enjoying each other's company on a holiday that none of us thought would ever happen.

As the sun begins to set, we all gather around the fire to watch the sky turn orange, then pink, then it starts to get dull. When the natural light show is over, my other senses feel extra-sensitive. It's like the volume has been turned up. The sound of the waves, the crackling of the fire – it all soothes me into a state of complete and utter relaxation.

'Honestly, Clarky, thank you,' Maxi says. 'This has been unreal and I'm absolutely stuffed – all the food we brought is gone – I'm not sure I could eat dinner tonight.'

'Maybe dessert,' I joke. 'I always have a place for dessert.'

'Oh, me too,' she says with a smile. 'What time is the boat coming back for us?'

'Erm, four, I think,' Clarky says, scratching his chin thoughtfully.

Maxi thinks for a moment.

'It's way past four,' she points out, her voice wobbling slightly.

Clarky picks up a stick and pokes at his fire.

'Not this four,' he says quietly.

'What?' Mike asks, raising his voice.

'Not this four,' Clarky says again, loudly and clearly this time.

'Do not tell me the boat isn't coming until four a.m.,' I say.

'Don't be stupid,' he replies. 'Four p.m. Four p.m. in a few days.'

'Excuse me?' DJ says. He pulls himself to his feet and walks over to Clarky. 'What did you say?'

Clarky exhales deeply as he stands up.

'Okay, listen, I haven't been totally upfront with you about this trip,' he starts.

I almost don't need to hear another word. This is Clarky. This is what Clarky does. This isn't going to be good.

'This isn't the relaxing day boat trip to a private, untouched island that I pitched to you earlier,' he continues calmly. 'This is a shipwreck experience.'

'What does that mean?' Maxi asks.

'It basically means we're stranded here,' Clarky explains as a grin creeps its way across his face. 'We have to survive on this island for the next few days, until they come to rescue us.'

Panic surges through my body. I know Clarky, and he does love to play practical jokes, he's a total wind-up merchant, but that's not what this is. I can just tell from the look on his face that this is 100 per cent real. And yet I just can't quite allow myself to believe that even Clarky – and a version of Clarky in his thirties, no less – would do something so stupid without telling anyone. I must be wrong. He must be kidding around.

'Oh, tell me you're joking,' Maxi says, her voice trembling.

Clarky shakes his head.

'Is this *Naked and A-fucking-fraid*?' Mike asks angrily.

'Well, we're not naked,' Clarky replies. 'But kind of, yeah.'

'Whoa, whoa, what the hell is a shipwreck experience?' Maxi asks, panic building in her voice.

'So, we're here, on this totally natural, untouched island,' Clarky explains. 'And we basically get to live out the fantasy that we're shipwrecked here. So, really, DJ was right, when he said it was like *Lost*. We need to build shelters, find food and save water – we get to live off the land, come on, it's going to be fun!'

I hurry to my feet and check our supplies.

'We have a bag of biscuits and four cans of Lemonsoda left,' I announce. 'And that's it. Clarky, you're pranking us, right?'

'Squad, come on, it's an adventure,' he insists. 'This is our chance to prove what we're made of.'

'I'm made of fear and anxiety and a love of sleeping indoors in a bed,' I point out, unable to hide my frustration.

'Yeah, I'm not doing this,' Cam says, taking his phone from his bag. He holds it normally, then up high above his head, then he turns around. 'There's no signal.'

'Obviously,' Clarky says. 'We're shipwrecked.'

'Will you stop bloody saying that,' Maxi insists.

'It's true,' he says with a nervous laugh.

'Did you know about this?' Cam asks Drea.

She stares at him for a second before tapping the AirPod in her ear, so she can hear.

'Huh?' she says.

'Did you know about this shipwreck experience?' Cam asks again.

'Yeah, whatever,' she replies. 'I'm just happy listening to my music, ta.'

'You don't have a problem with this?' Maxi asks her.

Drea shrugs and taps her ear again.

'Teenagers,' Mike jokes, trying to lighten the mood.

DJ starts looking around on the floor. Eventually, he finds a pile of stones which he starts arranging on the floor. He's made an S in no time.

'Is that going to be an SOS?' Clarky asks.

'No, it's going to be a "sorry we murdered our friend but he's a wanker",' DJ replies, before snapping: 'Of course it's going to be an SOS.'

'You've nailed the S,' Clarky says, impressed, nodding his head and clapping his hands. 'But it's a waste of time. Everyone knows this island is a shipwreck experience, so they won't pay any attention to any distress signals. So, yeah, a great job, but ultimately pointless – conserve your energy.'

Maxi looks like she's about to faint. She walks over to the sea and slumps down on the floor dramatically.

'I just cannot believe this is happening to me,' she says, sinking to the sand. 'I refuse to believe this is happening to me. This is some sort of sick joke. The boat *is* coming. I'm just going to sit here and wait, it will be here any minute. This is just a sick joke.'

I glance over at Clarky. He just shakes his head.

'Can we kill him?' Mike asks, sounding completely serious, but we know he's joking.

Clarky laughs.

Is there a chance Clarky is playing some kind of elaborate, unfunny practical joke on us or is this for real? And if it is real, how are we going to survive for several days – and nights – on this island without any food, water or shelter?

I walk over to Maxi and sit down next to her, wrapping an arm around her. Bless her, she's shaking – probably a combination of cold and scared.

'He's joking, isn't he, Jas?' she says. 'Tell me he's joking.'

DJ sits down on the other side of her and wraps an arm around.

'DJ, tell me he's joking,' she says to him. 'Surely we'll all die on this island if he isn't.'

'Clarky reckons he's a survivalist,' DJ says with a roll of his eyes, trying to lighten the mood.

'He's a wanker,' Maxi insists.

She's not wrong.

'Listen, I know this is going to sound silly,' she says, lowering her voice, glancing around to make sure no one else is listening. 'I saw a psychic, a few months ago, and I know, take everything they say with a pinch of salt, but she said she could see me waiting for something at the edge of a large body of water – she didn't know what I was waiting for, but she said it was important.'

'She probably looked you up online,' DJ reasons. 'That's what they do. She probably saw that you travelled a lot.'

'Hmm, maybe,' she replies. 'But she also told me that, if I hear drums, I'm in serious danger. Any time I hear any sort of noise, for a split second, I'm paranoid it's drums, that this is the end.'

'Psychics say all kinds of things,' I tell her. 'Not all of it is right, or as literal as they make it sound.'

I don't want to tell Maxi what to think, or what to believe, but going down this path is only going to scare her stupid.

I rub Maxi to try to warm her up and calm her down. I guess we'll just sit here for a bit, see if the boat turns up – and I'm really hoping and praying that the boat turns up tonight. If it doesn't, well, we'll cross that bridge when we come to it.

12

THEN – 2 AUGUST 2006

For some reason, I always know that when Clarky is in charge of making the plans, not only are we going to be doing something I don't enjoy, but it's probably going to go horribly wrong. Clarky's problem is that he acts first, thinks later. By the time his brain has caught up with his actions, it's too late to do anything about it, and he's either too stubborn to admit when he's wrong, or he always believes he is right.

I suppose we were thrown together as a friendship group, because we all wound up on the bus together, meaning we might not be friends if we had met in any other circumstances. But we are friends now, there's no turning back, so we have to take it in turns at deciding what we do for fun, so that everyone is happy.

Today it's Clarky's turn to decide what we're doing for fun, and Clarky has decided that we should go camping in a local beauty spot. I've never been camping before, it's never really appealed to me, so I can't say I've been looking forward to it, but now that we're here, I'm even less enthusiastic.

We're in one of the woods, near where we live, and although not officially a camping spot, Clarky seems to be firmly of the opinion that teenagers are allowed to camp wherever they want. I am humouring him with extreme caution, as I always do, until Clarky being Clarky pushes it too far.

It's beautiful here. As we walk with our things, we're surrounded by towering trees that provide a natural canopy overhead. The sunlight filters through the branches, dappling the ground with patches of light and shade. A gentle breeze rustles through the leaves, carrying the scent of the trees and the earth. It's so relaxing – for a walk, at least.

But then we arrive at our destination.

The clearing in the woods where we're actually camping is not so beautiful or relaxing. The trees are so tall and thick that they block out all but the faintest slivers of light, leaving us in a perpetual twilight that's about as eerie as it is depressing.

'Piss off, Clarky!' Mikey exclaims at the sight of our digs for the night.

'What?' Clarky replies innocently.

'You couldn't have picked a worse spot,' Mikey replies. 'The ground is uneven, covered in sharp rocks and tangled roots – never mind all the broken glass and litter. It's going to be impossible to find a comfortable spot to set up our tents.'

'It has to be here,' Clarky insists, his hands firmly on his hips, showing us he means business. 'This is the only bit that isn't patrolled.'

'How do you know that?' DJ replies.

'Because it's where the cool kids come to smoke and drink,' Clarky explains. 'And they're never bothered here.'

'Incredible,' I blurt. 'You've taken us for a camping trip at our local antisocial teenager spot.'

'*We* should be antisocial teenagers,' he insists excitedly. 'You're all so boring sometimes. And, look, it's the anniversary of my parents' divorce, so the last place I want to be is at home.'

I feel sorry for him, and mentally remind myself, as I so often have to, that we are the only friends Clarky has. What hope does he have, if we abandon him?

I stroll away for a minute, taking in our surroundings, only having to walk for a few seconds before I find a stream. It's hardly the clear, babbling brook we were expecting. It's choked with empty plastic cider bottles and crisp packets and stagnant pools of water – now I know where the awful smell is coming from.

'Hi,' Cam says, making me jump, not intending to sneak up behind me, but the atmosphere here has me on edge.

I exhale deeply.

'Hi,' I reply. 'So this is awful.'

'It is,' he replies. 'But I'll stick it out for a bit if you do.'

I smile. I'd probably hang out with Cam anywhere.

'Deal,' I reply. 'I don't think camping is for me.'

'I agree,' he replies. 'But I'd love to do it properly. I would travel to somewhere beautiful, somewhere I'd never been, fully stocked with everything I needed. Doesn't that sound like a cool way to see the world?'

I stifle a sigh at just how dreamy I found all of that.

'It really does,' I agree.

'Maybe one day we—'

'What are you two whispering about?' Mikey interrupts.

'We're just planning our escape route,' Cam jokes.

'Only Clarky would bring us camping to a shithole like this just as the sun is starting to set,' Mikey replies, shaking his head. 'And I hate that we're all relying on him, because none of us know how to camp.'

'Does Clarky actually know?' I ask curiously.

The three of us all glance back over at the group. DJ is struggling to put a tent up while Clarky messes with a campfire. I don't have a good feeling about this at all.

'...and Vicky Stubbs lost her virginity here.'

We just about catch the last part of whatever Clarky is sharing with Maxi and DJ.

'As if,' Maxi replies. 'I can't imagine Vicky here.'

'She did,' Clarky insists as he frantically rubs two sticks together to try to start a fire. 'To Spiller Hardaker.'

Ahh, one of Clarky's idols, the vile Hardaker brothers.

'I doubt it,' I add. 'I've never even seen Vicky talking to Spiller.'

Clarky shrugs. 'Maybe they tell me things because they like me more than they like you,' he reasons.

'They don't even know my name and I'm more than happy with that,' I insist.

'Maybe they tell you things because you're gullible,' Mikey jokes. Then he turns to DJ. 'Are you making that look hard, or is it that difficult?'

'It's that difficult,' DJ says, frustrated, as he throws two tent poles down on the floor.

'We'll be fine, mate, Clarky says he knows how to put a tent up,' Mikey reassures him.

'No, I said I know how to put my tent up,' Clarky replies, almost under his breath.

We all turn to face him, to see that he's abandoned rubbing sticks together to start a fire and is using a plastic lighter instead.

'What?' Mikey replies, his face suddenly so serious.

'I know how to put *my* tent up,' he says again. 'It's probably easier if I just show you.'

Clarky takes his tent out of the bag, only to reveal that it's some sort of pop-up tent, pre-assembled, that just sort of springs into shape.

'Oh, you tosser,' Mikey blurts. 'You know we've all got normal tents, and no idea how to put them up?'

Clarky pulls a face and laughs slightly.

'Gutted,' he jokes.

'You will be when we all go home,' DJ threatens.

'Okay, okay, look, mine is big enough for all of us,' Clarky reasons – it definitely isn't. 'Let's just have something to eat and calm down. I got the fire going.'

Maxi and I glance at each other nervously. By the time I'm looking back over at Clarky, he's pulling tins of baked beans with sausages from his bag. Then, finally, a box of frozen fish fingers – well, formerly frozen fish fingers – and a bottle of salad cream.

'No!' I blurt. 'Sorry, that's just... what is that?'

'My favourite,' he replies proudly. 'I'm going to make it for all of us.'

'Can you even cook fish fingers over a fire?' I ask.

'Generally? Or can *I*?' he replies.

'Both,' Maxi quickly insists.

Clarky shrugs. 'Of course,' he says, although not at all convincingly.

'I'll have some beans,' I reason. 'But I'm fine for fish fingers.'

'Me too,' Maxi insists.

'Okay,' he replies. 'But don't be jealous when you see how good mine looks.'

'Jas, have you got a minute?' Mikey asks me, nodding to one side, for me to follow him.

'What's up?' I ask. 'Well, apart from all of this.'

He laughs.

'I was just wondering if you wanted to go for a walk with me, back towards the village, to the shop?' he suggests. 'We could ditch this lot, grab some real food – we don't even have to come back, we could go do something else, something normal.'

'Come on, we can't abandon the others now,' I tell him with an encouraging nudge. 'If anyone can do this, you can. You're outdoorsy.'

'No, I'm sportsy,' he insists. 'There's a difference.'

I like that the boys in our group are all different. Mikey is the sporty one – watching, playing, talking about it, anything – whereas DJ is more into watching TV and movies and playing video games. Then we have Cam, who shares DJ's love of TV and movies but also loves reading, writing and drama. And Clarky, well, Clarky is just a thing of his own – a thing I'm currently watching trying to cook soggy fish fingers over a campfire.

Once Clarky has eaten – given that he was the only one who found it appetising – and the day has turned into night, we're all sitting around the campfire, trying to warm ourselves up and forget about how horrible all of this is. Clarky is poking at the fire with a stick – as though he knows what he's doing – while Maxi and DJ are cuddled up together, just inside the tent, looking out over the fire. Mikey is hovering around me, trying to make small talk, and Cam is on the other side of me, not really saying much. I keep trying to think of things to say to him but then I'm distracted by the sound of DJ's voice, and – more specifically – what he's saying.

'Have you guys heard about the two inmates who escaped from the local prison?' he asks, his voice low and creepy.

We all turn to look at him, some of us intrigued, others horrified.

'They were serving life sentences for attacking unsuspecting teenagers – luring them out into the woods and then murdering them in cold blood,' DJ continues, his eyes gleaming with excitement.

A cold chill washes over me – even though I know we don't have a local prison. I look at Maxi, who seems genuinely terrified, so I roll my eyes at her stupid boyfriend.

'DJ, that's ridiculous. There's no way that could be true,' I point out.

DJ just grins at me menacingly.

'Oh, but it is,' he insists. 'And they say that when the moon is full and the stars are bright, you can hear their screams echoing through the woods.'

Maxi gasps and clutches at DJ's arm.

'Stop it, DJ, you're scaring me!' she begs him, but DJ just laughs and leans in closer.

'And you know what the scariest part is? They're still out there, somewhere, waiting for their next victim.'

Clarky snorts. 'Yeah, right. Like anyone would be stupid enough to come out here and camp when there are serial killers on the loose,' he says.

Cam and I exchange glances, both of us in silent agreement that if anyone was going to come out here to camp when serial killers were on the loose, it would be Clarky.

I glance back at Clarky to see a flicker of fear in his eyes.

Maxi really seems to be taking DJ's story seriously. She's pale and sweaty, and she keeps glancing around, as if expecting to see the two escaped inmates lurking in the shadows.

'DJ, Maxi really isn't finding this funny,' I tell him, as I try to ignore the sense of unease that's creeping up my spine. It's just a stupid story, but being here is making it so creepy nonetheless.

DJ looks at Maxi, his expression changing as he realises she is actually terrified, not actually playing it cute.

'Shit, sorry,' he says. 'It's just a—'

DJ is interrupted by the sound of a man – no, two men – laughing. It's distant, but not too far away.

'Can we all just get in the tent and close the door, please?' Maxi insists.

Clarky puts the fire out, plunging us into darkness.

'What did you do that for?' I ask him.

'We don't want to give our position away to the murderers, do we?' he replies, as though that's a perfectly reasonable thing to say.

'There are no murderers,' DJ tells him. 'I was telling a spooky campfire story.'

'Well, someone is out there,' Clarky replies. 'So, come on, in the tent.'

We all hurry inside, Clarky zipping the door closed behind us. I cuddle up to Maxi, using the light from my phone screen to make things a bit less creepy for her, although the dim glow only gives everyone a sort of spooky, shadowy face.

Now that we're all in here, squashed together, it confirms that there is no way on earth we can all sleep in here. We can all just about sit, but that's it.

I'm about to point this out when we hear the voices again, growing louder, cackling with laughter, then the sound of glass smashing.

'Oh my God, we're all going to die,' Maxi sobs quietly.

'Ay-up,' one of the voices says, right outside the tent now.

You can just about make out a hand, on the outside of the tent, as someone reaches for the zip to open the door.

I can't tell you how many of us let out screams – more than just me and Maxi, though – as the door opens, only for Spiller and Tommy Hardaker to be staring in at us. They both laugh wildly to have discovered us all squashed into a dark, dingy tent like this.

'What are you losers doing?' Tommy asks.

Clarky springs to his feet, into action, looking cool once again his number one priority.

'I was just scaring this lot shitless with a ghost story,' he tells them.

'It looks weirder than that,' Spiller points out. 'This spot is for having a laugh, not orgies.'

'We were just going home anyway,' Mikey tells them, pulling himself to his feet, offering me a hand to help me up.

'Dorks,' Clarky jokes. 'Past their bedtime, innit?'

We all grab our things and head off back in the direction of home.

'Let's never go camping with Clarky again,' Cam says as we make our way back through the dark, creepy woods.

'Yeah, if we don't get murdered before we have a chance to make that decision,' Maxi replies.

13

NOW

'This is a nightmare,' sobs Maxi. 'A full-blown nightmare.'

I'm doing my best to calm her down, but I'm concerned too.

'We'll be fine,' I reassure her, trying to sound like I believe it. 'We're strong, we're creative, and we have each other – and, not to sound like a bad feminist, but the boys will take care of us. We'll get through it.'

Now that it's late at night and the boat to take us back to the villa clearly isn't coming, the gravity of our situation has begun to sink in.

We're stranded on a deserted island with no food, no water, no shelter, but even more infuriatingly, Clarky is clearly having the time of his life, laughing and joking and running around like a cheap Bear Grylls.

'This really isn't funny, Clarky,' Maxi says emphatically, her voice trembling with fear and anger. 'We're probably all going to die on this island.'

'In theory, we could die,' Clarky responds, stroking his chin. 'But, trust me, I know what I'm doing.'

'He's seen every season of *Naked and Afraid*,' I joke angrily.

'I *have*,' he replies, sounding pretty pleased with himself. 'I'm ready for this adventure.'

'Mate, stop banging on about adventure, like this is a bit of fun,' Cam tells him. 'You're upsetting people.'

Cam subtly nods towards Maxi.

'But—'

'Okay, let's not panic,' Mike cuts Clarky off, his voice calm and steady – exactly what we need right now. 'First, we need to come up with a plan. We need to think about how we're going to sort shelter, food and water.'

Mike has always been the leader of the group, the one who calls the shots – for better or worse. Today it feels like a good thing.

'Where do we even begin?' DJ asks, frustrated. 'We don't know how big this island is. It's dark – we don't know what's lurking beyond the trees, over the rocks.'

'We've got lemonade and biscuits to get us through the night and into the morning,' I reason. 'We don't need to start venturing deeper into the island tonight.'

'I know what to do,' Clarky says proudly. 'Every good survivalist knows that you can get water from plants that grow near the shore. I bet we could find some, if we search along the beach – I think that's our best bet.'

'That's a fantastic idea, Clarky,' Mike says as he pats him on the back with faux encouragement. 'How about you go do that?'

Mike is clearly trying to get rid of him for a while to give Maxi a chance to calm down, but Clarky chooses to ignore the hint.

'If we work together, we'll have more luck,' Clarky insists. 'We need to try to find some sea purslane. It's a succulent that can live in salty water. We can drink from it to quench our thirst.'

Who knows if Clarky has any idea what he's talking about. He could have fully made that up and I wouldn't have a clue.

'I'll stick with the lemonade, thanks,' I say, pulling a face.

Now that the sun has set and darkness has enveloped the island, everything has changed. There is no escaping the chill in the air now that the temperature has dropped. The warm breeze that was once so comforting during the day now feels cold against my skin. I wrap my arms around myself, wishing I had brought a jacket. We're in the exact same spot as we were earlier, but it's as though everything that felt good about being here has been switched off, as if the entire island is holding its breath.

'It's so cold,' Maxi says. 'So, so cold. Clarky, you tosser, you could have at least told us to pack appropriate clothing.'

'That's not really how shipwrecks work,' Clarky explains.

'*Neither is this*,' Maxi snaps hysterically.

Oh, poor Maxi. I think it's fair to say that none of us – excluding Clarky, the mastermind behind today's activities – is dealing with this all that well, but Maxi is falling to pieces before my eyes. I need to do something.

I gesture away from the group with my head, to tell Clarky to follow me to one side so we can talk – well, that's the best I can think of, as far as getting some privacy goes, without venturing into the trees, or trying to climb over the rocks that surround us.

'Right, come on, there must be a way out of this,' I say quietly when it's just the two of us. 'Just let us go home – you can stay. This is totally your thing, but I don't think the rest of us are cut out for it. There must be some way to, I don't know, tap out?'

Some kind of *something* makes a noise. It must be an animal but I couldn't tell you if it was a bird or a wolf or a bloody Minotaur. Clarky turns an inquisitive ear to the sky, like a dog hearing a squeaky toy. He nods, as if to say he has determined that whatever made the noise is no threat to him, then he turns his attention back to me.

'There really isn't any way to drop out now,' he replies. 'So you may as well enjoy the ride.'

'Okay, but legally speaking, they would be liable if something bad were to happen to us,' I point out. 'They can't just leave us here to fend for ourselves.'

'Don't worry, I signed some paperwork, basically a waiver to say that whatever happened to us, we would take full responsibility for,' he explains.

'Don't worry?' I repeat back to him. 'You think knowing the company who organised this will be in absolutely no trouble if one of us dies is going to stop me worrying?'

Clarky shrugs.

'You're an idiot, do you know that?' I say, my final thought on the subject before I head back to the gang.

Cam looks at me. He raises his eyebrows briefly. I bite my lip and shake my head slightly. A completely silent conversation that says so much. We're stuck here for the foreseeable future and completely screwed.

'Right, okay, listen up,' Clarky shouts with a clap of his hand. 'As our survival coordinator, I'm going to tell you what you need to do to survive – listen to me and you'll be fine.'

Mike scoffs. Clarky ignores him.

'Maxi, good work bringing blankets,' Clarky tells her.

'They were for the picnic, you complete and utter tosser,' she claps back.

'Good work anyway,' he says, shrugging off her insult. 'It's gotten quite late, dark and cold. I've assessed the situation and I believe that we will be safe to sleep on the beach tonight, but tomorrow when it's light we need to go inland, build bunks, sleep on beds raised from the floor – otherwise the insects are going to eat us alive – and we're going to need to find food, and we're going to need to filter water through the soil so we don't get ill.'

'Soil water?' DJ replies. 'Have you lost your mind?'

'*Trust me*,' Clarky insists. 'I know what I'm doing.'

'You don't, mate,' Mike tells him. 'You really don't.'

Clarky ignores him and continues to bark instructions.

'Also it might be a nice idea if each of the guys cuddles a girl tonight,' he adds. 'The girls will feel the cold more than we will.'

'Oh, Clark Clarkson, you're my hero,' I sing sarcastically.

'Honestly, mate, I would kill you, cook you and eat you to stay alive but I'd be too worried it would make me dumber,' Mike tells him.

'Anyway, I'll take Drea,' Clarky concludes.

'God, Maxi, this is just... you can sleep next to me, if you like,' DJ babbles. He sounds stressed, exhausted, and apologetic even though none of this is his fault.

'Thanks,' she replies. 'Honestly, I'm so cold. Is it only going to get worse?'

Clarky stands proudly with his hands on his hips. You can tell he feels like the big man.

'The temperature always drops at night,' he informs us.

Suddenly, it occurs to me, hitting me all of a sudden, giving me a mental jolt: Clarky is sleeping with Drea, DJ is sleeping with Maxi. That just leaves me, Mike and Cam. God, this couldn't feel any more like the old days if we tried. What the hell am I supposed to do? It's like the old, messy love triangle we were trapped in when we were teens only now it's so, so much more awkward, and in such a stressful scenario. Whom do I sleep with? What is the least uncomfortable option for everyone? Perhaps I should just ask them to sandwich me between them, I'd certainly be warm then, and, oh, not uncomfortable wishing that a huge tidal wave would come and wash us all out to sea, putting us all out of our misery, no, *not at all.*

Now I'm losing my mind.

'Go on then, I'll be a gent,' Mike says. 'Jas, what do you reckon? I'm always boiling at night. Fill your boots.'

'Thanks,' I reply. 'That would be really helpful.'

Maybe that's the best way to play it, casually, gratefully, like it's a necessity and I'll take what I can get.

'Cam, mate, don't be on your own,' DJ insists, noticing him standing alone, keeping quiet. 'Sleep next to me. We've only got three blankets anyway.'

'I'm sure I'll be fine,' Cam insists simply.

'Honestly, mate, we've got to do what we've got to do, it's all good,' DJ persists.

'Come on then,' Clarky insists brightly. 'Let's get in bed, conserve body heat and energy, we've got a big day ahead of us tomorrow.'

Maxi starts crying.

'We're going to die, we're all going to die,' she sobs.

DJ takes her face in his hands and looks into her eyes.

'Listen to me, Max, I'm not going to let that happen, okay?'

Maxi sniffs hard and nods.

Mike takes one of the blankets and clears an area of sand of anything that might be uncomfortable to lie in.

'Here, do you reckon?' he asks me, nodding towards somewhere near the fire, but not too close.

I shrug.

'I guess,' I reply.

Honestly, however awkward you're thinking this is, it's so, so much worse. Mike lies down on the sand, pulling the blanket over him before peeling it back for me to 'get in'.

I smile as I get down and roll onto my side and lie facing away from Mike. He spoons up behind me before covering me with the blanket.

Okay, so I am much warmer, for having someone close, but

Mike and I were teenagers, still in school when we were briefly a couple. We never even really kissed, not properly, we didn't get beyond holding hands, pecks on the lips, and standing hugs. This feels so intimate, so strange.

'And I thought I'd never get you into bed,' he jokes.

I laugh.

'It's just how I imagined it,' I reply playfully.

'The stars twinkling above us, the roaring of the ocean, the beautiful beach,' he says with a sigh. 'If you forget that our friends are only metres away, we don't have enough food or drink, and we're all going to die, it's actually quite romantic.'

My laugh is interrupted by a blood-curdling scream. We both sit up and look around to see Drea freaking out.

'What?' Clarky asks. 'What? What? Is it snakes?'

'Snakes?' Maxi cries. DJ hugs her tightly. 'Oh God...'

Drea – who, up until now, has been listening to music, silently unbothered by everything that is going on – screams.

'My AirPod batteries have died,' Drea wails.

Oh, boy, now we really are in trouble.

14

I wake up with a start, my heart beating hard and fast in my chest. Oh, thank God, it was a nightmare. I dreamt that I was back at school, in one of the classrooms, crying for help because the place was on fire and I couldn't find any of my friends. But it was just a dream. Just a horrible dream.

For a moment I'm disorientated, unsure of where I am, but as I shiver in the cold night air, I remember that I'm stranded on an island. You've almost got to laugh – somehow my nightmare seems less scary than my reality.

I glance at Mike, who is sound asleep beside me. He's sleeping so peacefully and I'm so jealous. How on earth is he doing that?

I glance around. It's hard to see much, beyond Mike, because the fire has gone out. Ah, and even though Clarky had the sense to bring a lighter, he unfortunately didn't possess the required set of skills to not drop it into the fire, destroying our only source of light and heat. Oh, I can't wait until tomorrow, to watch the clown rubbing two sticks together, trying to get a new fire going.

I tell myself that it was my bad dream, the low temperature or the extreme discomfort that woke me up with a start but then I hear it again: a noise from behind the trees. Rustling and, I don't know, some kind of animal noise maybe. I slowly sit up, my eyes scanning the darkness, but there's nothing I can make out. Oh God, what is it? Is it an animal? I wouldn't even know what kind of animals they had and thanks to DJ I can't stop thinking about *Lost*. I'll allow myself to rule out smoke monsters, but boars maybe?

I grab my phone but the battery is flat. Fantastic. But as I'm feeling around in my bag, I find my camera. Perhaps I could sneak over there, stay out here on the beach but use my camera flash to take a picture of what is lurking beyond the trees. At least then we'll know what we're up against and, with a bit of luck, the flash might scare it away.

The thumping in my chest spreads to my ears as I creep across the dark beach, clutching my camera tightly in my sweaty hand. At the minute, my heartbeat and the water lapping against the shore is all I can hear.

I pause but then I hear it again. Grunting. Definitely some kind of boar. Well, Clarky wasn't wrong about this being exciting, because while I do constantly feel like I'm about to die, I'm never quite sure from what. There are so many weird and wonderful options, although knowing my luck it will be something stupid.

As I get closer to the trees, I start to feel uneasy. I know I shouldn't be out here by myself, there can't be anything out there in the shadows that isn't bad news, but I'm here now. I need to stick with the plan.

I can't see anything in front of me, the darkness is practically suffocating. But I keep going, my gaze fixed on the spot where I heard the noise. Someone needs to protect the camp right now, even if it's me. To be honest, I'm as qualified as anyone else here.

As I approach the trees, I raise my camera, ready to use the flash. I know it's dangerous, and stupid, and that it could expose my position to any potential threats. Too scared to get too close, or reveal my exact location, I press my body up against a tree for camouflage and cover, I stick out my arm, my camera held tightly in my hand, and press the shutter.

Flash.

For a split second, the flash illuminates the darkness, then I hear a voice say, 'Shit.'

My heart stops as I realise we might not be completely alone out here.

'What was that?' the voice says again. It's female, familiar – it's Maxi.

Oh, God, she must be going to the toilet behind the trees and here I am, freaking her out and potentially embarrassing her.

I dash back to bed, my feet slipping all over the sand as I run, not wanting to make an already strange situation any more awkward. I drop my camera on top of my bag and lie down next to Mike, tucking in close. He drapes his arm across my body in his sleep, almost like a reflex. I close my eyes tightly, my heartbeat as loud as it can be in my ears, and pretend to be asleep.

It's a sorry state of affairs when you want to go back into your nightmare, isn't it?

15

THEN – 14 FEBRUARY 2008

I'm last to arrive at the park where we often hang out – it's not surprising that I'm the last here, not now that Clarky is away at uni in Leeds – but it's unusual to see Maxi running over to greet me, waving frantically as she bounds over excitedly, cutting me off before I can get to the rest of the gang.

'Jas! Oh, Jas, do I have some juicy gossip for you!' she whispers, her eyes sparkling.

I raise an eyebrow curiously. It must be good, if she's this excited.

'Oh, really?' I reply. 'Go on then.'

It's Valentine's Day today, but, for some reason Maxi and DJ are still choosing to hang out with me, Mikey and Cam after sixth form. They've been together for years – for as long as I can remember, really – but they've not taken their relationship to the next level yet, and I think they're finding it kind of awkward. I'm not surprised. We're that sort of age where some of us are ready for sex and some of us aren't – and even the ones who are ready don't know how to actually initiate doing it for the first time. I know Maxi isn't sure if she's ready, but she says that half the problem is that it's because they have nowhere to do it. She recently confided in me that they had discussed doing it for the first time on our ill-fated camping trip last year, when DJ couldn't get his tent up (no pun intended), and we all know how that ended, so it never happened. But with Maxi's dad being quite old-fashioned and DJ's parents being super-religious, they never get a chance to give it a go, so they're probably here to distract them-selves from it on the most romantic day of the year, or avoid the concept altogether.

'Mikey's going to ask you to be his girlfriend!' she blurts, a full beaming grin finally erupting across her face.

I feel my stomach drop.

'What?' I reply, gobsmacked. 'That's awful. I don't want him to.'

Maxi looks confused.

'Why on earth not?' she replies. 'He's the most popular guy in our year – and, don't tell DJ I said this, but he's so fit!'

'I know, but I don't like him like that,' I explain. 'Wouldn't it ruin our friendship group, if he asked and I said no, or if we gave things a go and they didn't work out? And, anyway, I like someone else.'

I don't say who, but Maxi looks at me as though she knows exactly who I like.

'Ahh. Well, look at it this way, if this someone you like, this mystery person I couldn't even guess the name of,' she continues sarcastically, 'if he liked you the way you liked him, wouldn't he have asked you out by now? And if for some strange reason he was too scared to do so, then don't you think another boy asking you out might be just the push he needed to make him do some-thing about it?'

'In what universe will me saying yes to boy number two make boy number one ask me out?' I reply in disbelief.

'I'm just saying, if he knows someone else is interested, maybe he'll do something about it,' she says. 'But if Ca... I mean boy number one isn't interested, don't you think you should give things a go with Mikey? Your friendship could grow into something so much more, and you've been holding out for someone else all this time – I think you owe it to yourself to give something new a try.'

I sigh. Perhaps Maxi is right. If Cam doesn't want to be more than friends, then maybe I do need to give other boys a chance. They're not exactly knocking my door down – in fact, I can't even believe Mikey is interested, I thought he only saw me as a friend. Do I see him as more than a friend? I'd never really given it any thought, until just now. Maxi is right, he's fit, he's funny, he's definitely one of the coolest boys in our year. I would have to be crazy to turn him down – but the problem is that I'm crazy about Cam. I just wish I could know for sure if he was interested in me or not. Either way, what I need is time to figure this out.

'Whatever you do, don't leave me alone with him,' I insist to Maxi, hooking my arm with hers as we go to join the boys at the swings.

'Okay, whatever you say,' she replies. 'But you know I'm right.'

I nod, feeling a mix of excitement and nerves.

'Yeah, I guess you are,' I reply. 'I just need to think about it.'

'Finally,' Mikey says. 'I was beginning to think you girls were going to run off and leave me to spend my Valentine's Day with these two muppets.'

'In your dreams,' DJ jokes, blowing him a kiss. Cam doesn't say much, though.

'Jas, can I have a word with you?' Mikey asks me. 'In private.'

Wow, he isn't wasting any time in cutting to the chase.

I look to Maxi, my best friend, the one who is going to save me.

'She's all yours,' she replies with a smile.

I subtly widen my eyes at her as she pulls me close for a hug.

'No point overthinking it,' she whispers into my ear.

I feel my heart rate pick up as I follow him in the direction of an old oak tree we sometimes shelter under when it's raining. I appreciate Maxi giving me the heads-up, tipping me off to what Mikey is going to ask me (I don't appreciate her not sticking to her promise of making sure I don't wind up alone with him today, though) but it's still difficult. What am I going to say to him? How am I not going to make this weird?

'Sorry to be odd,' he tells me. 'It's just, I really wanted to talk to you in private, to tell you... well... to tell you that I like you.'

'Aw, I like you too,' I reply. 'I'm so lucky, to have such wonderful friends.'

I swear, this makes Mikey flinch.

'Well, more than that, really,' he continues. 'I really like you, actually. We've been friends for years now and those feelings have only grown. I think you're smart and you're funny and you're fun to be around. I'd love to spend more time with you, just me and you and, I suppose what I'm trying to say is...'

Mikey pauses for a second before shouting to the group over my shoulder.

'Guys!'

I turn around and see that Maxi, DJ and Cam are holding up two pieces of paper – one in each hand – with a large letter drawn in permanent marker on each one. Maxi's say 'B' and 'E'. DJ's say 'M' and 'Y' and Cam's say 'G' and 'F'. BE MY GF. Oh my God, 'Be my girlfriend'.

'So, Jasmine, what do you say?' Mikey asks me. 'Will you be my girlfriend?'

I feel a heavy sinking pain in my stomach.

'Oh my gosh,' I blurt, buying myself some time. 'All of these guys were in on it?'

'Yep, all three of them,' he says. 'Especially Cam, my best buddy. He's been really supportive.'

Oh, so there it is. Cam isn't interested in me, not like that. It hurts – of course it does – but what was I expecting? I think over what Maxi said, about how I need to move on with my life, and give other boys a chance. Maybe Mikey could be the right guy for me? Maybe our friendship will turn into more if I just give it a chance? And, if I say no, what will that do to the group? If I do say no, I need to be damn sure I mean it, and if I do say yes, it needs to be for the right reasons. Not just because I can't have Cam, but because Mikey could be good for me. I already trust him, so that's a good start. I know him well, I know we get on.

'Come on, Jas, don't leave me hanging,' he says almost nervously.

'Okay,' I reply.

'Okay?' he says.

'Yes,' I say, more like I mean it this time.

'She said yes,' he calls out to the rest of our group. 'Oh my God, I was so nervous, asking you, worried you might say no.'

It's nice, seeing him let his cool guard down, it makes me smile.

Mikey leans in and gives me a very brief peck on the lips – my first ever kiss with a boy.

'Let's go join the others then,' he says as he takes me by the hand.

'Okay,' I reply.

Wow, this feels so weird. Not bad weird, just unusual. I've never held hands with a boy before, never kissed a boy before – obviously never had a boyfriend before. I can't believe it's all finally happening. I just need to shake that feeling that I wish it was happening with someone else.

16

NOW

My eyes snap open as I hear a scream. Why do I feel like this is going to happen often while we're on this island?

I allow them a second to adjust to the bright sunshine before I can take in my surroundings.

I realise I'm staring at the back of Mike's head, meaning I've spooned up to him in my sleep. I'm terrible for that when I'm cold, my body gravitates towards the warm person next to me, it's just usually whenever I've shared a bed with someone it's been in the usual way – and in an actual bed, for that matter.

I feel Mike's body tense up as he hears the scream. We both hurry to our feet, heading in the direction of the commotion.

'Shit,' Clarky shouts. 'Shit!'

'Mate, what's wrong?' Cam asks, pacing back and forth with him, trying to put a calming hand on his shoulder.

I notice Maxi, sitting on her blanket, hugging her knees. She doesn't look good at all, like she's hardly slept a wink. DJ is standing next to her.

'Clarky, what's wrong?' I ask him calmly.

'It's Drea,' he says. 'She's vanished. I woke up and she was gone.'

'Gone where?' Mike asks.

'I don't know, do I?' Clarky replies. 'She's disappeared.'

Clarky drops to the floor, examining the sand. More than sounding panicked, he seems to be more excited about the opportunity to flaunt more of his dodgy survivalist skills.

'No signs of her being dragged,' he confirms. Then he thinks. 'Unless she was carried away. Pirates?'

I roll my eyes as he wonders out loud.

'Clarky, we're in Italy, they're not exactly known for their pirate population, are they?' Mike reasons. 'Maybe she's gone to the toilet.'

'Drea?' Clarky shouts out. 'Drea!'

His voice gets more hysterical, but she doesn't call back.

'We need to form a search,' he concludes.

Just when you think things can't get any worse – it's almost as though a shipwreck experience is not a very good idea. Funny that.

It's strange, because even though the sun is shining and the weather is warm again, the island doesn't have the same sparkle it did yesterday, it feels creepy, empty, dangerous.

'Wh-what's that?' DJ blurts.

'What?' Maxi replies, panicked.

'My S, the one I made from stones in the sand,' he continues as he approaches it. 'It... oh my God. It says DJ now. Who did that? That's not funny.'

'That really isn't funny,' Cam says as we all hurry over there.

'Why would someone write my name?' DJ asks, completely freaked out. 'Wait a second...'

As we all approach the arrangement of stones, we realise that, just beyond them, further along on the sand, there's a longer message.

The fire was my fault

'The fire?' DJ says. 'What fire? The... wait...'

Oh, God. Ohhhh, no. Who has opened that can of worms? And why?

'The fire at my house?' DJ asks as he turns to us all. 'Someone else started it?'

'Okay, I think we all just need to calm down for a second,' I reason, but DJ is incensed.

'How can I calm down?' DJ replies. 'It's obvious what's going on here. This situation has got to someone, it's made them crack, brought out their guilty conscience. Someone knows I didn't start that fire – I never understood how I caused it, I put the fire I started out. There was no way it could've started again. I knew it. I knew it. Come on then, who started that fire? Who ruined my life?'

'This is obviously someone's idea of a practical joke,' I point out, unable to resist a side glance at Clarky.

He frowns at me.

DJ's parents were away at their caravan, the day we got our A level results, so DJ decided to throw a house party. His parents' house was so cool, the perfect place for a party. Next to the main house they had a sort of granny flat. Downstairs there was a large double garage and his dad's workshop and upstairs there was DJ's bedroom, a bathroom, and a living room with a kitchen. Thankfully, it was next to the main house, but not joined on, or the entire house might have been destroyed too.

There was so much going on that night, but DJ had one goal, one thing motivating him to throw the party, and it wasn't to celebrate his As, it was so that he and Maxi could finally have sex for the first time. Well, isn't that why every teenager throws a house party?

The official story was that DJ lit a candle, trying to make things romantic, but then knocked it over and caught one of his curtains on fire. He says it was nothing, that he put it out, but Maxi being Maxi took this as a sign that they shouldn't have sex and ran off. DJ ran after her. Next thing we all knew, the place was on fire and we were all running for our lives. DJ assumed the fire he caused had restarted somehow, but now it's seeming like that's not what happened. Someone else started it.

'Right, I need to know where everyone was, when the fire broke out,' DJ insists.

'Come on, mate,' Mike tells him, reaching out to comfort him, but DJ slaps his hand away.

'Where were you, huh?' he asks him.

Mike laughs awkwardly. 'I don't know, it was a party, I'd been drinking,' he replies.

'What about you?' he asks Clarky. 'Or you, Cam? Jas, where were you?'

'I don't know,' I tell him, although that's not strictly true. Well, it's not true at all.

'Someone here ruined my life,' DJ says again.

'Okay, listen, we all need to calm down,' Maxi says, trying to be more like her usual self, but her voice still wobbling.

'It didn't ruin your life, though, did it?' Clarky chimes in.

Oh, God, Clarky, not now.

'Leave it, Clarky,' Cam tells him, reading my mind.

'Of course it did,' DJ replies. 'What are you talking about? I lost my girlfriend, I lost my friends because I wasn't allowed to see any of you any more – I was grounded indefinitely, at eighteen, do you know how mortifying that is?'

'No one can ground you at eighteen,' Clarky reasons.

'I burned half my parents' house down – at least I thought I had – I did whatever they wanted,' DJ replies. 'They sent me to Catholic uni, for crying out loud. I lost everyone I knew, everything I'd worked for, I didn't get to go to the uni I wanted. My life changed in every way it could.'

DJ's parents were very religious so it made sense that, when they thought he'd caused a fire by throwing an out-of-control party behind their backs, they decided he needed some religious direction in his life to get him back on the straight and narrow. They made him go to one of his backup universities – a Catholic university, on the edge of a town on the outskirts of Leeds, miles from the city centre. I think they thought he would spend time in the chapel, miles away from anything fun, not really considering that it was a university like any other. More than anything, though, I think they just wanted to keep him away from us, from Maxi. If ever there was ammunition for parents to be able to warn their children about the very real dangers of sex then, boy, was that it.

'Right, a uni where you met your business partner, or whatever,' Clarky points out. 'Who you made a packet with. So why are you complaining?'

DJ sits down on the floor and places his head in his hands.

The sun is beating down on us, I can feel sweat forming on my brow – I never thought I would miss the chilly weather we had last night, but it suddenly feels like keeping warm is always a lot easier than staying cool. I wonder how much sun cream we have, how long it will be before the hunger and thirst gets too much...

'Jas, can I have a word?' Cam says.

I nod, happy to be snapped from my thoughts.

'I'll be in the sea,' Maxi says dramatically.

She strides into the water, like something out of a movie, and drops to her knees. She toys with the water, almost menacingly, as though she's trying to cast a spell – hey, if she can part the sea, I'm all for it. I'll do anything to get off this island.

'How was last night?' he asks me once we're alone.

'I don't even know how to answer that,' I say with a bemused laugh. 'Fine, I suppose. About what I expected.'

'It must be awkward,' he says. 'With Mike.'

'Just a bit,' I reply. 'I suppose this would be awkward with anyone.'

'Maybe we can rotate sleeping together,' he suggests. Then he laughs. 'You know what I mean. I don't think I can do another night under the same blanket as Maxi and DJ. It was... odd. I felt like they were, I don't know, snuggling? They weren't still enough for my liking. At one point I had to clear my throat, to remind them I was there.'

'Come on, we all know how much Maxi loves Rupert,' I remind him.

'Oh, no, I know,' he replies. 'But I guess old habits and all that. Anyway, that's not why I called you over here. Look at this.'

I glance down at the picnic basket we brought with us yesterday. There are maybe five or six biscuits in the bottom of the bag, someone has had a good go at them, but the situation with the drink is even worse. All of the Lemonsoda cans are empty, discarded next to the picnic basket.

'Well, that's not good,' I say pointlessly.

'Maybe a biscuit each, if we're lucky, and not a drop to drink,' he replies. 'Honestly, I didn't expect this to go from nought to *Lord of the Flies* so quickly but I think we're going to have a big problem on our hands when the others see this.'

'Maxi really isn't coping, is she?' I say, nodding towards the ocean, where Maxi is doing some kind of bizarre dance. 'And while I'm sure we all would have been absolutely fine with

Clarky's brilliant survival skills, now he's all whipped up about Drea vanishing, I fear he's not going to be as much use as we thought.'

'Which was no use at all,' Cam agrees. 'But at least he was trying, keeping himself busy. What do you think has happened to Drea?'

'I mean, wherever she's gone, she's taken her bag,' I point out. 'Everyone is going mad. DJ is beside himself.'

'What was that message all about?' he asks quietly.

'I think he's right,' I say. 'Someone's guilty conscience got the better of them last night. To him, we're all suspects.'

'Who do you think it is?' Cam asks.

I glance over at our friends.

'Your guess is as good as mine,' I reply.

'What will you say, if he pushes you on where you were?'

I shrug. 'Anything but the truth,' I reply. 'You?'

'Same,' he says. Then he smiles. 'Funny, that we're each other's alibi.'

'Oh yeah, I'm sure certain people here would be thrilled if they knew the truth,' I say with a laugh.

Cam sighs. 'Do we have to go back over there?' he asks.

'Unless you have a better idea,' I tell him. 'Come on.'

Clarky is pacing back and forth across the sand, murmuring to himself. He is understandably rattled by Drea's disappearance, and obviously I feel terrible for him – and concerned for her – but he doesn't seem to realise that he's the reason we're all in this mess.

I pull as much air into my lungs as I possibly can and then blow it all out again. I need to concentrate, to focus on what I can do to help because I can't fall apart too. The problem with Maxi and DJ is that they're so similar, both so in tune with their emotions, both struggling not to wear their heart on their sleeve.

Cam and I, on the other hand, have years of experience when it comes to bottling things up, hiding how we feel for the greater good. And Mike, well, he's always fancied himself as the daddy of the gang. He always tries to do what he can to look after everyone.

I feel like Clarky is being purposefully vague with the timeline but, as far as I can tell, we've got at least another two nights here before the boat will be coming back for us. So that's the best part of three days and two nights. There is no way we'll survive that. If the dehydration doesn't get us, we'll surely kill each other.

I make my way over to Maxi, stopping short of getting in the sea with her. I'm so thirsty, the water looks somehow so unappetising but so tempting to drink – but even I know that you don't drink the salty sea water.

'Maxi, let's have a chat,' I suggest. 'Let's make a plan, just us girls. You know what the boys are like, all charged up, thinking like men. We need to do what we used to do at school and work them like puppets without them realising.'

I smile but she's unresponsive.

I glance back and can't help but notice Mike and Cam walking off to the side, away from DJ. I wonder what they're talking about. Cam is probably filling him in on the situation with the supplies – or lack thereof. My gosh, I never signed up for this. I know Clarky didn't want a relaxing holiday but there's a whole world between relaxing and the single most stressful experience of my potentially short life.

'Hey, Maxi,' I say quietly, wading into the water next to her. 'Are you okay?'

Maxi looks up at me with tears in her eyes.

'I'm not sure how much longer I can take this,' she admits.

I wrap my arm around her and comfort her.

'Life at the minute is not...'

Maxi's voice trails off and her eyes widen.

'What's that?' she asks me. 'Is that... is that drums? Oh my God, is this it? Is this when I die?'

'Hey, hey, calm down,' I insist softly. 'You're just whipped up and paranoid and...'

Bloody hell, now I think I can hear drums.

I glance back at the boys again. Suddenly, they're all scrambling, DJ is springing to his feet, joining Clarky, Cam and Mike. Mike is pointing at the rocks that surround us on three sides.

'What?' I call out.

'We can hear something,' Cam calls back. 'Drums.'

'Oh my God,' Maxi cries as she realises we can all hear it, making it real.

'Hey, come on, it's okay, let's go stand with the boys, they'll keep us safe,' I reassure her, sounding far more confident than I feel.

'Wh-what's that?' Clarky asks, his voice wobbling. 'Oh, shit, someone else *is* here, someone that wants to kill us. They're battle drums, if ever I've heard them.'

'You've never heard battle drums, soft lad,' Mike tells him. 'Come on, calm down.'

Maxi holds me tightly as we stand with the boys. I look to Mike for the answers.

'What I'm going to do is I'm going to climb up the rocks – there's a bit of a pathway – I'm going to peer over the top, and I'm going to see what I can see,' he says.

'Is that a good idea?' Clarky asks.

'I thought you were all for exploring the island,' Cam reminds him.

'Yeah, when I thought it was deserted,' Clarky replies.

'Be careful,' I tell Mike.

He smiles, nods, then heads into the trees. It doesn't take long before we see him, carefully making his way up the rocks, climbing all the way to the top. We watch as he peeps over, then he allows his head to stick up some more. Then, all at once, he climbs up and stands tall at the top.

'Ha-haaa!' we hear him shout. 'Wooo!'

'What is it?' I shout up to him.

'You guys are not going to believe what's up here,' he calls down to us. 'Come on up, you have to see. DJ, Clarky, bring our things. I've found a better spot for us.'

The boys do as instructed, grabbing our belongings, before the four of us excitedly – but carefully – make our way through the trees and up the rocks to join him, to see what Mike can see that's got him so giddy.

My head throbs from the exercise. Am I that unfit or is it a combination of hot sun and me not having anything to drink yet this morning? Hopefully it's the latter, although I'm not sure how we're going to go about getting something clean to drink. I don't much fancy Clarky's soil-purified water.

I don't know what I'm expecting, when I look over the rocks – nothing but trees, mountains, stuff like that. Best-case scenario is that it's a paradise, with a big lush waterfall, beautiful open spaces, and all the fruit trees we could hope to eat from, and drink from, I suppose, if they're the kind you can get juice from – that would be the answer to all our problems.

But as I finally peer over, my jaw drops. Cam and I glance at each other, our eyes wide with amazement, then I look at Mike.

'So, there's that,' he says casually.

'Now we know what happened to Drea then,' Clarky adds – I think he's in shock.

Maxi grabs my arm and squeezes it tightly.

'Tell me you can see that,' she begs. 'Please, God, tell me I'm not hallucinating.'

'If you are then we all are,' I practically laugh.

At the bottom of the rocks there is a sort of forest, not unlike the one on our side, just much bigger. Then, at the other side of the forest... oh my gosh, I still can't believe I'm saying this... at the other side of the forest is what looks like an enormous holiday resort. It isn't drums we can hear, it's music, in the distance.

From up here, I can see a massive hotel complex, multiple swimming pools, beaches – there's even a mini theme park on one side. Right as I'm looking at it, I notice one of those seats that they strap two people into, attached to elasticated ropes, where they fling you up high into the air. My gut response to something like that would usually be to say that's the last thing on earth I would want to do but right now I'd probably go on it just to be able to sit on a chair. If they gave me a bottle of water and pizza, I'd sit on it all day.

'Let's go take a closer look,' Mike says.

'Let's go eat something,' Maxi adds.

DJ exhales deeply.

'Don't think I've forgotten about the fire,' he warns us all. 'But I do really need a drink.'

We share out carrying the items we have, not that we have much, and carefully make our way through the forest – something that would have been scary but now I know that there's a resort at the other end of it, I'm not so worried. Thankfully, we don't have far to go – somehow, I get the feeling the shipwreck experience might be in need of a new location.

'Well, this explains why I got such a good deal on the shipwreck experience,' Clarky moans.

'Oh, who gives a shit,' Maxi replies.

'I'm just saying,' he persists. 'You can't have an authentic shipwreck experience if there's a hotel next to you.'

As we finally arrive at the resort after a brief walk none of us really had the energy for, we realise there are balloons and banners everywhere. Everything looks so clean and new.

'I think it's opening day,' I point out.

'Yep, that will be why it was so cheap then,' Clarky says.

'I do hope you're going to put in a complaint,' I reply sarcastically.

'Oh, absolutely,' he says, not picking up what I'm putting down at all.

'Right, that's it, I'm booking us some rooms,' Maxi says, suddenly seeming like her old self again. There isn't a glimmer of emotion or upset – even her posture is different. 'We exhausted, we're starving, the boat isn't coming back for us until who knows when, and, frankly, some of you stink.'

I'm sure we all stink. The heat, the dry sea water on our skin, sleeping on the sand – I'm even picking sticks from my hair, since our walk through the forest. We definitely need showers.

'We could stay here at least two nights,' Clarky says excitedly.

'I thought you wanted a shipwreck experience,' I remind him.

'No, I wanted a wild holiday,' he replies. 'Look at this place – it's a party resort. Everyone is late teens/early twenties.'

'Oh, just your type then,' Mike jokes.

'Which reminds me, I need to find Drea, she must be here,' Clarky muses. 'Look, it's this or the beach, and we can have some serious fun here. You can still relax, if you want, but I need this, guys. Come on, when in Rome, right?'

'Well, I have no idea where we are,' Maxi replies. 'Certainly not Rome. But civilisation definitely suits me. Let's find reception, book some rooms, and get settled in. And don't worry about the money, it's all on me. Let's just stay here, have some fun, enjoy the facilities, and then we'll take the boat back to the villa. But then I want to relax, Clarky, all of us, deal?'

'Deal,' he says, dancing on the spot like an excitable little boy.

I suppose this is like Disneyland for adults.

'Excuse me,' Cam says politely, flagging down a young woman walking past him. 'Where are we?'

'La Fine del Mondo,' she screams before lifting up her bikini, allowing her boobs to fall out with a big flop.

Cam's eyebrows shoot up. He quickly turns back to us.

'La Fine del Mondo,' he tells us.

'Well, "fine" means "end" and "mondo" is world... The End of the World,' Maxi eventually figures out. 'That's what that means.'

'Sounds... ominous,' DJ replies.

'Oh, who cares, let's go book some rooms,' Maxi replies.

Maxi is right. I know this isn't the holiday we planned but it's only for a few days and it's civilisation. Last night, all of us on the beach, thinking we were stranded, that was the end of the world. This place, this place seems amazing.

But at this point, so long as there's food and beds, who cares?

17

'I always land on my feet,' Clarky thinks out loud as we make our way along the hotel corridor.

Obviously, we don't have any luggage but there was a cheap and cheerful fast fashion shop downstairs – Maxi dubbed it Primarko – where we all stocked up on essentials. Well, sort of. Essentials in that it is essential we wear clothing, but everything was bright, loud, revealing or all of the above. But right now, clothes are clothes. I just want to have a shower, put something clean on and climb into bed.

'Oh, really?' Mike replies with a laugh.

'Yeah, I mean, look at me, bags full of new clothes, strolling through a fancy resort on my way to the biggest suite the place has to offer,' Clarky points out.

'You're not being rewarded,' Maxi corrects him. 'I still very much want to kill you. You're only getting in the suite because this place was fully booked – apart from this fancy suite – so we're sharing it out of necessity. We're lucky it sleeps six, I'm hoping I can avoid you for the rest of the trip, but on the off-chance I can't, that's what the clean clothes are for.'

Maxi scrunches her nose, as though she's caught a bad smell.

Clarky doesn't care. He's just so over the moon to be finally getting the holiday of his dreams.

'I wonder how fancy the suite is,' DJ says, perking up a little.

'Very, I'm hoping,' Maxi replies. 'The girl at reception kept saying the name. I think she said it was the Scambisti Suite. I can't say I know that word, although my Italian is limited. Perhaps they're someone rich and famous in Italy. Ah, here we are.'

Maxi unlocks the door. We all follow her inside. The shutters are closed, making it really dark.

'Oh, fancy,' Clarky says sarcastically.

'I'll find the light switch,' Mike says.

'Honestly, I don't care how fancy it is,' I say, filling the silence while Mike finds the lights. 'I think I could sleep on just about anything right now.'

Right on cue, the lights turn on.

I take in a short, sharp breath. No one else makes a peep. No one moves a muscle.

'What the—'

'Well, thi—'

Mike and Cam blurt over one another after what feels like an eternity of us just staring, trying to make sense of what we're looking at.

The décor is interesting. Everything is red or black – deep, dark colours instead of the natural, Mediterranean villa vibes I've found elsewhere. It's a large room, which you would think should be ideal, except that's one of the problems, it's just one big room with two super-king beds arranged not too far apart. Oh, and the other problem – and I feel silly even mentioning it really – is that this is clearly *some sort of sex dungeon*. Even the voice in my head sounds hysterical.

'Right,' Maxi says calmly. 'I suppose the red flags should've raised when she described it as a room for six very special friends – I thought it was just a language barrier thing but, yes, right.'

'I think you've got a bargain,' DJ jokes. 'There's some serious kit in this room.'

'I don't even know what most of it is,' I blurt.

'Well, this is a spanking bench,' Clarky says, taking a seat on the edge of… something that, had I seen in any other context, I would have assumed was school gym apparatus.

'It's also what you're going to be sleeping on,' Maxi tells him.

'Come on,' he replies with a laugh. Then he realises she's not joking. 'You can't sleep on it, look, this is how you use them.'

Clarky essentially positions himself on all fours on the bench. Mike can't resist grabbing a sparkly paddle from a table of tools and hitting him on the arse with it. No one asks Clarky why he's such an expert on spanking benches – no one wants to know.

'This room does sleep six,' Clarky reminds her.

'It doesn't sleep six,' she corrects him. 'There are two beds, that I imagine are supposed to, erm, host three people in each.'

'Right,' Clarky replies.

'So Jas and I are taking one,' Maxi informs him. 'And I don't imagine more than three of you boys will fit in the other – and you are the one who got us into this mess.'

'We could strap you into that thing,' Cam jokes, nodding towards a large black X-shaped structure standing between the beds, with straps for your arms and legs, essentially pinning you in some kind of kinky star-jump position.

'Or that,' Mike adds. 'We could hang you from there, it might keep you out of trouble.'

He's referring to the harness that hangs above one of the beds.

'My gran has one of these in her care home,' Clarky says, pointing to a red leather chair with a hole in the seat.

'No, she doesn't, buddy,' Cam replies, patting him on the back.

'Even the coffee table is kinky,' Maxi points out. 'Look at that, there's a cage underneath it. Perhaps we could stick Clarky in there?'

'I'll sleep in the bath,' Clarky replies.

He thinks for a moment.

'You know, I know we're not all going to be shagging...' You don't know how relieved I am to have him confirm that. '...but this is actually a really sick room.'

'Sick,' Mike repeats back to him mockingly. 'You'll fit right in here, with your young-person words.'

I can't help but take a peep at the table of tools. There's a large wardrobe behind it which, yep, is full of sex toys and naughty outfits.

'Wow,' I blurt.

'I would be interested to know about their hygiene procedures,' Maxi wonders out loud.

'At least you know we're the first ones to stay in here, if it's opening day,' DJ reasons. 'Not that we're going to be using it,' he quickly adds.

'Oh my God, guys, you've got to see this,' Clarky calls out from the bathroom.

We join him in the large bathroom. The first thing I notice is the group shower, with its multiple heads, kind of like you would find in a locker room. Next I notice the large Jacuzzi bath, for you and five of your closest friends. Finally, I notice Clarky, lying on a sofa that is positioned opposite the toilet. Back at the villa, I had no idea why you would ever need a sofa in the bathroom – here, I feel like I know exactly why.

'I'll sleep on this,' Clarky says happily. 'Best bed in the suite for privacy.'

'I don't think privacy is the aim of the game with that thing,' Mike points out.

'And you'd better hope no one needs the loo in the night,' Cam adds.

Clarky shrugs. Then he lies back and shakes his body around excitedly.

'Guys, I can't thank you enough,' he blurts, unable to hide his joy. 'This is just... the best holiday ever. Exactly what I wanted, just what I needed.'

'It's certainly not what I had in mind,' Maxi replies. 'But, while we're here, might as well make the best of it. Let's all have showers, get dressed, and explore.'

'Separate showers,' I quickly point out.

'Oh, gosh, yes, separate showers,' she adds. 'Sorry, that usually goes without saying. Does anyone mind if I go first?'

'Hey, it's your room,' DJ points out. 'Your S & M suite.'

'And it has everything you could possibly need except toothbrushes and toothpaste,' she points out.

'I'll go get some,' I tell her. 'I noticed a shop down in the lobby that probably sells things like that.'

'You're a star,' she tells me. 'Just charge it to the room.'

'Can I come with you?' Mike asks me.

'Sure,' I reply, grabbing a sarong. 'Back soon, everyone.'

Once we're out in the hallway, with the door firmly closed behind us, Mike exhales deeply.

'Are you okay?' I ask him.

He wipes his mouth with his hand, practically pulling the stress from his jaw, and then relaxes into a smile.

'It's been a night,' he concludes. 'And a morning. To be honest, it's a bit awkward in there, isn't it?'

'Nah, get your feet in the stirrups, relax a little,' I joke. 'Yes, it's incredibly awkward.'

'At least you don't need to sleep with me for warmth now,' he points out as we stroll back towards the lift.

'True, but we still get to share a bedroom, so it's still really odd,' I reply.

Mike laughs as he calls for the lift.

'At least Maxi has calmed down,' he says. 'But you can tell DJ is overthinking things.'

'I'm not surprised,' I reply. 'Hopefully he lets it go. There's not much point dwelling on the past, is there?'

Ha. I say that like I don't spend most of my time dwelling, wondering, worrying, trying to predict the future, having completely imaginary, anticipatory rehearsal arguments with people in my head, just so I'll be ready for the real thing – and the real thing rarely comes, but best to practise, and feel mentally drained like you would after a real argument, right? I really should practise what I preach.

The lift doors ping open. Inside there are two girls and a guy engaging in some sort of three-way kiss. The guy breaks loose, leaving the girls kissing for a moment.

'Are you coming in?' he slurs.

'We'll get the next one,' I tell him.

Mike very kindly reaches inside and presses the button to close the doors. Then he turns to look at me, his eyes wide and his eyebrows raised.

'How old are we?' he asks me.

'Younger than we feel,' I reassure him.

'I get the feeling this resort is aimed at people about a decade younger than us,' he points out. 'What were you doing with your life a decade ago?'

'Erm, let's think,' I say as we get into the next – thankfully empty – lift. 'I was probably doing my postgrad teacher training. Wild times.'

'At least you can answer the question,' he tells me. 'I can't even remember. I sometimes wish I'd gone to uni, instead of getting a job.'

'You did what was right for you,' I remind him. 'Uni isn't for everyone. I think lots of young people think it's going to be a wild time – weren't we all looking at York St John for that very reason? But it's what you make of it. Not everyone parties their way through it. Going there on my own, in the end, probably made me focus more on the work side of things – the real reason you're supposed to go.'

'Well, that's good then,' he replies. 'Imagine trying to do a degree with this lot, with all our shit.'

'Clarky handing over chunks of his student loan if you let him push you down the stairs in the auditorium,' I joke.

'Maxi and DJ planning their wedding instead of writing their dissertation,' Mike adds.

'I'm sure Maxi could write a dissertation on planning a wedding,' I point out. 'I know it sounds like a strange thing to say but she's... really good at her lifestyle. Throwing the best holidays, having the nicest house, being the brightest, most beautiful, confident person in a room.'

'I know what you mean,' he replies. 'It's hard not to feel like the least impressive person at the party, when you're competing with this lot. Even Clarky is head of his department.'

'Someone must be regretting giving him that job,' I laugh. 'Even Drea has done a runner.'

'Maxi is loaded, DJ is loaded, Cam must be loaded too – tell me you're not stinking rich,' Mike begs.

'You're one to talk, heir to your dad's empire,' I tease. 'I am most definitely the least impressive person at the party, to borrow your metaphor.'

'Drea,' Mike says.

'I'd take that victory, if she weren't practically a child,' I reply. 'And I'm probably not doing much better than her, to be hon—'

'No, I mean she's over there, look.' Mike points to a woman pinned against an ornamental pillar, her legs wrapped tightly around a man's waist and their lips locked. 'That is her, right?'

'It can't be,' I say, a second before I stand corrected.

Drea breaks for air and spots us out of the corner of her eye. She's manically excited to see us.

'Oh my God, my friends,' she tells the heavily tattooed man in the tiny pair of swim shorts holding her. 'My friends.'

Drea hops down and runs over to us.

'You guys, oh my God, it's been ages,' she slurs.

'I don't even think it's been half a day,' I tell her, accepting her hug. She's all warm and sweaty – unsurprisingly, really.

'This is, erm...' she thinks. 'Danny?'

She says her new friend's name as more of a question than a statement.

'Dennis,' he corrects her.

'I got the D,' she concludes. Then she snorts at her words. 'Denny is, erm, letting me charge my phone and my AirPods in his room.'

'Ah, nice,' I say. 'Well, we've got a room here.'

'Yeah, I think I'm just gonna hang with Denny,' she says with a casual shrug.

'Shall we tell Clarky where you are?' Mike asks her.

'Erm, no, probably not,' she replies. 'I'll let him know, when my phone is charged.'

With their relationship still not quite clear to me, and Clarky finally having fun on this holiday – coupled with the fact that he didn't seem all that bothered she was missing – it's probably not worth telling him we've just found Drea, here, like this. If he mentions her again then maybe that might be the right time, but while he's seemingly unbothered, probably best just to let him have fun. Where's the sense in letting her ruin his holiday?

'Okay, cool,' I reply, clapping my hands. 'Well, we'd better go, we'll leave you to your... yeah.'

'Laters,' Drea says as she leaps back into Dennis's arms.

'Yeah, I'm definitely old,' Mike concludes as we walk the last few metres towards the shop.

I glance around us. Everyone is so young, so fun, so full of energy.

I don't necessarily feel old, but I can't help but feel the tiniest bit envious. Drea has been here a matter of hours, and she's already found someone new to get off with – evidentially the biggest, hunkiest man at the resort. Then there's me and Mike, on a quest for toothpaste to avoid spending time in our sex dungeon. Maybe I'm not old, perhaps I'm just boring?

'I think we're all in a fish-out-of-water type situation here,' I reassure him. 'Perhaps we need to do what Clarky is trying to and lean into it. Well, stopping short of utilising the facilities in the room, but you know what I mean. Just have fun – your own kind – don't worry about what everyone else is doing.'

Mike stares at me for a moment. I can see the cogs turning in his brain, although I can't begin to imagine what he's thinking about.

'Before we go in, can I just say something, while it's just the two of us?' he asks.

'Of course,' I reply, suddenly feeling nervous about what he's going to say. He looks quite serious.

'I just want to apologise, for what I was like when we were together,' he says. 'I was immature, to put it politely.'

'Mike, you were a teenager,' I insist. 'We were all immature. Don't worry about it, okay?'

'No, I was out of order,' he replies. 'I think about it a lot, about how life could have been different if I'd made better choices, but the one thing I know for certain is that I owe you an apology. We had something good and I blew it.'

Wow, he's really dwelling on this. I get that he feels bad, our relationship didn't exactly come to the best end, but we were kids. He doesn't need to feel so bad, just because a teenage relationship didn't work out.

I give Mike's shoulder a rub, to show him that there's no hard feelings. I know that, for me at least, my feelings for Mike back then were platonic, no matter how hard I tried to get them to blossom into something deeper. I was a teenager, I didn't know what I wanted – or if I did know, I didn't know how to make it happen. If I'm being honest, Mike being so difficult towards the end of our brief relationship made it easier for me to end it – I'm almost grateful. But he clearly feels bad about the way he handled himself. I suppose it's nice, that he still cares.

'If you want me to accept your apology then I will,' I reply. 'But, honestly, it's all water under the bridge now. We're adults, it was more than a decade ago – let's just focus on having fun, yeah?'

'Yeah, you're right,' he replies. 'Let's just enjoy ourselves, see what this resort has to offer.'

'Follow me for coke, follow Loftie for K,' a guest with a strong Geordie accent announces as he and a small group of people shuffle past us.

'Well, maybe not quite everything the resort has to offer,' he quickly adds.

18

THEN – 26 APRIL 2008

I know that this is going to sound horrible but I'm so glad that Mikey can't make it today. We've been boyfriend and girlfriend for a couple of months now but things are just not working out. I know it's a cliché, to say 'it's not you, it's me' but it really is a me thing. Mikey's great but I just don't have boyfriend/girlfriend kind of feelings for him, and at least now I can say that I gave it a go. That day, when he asked me out, when I realised that Cam had helped him set the whole thing up and essentially given Mikey his blessing, I thought that was the writing on the wall for us but... I don't know... obviously, my feelings haven't gone away and I can't say I don't still pick up on the occasional vibe from Cam. But maybe I am just reading too much into it – it's just that we get on so, so well. I've never been more sure that someone was the right person for me, and he just makes me feel so good, just by me being in his orbit, so I'm excited to be spending time with him today, and relieved that Mikey won't be here because things are awkward. Seriously awkward.

'Has anyone actually ice-skated before?' Cam asks as we make our way up the stairs to the indoor ice rink.

'Nope,' I say, my nervousness showing in my voice.

'Never,' DJ adds.

'Neither have I,' Maxi says. 'I just really fancied trying it, and with it being my turn to choose what we do, you guys have to do as I say.'

She's joking but she's right. If Clarky can drag us camping, Mikey can take us to watch Leeds United play, and DJ can get us all to sit through *Transformers*, then we can all pop on a pair of ice skates and give it our best.

The ice-skating place is a large, open space with high ceilings and bright lights shining all around which, coupled with the pop music playing from speakers dotted everywhere, makes it feel a bit like a disco. The ice rink itself takes up most of the space and is already packed with people skating – people who make it look easy. The sound of the blades on the ice, mixed with laughter (and the occasional scream as someone loses their balance) gives the place a really fun atmosphere. There are little stands around the edge of the rink where people can sit and watch – so at least I know I can always default to that – but I'm here and I'm willing to try.

Maxi and DJ are eager, skating out across the ice the second they've got their skates on. I'm a little nervous so I'm taking my time. Cam must have noticed, because he's hung back with me.

'Maybe we can stick together,' he suggests. 'If I'm being honest, I'm a little nervous.'

I smile. I wonder if he really is nervous, or if he's just trying to make me feel better.

'That would be great,' I reply.

We join the others on the ice but I hold on to the side to start with – I don't care how dorky I look, I'd rather look like an upright dork than one flat on her back on the ice. Cam skates alongside me.

'You're actually pretty good,' I tell him, almost suspiciously.

'Well, I used to come here often when I was a kid,' he explains. 'My cousin was way into it. I didn't think I'd be any good at it now that I'm a gangly teenager.'

I laugh.

'Oh, I have actually done it one time, since then, when I was on holiday with my family in New York,' he recalls. 'But that was cut short because my mum wasn't feeling well and my dad was too scared to try – don't ever tell him I told you that, though, he'd be mortified.'

'His secret is safe with me,' I reply. 'New York is cool. I would love to go.'

'I would love to go again, as an adult,' he replies. 'Holidays with your parents aren't quite the same. I'd love to travel.'

'Me too,' I say excitedly. 'Where do you want to go?'

'I'd love to go to Japan,' he replies. 'Tokyo seems like such a cool city. I want to visit South America too, maybe go to Peru, hike the Inca Trail to Machu Picchu.'

'Sounds amazing,' I reply. 'Beaches are top of my list – I'm thinking Bali, Thailand – oh, and St Lucia, Barbados...'

'Wow, someone who wants to see the world just as much as I do,' Cam replies with a smile.

'Definitely,' I reply. 'Although I'm not sure I'll ever have the money to do it.'

'Well, let's make a deal, if either of us ever gets rich, we'll take the other person on holiday,' Cam suggests. 'What do you say?'

'Sounds great to me,' Maxi says as she and DJ skate past us arm in arm.

I laugh – until I realise I've let go of the side and I've been skating without holding on, albeit very slowly and cautiously, for a minute or two.

Cam (who I suspect had already realised) notices me coming

to the realisation that I'm not holding on to the side, and the subsequent panic I'm feeling.

'Don't worry,' Cam says, skating backwards in front of me. 'I've got yo—'

Of course, me being me, given licence to fall, that's the first thing I do.

I lose my footing and start to fall backward. But before I hit the ice, Cam catches me, holding me in his arms for a moment longer than he needs to. My heart races, and I can't help but wonder if he feels the same way I do, because the butterflies in my stomach are going mad, and as cringe as it sounds, I'd fall all over again just to feel him hold me like this.

'Thanks,' I say, feeling a little breathless.

'No problem,' Cam replies with a smile. 'All in a day's work.'

'We can't take her anywhere, can we?' Maxi jokes. 'Cam, go do boysie stuff with DJ, I can't keep up with him. I'll babysit this one for a bit.'

'Okay,' Cam says, skating off. He really is good at it.

'I don't think ice skating is my thing,' I confess to Maxi, holding on to the side with one hand, as she takes my other arm in hers.

'Do you know what I think is your thing?' she replies. 'Cam.'

'Shut up,' I say, unable to hide my grin.

'It's always been Cam, hasn't it?' she replies. 'Come on, you can tell your auntie Maxi.'

'I just... don't see Mikey as a boyfriend,' I say, simply. 'I've tried but I can't see him as more than a friend. I'm sure he must be starting to realise.'

'Just between us, he is,' Maxi replies.

'What?' I blurt. 'How do you know?'

'This is just between the two of us, promise?' she says,

squeezing my arm. 'Because DJ told me, and he said I couldn't tell anyone.'

'I won't say anything, I promise,' I reply – so keen to hear what she has to say I'll agree to anything.

'Mikey is going around telling people that you're frigid,' she tells me. 'He says you won't even kiss him properly.'

Wow, that's horrible. Why is he going around telling people anything about me?

'I mean... I won't kiss him properly,' I reply. 'Because I don't fancy him. But I would never go around telling people that.'

'Boys are horrible,' Maxi concludes. 'I always wonder if DJ tells people we haven't slept together yet, or if he lies and says we have – I don't know what would be worse. But Mikey is just being a baby, he thinks he's so fit, he probably can't imagine why any girl wouldn't want to kiss him.'

I furrow my brow, more angry than upset.

'I can't believe he's telling people I'm frigid,' I say. 'I'm not frigid, am I? Just because I don't want to kiss him.'

'Well, let's look at it this way,' Maxi starts. 'You don't want to kiss him, but do you want to kiss other boys? I would use Cam as an example, but I know you're not ready to own up to that, so let's just say any boy, you don't have to name him, but are there any boys you would kiss right now?'

I can't help but glance over at Cam, who is currently skating with DJ on his back. Gosh, he's so cute.

'Yes,' I reply.

'There you go then,' Maxi concludes. 'I feel kind of bad, because I convinced you to give things a go with Mikey. I thought it might work out, or that Cam might come to his senses – I think he might be, though. Cam talks to DJ too.'

I shoot her a look.

'I'm not saying another word,' Maxi insists. 'But I think it's time you started to think about what it is you want, and then you figure out how it is you get it.'

Maxi is right. Well, almost right. I know what it is that I want – who it is that I want, but now I feel like I'm in too deep, like our entire friendship group depends on how I act. The last thing I want is for everyone to fall out. But the first thing I want *is* Cam. I just need to work out how to get him.

19

NOW

You would never know today was La Fine del Mondo's first day open – were it not for all the balloons and banners saying as much – because everything is in full swing and running like a well-oiled machine.

With our friendship group understandably not feeling quite close enough to take group showers – I know, we're old-fashioned like that – we've been taking turns to get washed and dressed, ready for a day of... who knows what.

Tired of being cooped up in the room, those of us who are ready have made our way down to the pool area. Clarky is off somewhere being Clarky (honestly, the less you know about what he's doing, the more plausible deniability you have when it all goes tits up, and he still isn't mentioning Drea, so I think keeping quiet about seeing her is the right thing to do) and Mike was the only one left to shower and change so he encouraged us all to go ahead without him. To be honest, it is kind of bizarre, hanging out in that room. I don't know how to describe it other than to say it's like the room expects sex. It's well and truly set out its stall, with all the kit an S & M-loving swinger could possibly need, and we're just chilling around it, trying to pretend it's not there. It's hard to have a serious conversation when you're sitting on chairs with holes in them, under straps that hang from the ceiling. And, not to sound hysterical, but it feels like an accident waiting to happen. Take it from the person who had to find the key after Clarky handcuffed himself to the table. Suddenly, I can't understand why I didn't leave him there.

Maxi, unwilling to leave the relative sanctuary of the swingers' room just yet, ordered a breakfast buffet to be delivered to us – and, wow, did they deliver. I swear the smell of coffee hit me before the person bringing it even knocked on the door. Multiple trolleys arrived with a variety of drinks and foods for us all to help ourselves to. I swear, the boys' eyes turned to love hearts when they saw the cured meats arranged artfully on a platter. I usually prefer sweet stuff for breakfast but I had a slice of prosciutto and it felt like it melted in my mouth. In fact, it was such a visually stunning breakfast, with brightly coloured fruits creatively arranged on a platter, but – for me at least – the real stars of the show were all the pastries. Croissants, brioche, and my new favourite thing: cornetti. They're sweeter than croissants, I prefer the texture too, but the fillings, oh my God, Nutella or vanilla custard – I couldn't choose, so I had both, washed down with a coffee and chased with the freshest glass of peach juice I have ever tasted. Heaven.

After we ate, I slipped on one of my new bikinis – and a mini sarong, to help cover the bits it doesn't cover, that I really, strongly feel it should – and headed down to the pool area with the others.

'Pool area' feels too weak a title to describe where we are. Yes, there is a pool here, a massive one with a bar inside it that you can swim up to, and a water slide that twists and turns before spitting guests out in the pool. Every few minutes I hear the delighted screams of those who have just taken the plunge.

Beyond the busy surrounding area packed with sunloungers

there is a wide-open space, filled with even more sunloungers, tables and chairs of various shapes and sizes. I'm told this area turns into a club after dark. The space is surrounded by fancy lighting (not turned on; obviously, the sun is beaming down on us right now) and leads up to a stage housing an epic DJ booth. I notice a couple of people on the stage messing around with microphones and pieces of paper, as though they're just about to do something.

I'm relaxing on a sunlounger, sipping a large, fruity cocktail as I people-watch. Perhaps it's because yesterday I thought I was going to spend the next few days sleeping rough on a deserted beach, but I'm not sure I could be happier here. The sun is shining, the pool is sparkling, and the music is pumping all around us.

I've noticed a few things, in the short time we've been hanging out here. First of all, yes, we are absolutely the oldest people here. I get the feeling that, if we had tried to book a room here in the conventional way, someone probably would've had a word. I think we just got lucky – or confused the receptionist – turning up to book a room, given that this is an island and everyone else used a ticket to board the boat here. Groups of holiday-goers are all around us, everyone seemingly wasted already, drinking, dancing, dry-humping – the three Ds that make for a perfect holiday when you're young. I tick myself off – I'm in my early thirties, I'm not old. I could drink, dance and dry-hump with the best of them if I wanted to.

Another thing I have noticed is that most of the guests here are English, and a lot of the staff too. It feels like this resort exists to cater to Brits wanting to go abroad and have a wild time. Signs are in English first, then Italian, and everyone I overhear chatting has an unmistakeable accent from back home somewhere, to the point where every time I hear a Scouser, I panic that it's *my* Scouser, Clarky, up to no good.

No matter where you look, or what you see, you can't deny that this place has a good vibe. Maybe it's the sun, maybe it's the cocktails, but even watching a girl hold her friend's hair while she throws up underneath a palm tree makes me smile – what are friends for?

'Cam, that is a fantastic idea,' Maxi insists. 'You have to do it.'

'Do you think?' he replies. 'I'm seriously considering it. Now that I'm at a pause in my life, I can't think of a better time.'

Cam has just been telling Maxi and DJ about his plans to set up a creative hub for young people, to nurture their talents in English, art and drama.

'I wish we'd had something like that when we were younger,' Maxi says sincerely. 'You have to do it.'

'There's huge demand for tutoring at the moment,' I chime in. 'Especially in an area like where we grew up. Everyone just wants to give their kids the best start in life. The kids who aren't doing so well need extra support. The kids who are doing well want help to thrive in their favourite subjects. It could be a great thing for our community.'

'You'd be perfect, Jas,' Maxi says encouragingly.

'It sounds right up my street,' I reply.

'Hey, don't throw away a job you love because I've had a wild idea,' Cam insists.

Why did I go so hard on the job thing when – obviously – I don't have one, and something like this would be a dream come true for me?

'This idea could be a reality, though,' Maxi tells him. 'I have an investment that's about to pay off, I'm looking for a new one, something I believe in.'

DJ's ears prick up.

'You mentioned that maybe you would tell Rupert about my

distance-teaching tech ideas,' DJ reminds her. 'Do you still reckon he would be interested?'

'I have a video call with him later,' she replies. 'I'll see where he's at.'

Maxi's obvious attempt to avoid the question makes me smile. DJ, on the other hand, appears unfazed, as he continues to talk about his plans.

'We're on holiday from our holiday,' I joke. 'We shouldn't be talking about work.'

'If we're on holiday from our holiday, does that mean we need to go even deeper into holiday mode?' Maxi asks. 'Like, if we were taking a break from day-to-day life, and now we're taking a break from that... I think – and I hate to say it – Clarky might be right. We've ended up here, somehow, in this situation. Shall we just go for it?'

I just laugh.

'I'm serious,' she says. 'Fate has landed us here for a reason.'

'I'm all in,' DJ replies, banging his hands down on his sunlounger to show just how much he means it.

'Me too,' Cam says. 'When will we ever be in a situation like this again?'

'What do you say, Jas, are you down for a few days of seeing who can cause the most trouble?' Maxi asks, giving me an encouraging wink to help me with my decision.

I chew my lip thoughtfully.

'Assuming this doesn't involve the six of us having an orgy in our room, yes, go on then,' I say excitedly, throwing my hat into the ring.

'No, no orgy,' Maxi confirms. 'But if we were going to have one, you are the three people I'd choose.'

'Aww,' Cam jokes playfully. 'So sweet.'

'Mike's got pretty big arms,' DJ reasons and we all laugh. 'What? I'm just saying. He could be useful.'

'Well, okay, sure, in this hypothetical orgy, Mike can join in too,' Maxi tells him. 'I just felt bad saying everyone but Clarky.'

'Aside from – surprisingly – being the only member of the gang to admit to knowing how a spanking bench works, I don't think he'd be the best in an orgy,' I tell them. 'Did you see me have to take something off him earlier? He was sucking one of the jam sachets from the pantry because he was hungry. I had to tell him it was strawberry-flavoured lube.'

'You don't want him at your orgy,' Cam starts. 'I'd be more worried about him making me toast.'

We all laugh.

'Ciao, hello, English or Italiano?' a hotel employee hailing from Newcastle asks us.

The people who work here are easy to spot because they wear bright pink outfits, making them stand out in a crowd.

'English,' Maxi tells him. 'Are most people here English?'

'I would say mostly, yes,' he replies. 'Like Ibiza or Benidorm. This resort was definitely marketed at English customers, somewhere new and different for them to come for the usual summer holiday or drinking, dancing and, ahem, summer romances – they hired most of the staff from back home too. My name is Tom.'

'Nice to meet you, Tom,' I say politely.

'You too,' he replies. 'I am here to see if you guys want to join in with the group games?'

'More info,' Maxi says quickly. 'Always more info before I agree to anything.'

Tom laughs.

'Well, as you can see, party coordinators like me are approaching each group, to see who wants to participate,' he explains. 'I'm armed with a clipboard and a stopwatch. Geri is our gamemaster, she'll be up on the stage setting the challenges, and I would be assigned to your group, to score you. The winning group gets a three-thousand-pound bar tab, so it's worth rolling the dice – so to speak.'

'Should we wait for Clarky?' Maxi asks us.

'Are you talking about Clark?' Tom asks.

'Oh, God, what has he done?' I ask.

Tom laughs. 'Oh, no, nothing,' he replies. 'But he's with Amy's group. You see that gang of girls over there? I only ask because it's not every day you meet a Clark. We had a bit of a laugh because he's participating in an all-girl group.'

We glance over to see where Tom is pointing and, sure enough, there is Clarky with a gaggle of girls. He looks happy enough – more than happy, even. I'm glad I didn't tell him about spotting Drea.

'How's he managed that?' DJ asks no one in particular, sounding almost annoyed.

'Right, well, we should participate just to beat *Clark*,' Maxi says. 'Sign us up, Tom.'

I glance around the resort. Lots of groups are taking part, each with their own party coordinator assigned, in their bright pink outfits, with their pink visors. Suddenly, I'm getting quite a strong *Squid Game* vibe, but it's too late to back out now.

'Perfect,' Tom says. 'It's groups with even numbers only, so four is perfect. I highly recommend getting into pairs, it definitely helps.'

'Me and DJ, Jas and Cam?' Maxi suggests. 'Like old times.'

'Are you couples?' Tom asks.

'No, no, we're not couples,' DJ says quickly. 'Old friends.'

'I've run this game at one of our other resorts,' Tom tells us. 'Sometimes being in a couple makes it easier.'

'We were a couple when we were kids,' DJ tells Tom. 'Perhaps that will help.'

'I'm going to say not,' Tom replies, laughing in a way that makes me think the joke will soon be obvious.

'Ciao, hello, bonjour, hola, 'ow do?' Geri, who is now wearing a microphone, announces from the stage.

Geri definitely hails from our neck of the woods. She's tall and slim with short bleached-blonde hair. She's wearing the same pink casual attire as all the other employees with the addition of a pink glitzy waistcoat over the top – to make her stage-fancy, without making her too warm, I'd imagine. The sunlight pings off her clothes, making her twinkle like a disco ball.

'My name is Geri, I'll be hosting today's game,' she announces. 'The prize is a three-k bar tab – even that group over there will struggle to get through that – and the game is... Assume the Position!'

It's safe to say everyone else is more enthusiastic – or drunker, potentially – than us, because they cheer, woo, stand on their seats, inadvertently throw the contents of their drinks over one another.

'I'm guessing from that reaction some of you have stayed at one of our Spanish resorts and know what's coming,' Geri says. '*You*.'

I purse my lips and cock my head.

'Hmm?' I say to Tom.

'Geri will explain,' he whispers.

'For those of you who don't know, this is a fastest-finger-first game,' she explains. 'Fastest finger or whatever other appendage the game calls for. I will be reading out a series of limericks, leaving off the very last word or words and it's your job to guess the missing words. But here's the fun part, all of the missing words will be sex positions. And here's the really fun part, you should all be in couples in your groups – that's because you will submit your answer by getting into said sex position. You will see that each group has been assigned a hunk or a honey with a stopwatch. They will be timing you, to see which team is the fastest. My motto for this game is: you have to be right and you have to be tight. Meaning we want to see the correct sex positions and we want to see you and your partner up close and personal, as if you were doing the real deal. Sound good?'

Everyone cheers. I look to my friends.

'Well, you're going to get your dream-orgy wish,' I tell Maxi with a straight face.

She snorts.

'Okay, I know we all just gave it the big talk about going all in here – are we doing this?' she asks.

I just laugh.

'I'm in,' DJ tells her.

'Come on, Jas, don't make me do this on my own,' Maxi says.

I glance over at Cam, who just smiles and shrugs.

'Okay, fine, let's do it,' I reply.

'That's what we like to hear,' Tom replies. 'So Geri will read out the rhymes. Just work out the sex position and then get into it. I'll time you, write them all down, and then we go check which teams did it the fastest.'

'What happens if there's a tie?' I ask.

'We do it again, but naked,' Tom replies, completely straight-faced. Then he smiles. 'I'm joking – I don't think I've ever witnessed a draw. Both teams probably get a prize each. Don't worry about it.'

Geri goes through the aim of the game again, for a late-joining group.

'Play with your partner, play with your friend, play with a

stranger – the only thing you can't do is play with yourself,' Geri jokes. 'I'm looking at you, love.'

A man shouts something from further back in the crowd.

'What was that, love?' Geri asks him.

'I said speak up, we can't hear you, *love*,' the man heckles her.

Oh, there's always one.

'You can't hear me with a microphone, but I can hear you?' she points out.

'I'm shouting,' he replies.

'Well, there you go, dickhead, that's why you can't hear me,' she concludes, finishing him with a smile. 'Right, now, on to the quiz. Do you all have your partners at the ready?'

A wave of replies bounce around like beach balls. I take a deep breath.

'Okay, stopwatches at the ready, your first limerick is coming – maybe some of you will be too,' Geri jokes before pausing for dramatic effect.

> *There once was a man name Kyle,*
> *Who could get any girl with a smile,*
> *He'd be on to a winner,*
> *Wouldn't need to buy dinner,*
> *To convince them to do...*

I look to my friends.

'Didn't you two study English?' Maxi points out.

'Sex positions rarely came up,' Cam says with a laugh.

I think for a moment. They're limericks, not cryptic crossword clues, it's going to be some really naff rhyme.

'Doggy style,' I blurt quietly.

'Yes!' Cam says.

For a couple who were together for years but never actually

slept together, Maxi and DJ snap into simulated doggy style with a surprising ease.

I pull a dorky face and shrug my shoulders at Cam before kneeling down on my sunlounger. Cam takes my hips in his hands and presses himself up against me – as per the rules of the competition, it's nothing to get excited about, but it takes a minute for your brain to explain to your body that the person holding you in such an intimate position – the person you've had a crush on for decades, a crush that doesn't seem to want to wear off – is only doing this out of a combination of the desire for free drinks and peer pressure.

'Wow, look at you all,' Geri says to the crowd. 'I doubt this will be the last time many of you will be in this position this holiday – and I doubt it's the last time I'll see you in it, you dirty beggars. The answer was, of course, doggy style. Give your partners a pat on the back.'

'Not bad,' Tom tells us. 'You guys need to be quicker, though.'

'Words I never thought I'd hear in this position,' Cam jokes as we awkwardly separate.

'It's okay, I feel like it will be easy now,' I reply. 'I think I was expecting something more sophisticated from the limericks.'

'A round of shots, to loosen up our already loose friends,' Geri announces as waiters and waitresses with trays full of shots do the rounds.

'Only one?' DJ jokes as he takes one.

'You only need one of these,' the waitress warns him.

I knock it back. Well, when in… an unknown place in Italy. Oh my God, it's so strong, I don't even know what it is.

'Blergh,' I blurt.

'Whatever it is, it's gone straight to my head,' Maxi announces. 'Especially on top of the strong cocktails.'

The drink – whatever it was – warms my insides all the way

down. You know what, I do feel a little looser, and like I want to win this competition. Come on!

'Ready for another?' Geri asks. 'Okay, here we go.'

> *There once was a girl named Pearl,*
> *Who loved to bounce, twirl and swirl,*
> *She didn't know why,*
> *It felt so good on her thigh,*
> *But it's the reason she loves reverse...*

'Cowgirl,' we all say at the same time.

The boys drop to the floor, flat on their backs. Maxi is on DJ like a shot. I hesitate slightly but I'm pretty quick off the mark too, sitting down on top of Cam, facing his feet. I'm grateful these are – so far at least – positions where I don't have to look him in the eye.

'A lot of muscle memory there,' Geri says. 'Everyone was fast then. Hey, if you fancy your partner, give them a little bounce.'

As people all around us wiggle and grind, I turn around, to look over my shoulder at Cam.

'I'd never squash you like that,' I joke. 'Your cocktails will come back.'

As he laughs, I look over at Maxi and DJ – the two of them gleefully going through the motions. DJ has his hands on Maxi's hips as she grinds back and forth on him, throwing her head back, laughing, running her hands through her hair.

I nod towards them, gesturing for Cam to look. He rolls his head back to see.

'Wow,' he mouths at me.

Obviously, this is just a game, and no one is naked, but the fact most of us are wearing little more than bikinis and swimming shorts makes it feel so much more intimate than it would if we were wearing jeans.

Geri pushes on.

> *A good girl who liked to drink wine,*
> *Said of sex, it just wasn't her time,*
> *But when she swapped wine for brandy,*
> *She got quite randy,*
> *So she found a guy to...*

Not the best limerick – not that the aim of the game here is to critique the poetry – but from the second I hear the word 'wine', it's obvious.

'It's sixty-nine,' I whisper, before Geri has even finished.

As Cam and I lie down on our sides, before we fully assume the position, I notice DJ lying on his back, and Maxi about to lie down on top of him. Bloody hell, I'd say get a room, were we not sharing their room with them.

I rest my head on the inside of Cam's thigh, like it's a hard pillow. You would think this would feel the most uncomfortable, oddly it feels like the most sexual, but it's a little easier to keep your distance, and it's always better not making eye contact with anyone – she says, as though there's usually an audience for this sort of thing (although I suppose there is in our hotel room).

'Oh, very good,' Geri says. 'I can tell it's no one's first time doing that. It's interesting, to see the different interpretations – I'll be making a note of that one, if I ever get a bloke with the arms for it... and the stomach.'

We all make that semi-awkward shuffle to our feet again.

'It's hard to tell if you're doing a good job,' Cam says to me.

'Story of my life,' Tom jokes. 'You guys are doing great, though – seriously quick off the mark. You either know your sex positions or you're just really good at English.'

'The second one,' Cam and I both reply, almost in perfect sync.

'Your final dirty ditty,' Geri announces. 'Here we go...'

> There was a young woman called Mary,
> Who thought her lady garden was too hairy,
> If any man saw,
> He would run for the door,
> But she could hide it shagging in...

I wince and cringe but only for a second because right now I care about winning more than I would have ever imagined.

'Missionary,' I whisper to my teammates, on my way down to the ground, lying flat on my back, my legs splayed apart waiting for Cam, like it's the most normal thing in the world. Either four rounds of this game is the number it takes to stop caring any more, or it has something to do with that shot. Either way, I'm oddly disappointed this is the last one.

Cam gets on top of me, some of his weight rested on his fore-arms but the rest is pressing down on my body. This is purely a move of comfort, I swear, but my legs feel crampy just kind of vibing at the side of him, so I wrap my legs around his waist and hook my feet together. I do the same with my arms around his neck.

It's funny, people always think of this position as so basic, so standard, nothing special at all. But let me tell you, as someone who is getting a whole new perspective on these things given that I'm in this position with someone I'm not actually having sex with, this is the most intimate by far. Obviously, we have the most body-to-body contact with this one but that's not why, it's the eye contact, our faces being inches apart. Suddenly, our bodies touching feels like no big deal. It's our lips, so close, our breath tickling each other's lips, and our eyes focused on each other, almost looking into one another's minds, except Cam is hiding it all behind his gorgeous eyes and his cheeky smile. Can he tell what I'm thinking? God, I hope he can't.

'Good work,' Geri says. 'An oldie but a goodie. Now, don't move just yet. It's going to take us an undisclosed amount of time to check all of your times to see which group are our winners so I'm going to give you an opportunity to win bonus points. All you have to do is hold this position while we check the scores – and thank your lucky stars we let you do it in the missionary position and not the maypole or the wonky wheelbarrow.'

'I don't even know what they are,' Cam tells me.

'I feel like any wheelbarrow would be wonky with my total lack of physical fitness,' I reply.

'I don't know about that,' he replies. 'I've never had anyone wrap their legs around me so effortlessly.'

Cam flashes me a cheeky smile and I just can't take it any more. Looking into his eyes is like looking into the sun. It's too much to handle, I need to look away.

I giggle and avert my gaze, looking to the right, towards our sunloungers. I gasp when I see Mike sitting there, watching.

'Oh, hello,' I blurt like an absolute dork. 'How are you? Did you have a nice shower?'

'Yeah, it was good,' he replies, lacking any kind of emotion.

'Good, good,' I say. 'Are you going to have a drink?'

Mike holds up a beer bottle so I can see it.

'Nice,' I reply. 'You need to try the cocktails, they're incredible. We had some kind of shot too...'

Look at me, chatting away to my ex, like I don't have another man wedged between my thighs.

'How long have you been watching?' I ask.

'Not long,' Mike says.

'It's not what it looks like,' Cam dares to joke.

'We're trying to win a bar tab,' I tell him.

It feels like time is standing still now that Mike is feet away from us, watching us. This feels like some sort of betrayal, which obviously it isn't, but I feel like Mike is giving off a vibe, as though he thinks I'm doing something wrong too.

'There's a lot of people playing,' Mike tells us. 'I don't fancy your odds.'

'Is that Mike?' I hear Maxi call out. 'Hello, Mike. You've missed such a fun game but apparently there are others. You might need to find a partner, though, if you can.'

Oh, boy.

'Okay, campers, we have our winners,' Geri announces. 'If it's your team then your party coordinator will let you know. If not, don't worry, there are plenty more games to come. Thanks for playing.'

'It's you guys,' Tom tells us. 'You won.'

'What?' I squeak.

Without thinking, overjoyed to have won, I squeeze Cam tightly, pulling him down on top of me.

'We won?' Maxi squeaks. 'Oh my God, we won!'

It's funny, the money means nothing to Maxi, but the victory means everything.

'We're playing another game later, similar kind of thing, perfect for groups like yours – fancy it?' Tom asks.

I look to my friends – everyone looks up for it, nodding, giving me the thumbs up.

'Count us in,' I say.

'Perfect, I'll come and find you when it's time – I love a winning team,' he replies. 'And as for now, you haven't just won the bar tab, you've won another round of shots. And I've asked for an extra one, for your friend.'

Right on cue, a young man turns up with an extra shot. His enthusiasm is no match for the leg of the sunlounger and he trips, spilling the shot all over Mike's flip-flops.

'I'm so sorry,' the young man says. He grabs a resort towel from one of the sunloungers and dabs Mike's feet.

'You want to watch what you're doing,' Mike snaps at him, snatching the towel from his hands to clean his own feet.

'So sorry,' the young man says again. 'I'll get you another.'

The mood suddenly shifts from giddy celebration to sobering silence.

Mike's always had a temper. I thought he might have grown out of it by now. Still, let's not let it ruin a victory. We won the bar tab, so tonight should be interesting. Now that we've decided to lean into this place, to let our hair down and have fun, if this is how things have started then I'm terrified to see what tonight will bring. Terrified, but in the best possible way.

I can't wait.

20

During the day, lounging by the resort pool is for enjoying the warmth of the sun on your skin, and sipping cool, refreshing drinks, taking dips in the pool in a very typically daytime atmosphere. Of course, you are still surrounded by the same young, drunk, horny clientele you see everywhere else here, but chilling is what the space is for at least – if you're into that sort of thing.

At night, things are very different. As if from nowhere, the area is packed with large speakers and bright lights – it's still only evening, and time for more party games – so I haven't seen what the full nightclub transformation looks like yet, but I'm eager to see it. It sounds amazing.

Once again, seating areas are laid out in front of the stage, clearly ready for the next round of games to start, so we're all gathered together, already hitting our free bar tab hard. The water in the pool is so still and so flat it almost looks like glass reflecting all the twinkling lights around it. The night sky beyond us is dark, but everything here is illuminated, like we're in our own little bubble of fun.

The atmosphere is alive with laughter and chatter. All of the seating areas are full, with people waiting to take part in the competition, everyone already enjoying themselves with drinks in their hands. It's almost as though no one ever finishes a drink here, because another one replaces it the second it's finished, like some sort of boozy magic trick.

'So, whatever this is, we're doing it, right?' Maxi says.

'Okay, calm down,' I joke.

'I just mean that, if we're playing, we're playing – agreed?' she continues. 'If the game is anything like the one earlier, and Tom makes it sound like it is, then I think we need to set our stalls out, and say if we're playing, or if we're watching.'

'I'm in,' DJ says excitedly.

'Obviously I'm in,' Clarky adds. 'This is all I've wanted for this whole trip.'

I rarely believe a word that comes out of Clarky's mouth, but I definitely believe that.

'I'm down for whatever,' Cam adds.

'Then so am I,' Mikey replies, almost competitively.

And that just leaves me, and everyone staring at me, waiting to see if I'm game.

'That's all of us then,' I announce.

I am a little apprehensive, given the nature of the competition earlier, but if I can get through that, how bad can it be?

'Okay, kids, this evening's game is...' Geri pauses suspense-fully. 'Premature Evacuator.'

Then again, maybe I'm wrong.

Geri is all glammed up for the evening, standing on the stage in a full-length gold dress, occasionally flashing an enormous pair of heels underneath. The spotlight pointing at her makes the little sequins on her dress twinkle, turning her into a sort of human disco ball.

The sound of clinking glasses mixed with the beat of the music filled the air until Geri spoke, now everyone is quiet. Who knew it would be such a competitive crowd?

'Are you all sitting comfortably in your groups of friends?' Geri enquires. 'Well, you won't be for much longer.'

She says this in an almost threatening tone. I glance to Cam, in that way you often turn to look at someone when something happens, when you hear a joke – anything. Don't they say that when you find something funny, you always look to the person you like the most to laugh with? I don't know how true it is, but I do find it interesting, seeing who looks to me if I'm watching a comedy on TV with friends or family. It's even more interesting to see people looking at other people, though, trying to work out what their relationships are.

'Your party coordinators are watching over you,' Geri continues. 'They'll be timing you, once again, to see who is the fastest – and our winning team tonight wins a whopping ten per cent off their final bill.'

The crowd woos. Everyone loves a discount, but I doubt everyone here has had to fork out for the swingers' suite. It would be good to win this for Maxi – she must have spent a fortune on us so far.

'So what's the aim of the game?' Geri says. 'I will read out a series of instructions and the appropriate members of your team need to follow them. When your party coordinator is satisfied you've completed the challenge, they will give you the go-ahead to throw back a shot each. There will be a point for each team who completes a challenge the fastest. So simple even a bunch of drunks like you can do it, right?'

Everyone cheers.

'Okay, here we go,' she says.

Maxi looks to Tom, who has just finished spreading shots out on the table, and is now brandishing his stopwatch, ready to begin.

'Will it be obvious what to do?' Maxi asks him.

'Definitely,' he replies.

'Keeping in mind, in this competition, when we say kiss, we mean really kiss... The youngest boy and the youngest girl should kiss,' Geri commands.

We all glance at one another as our slightly drunk brains try to compute her command. Well, Maxi is younger than me, and the youngest boy is...

Maxi and DJ jump to their feet and snap together like magnets. Honestly, it's like they've never been apart, like muscle memory, the way their lips meet before their entire body follows suit, Maxi locking her arms around DJ's neck while he grabs hold of her bum, squeezing it with both hands, like he's trying to stop it getting away from him.

Cam and I exchange another glance. Okay, this is definitely kicked up a gear from the game we played earlier.

'Go on, lad,' Clarky cheers DJ on. 'This is what we're here for.'

This is not exactly what you would call a game for your typical married person – then again, Maxi is clearly having the time of her life.

'Okay, shot,' Tom commands.

Maxi and DJ both sink their shots. DJ cheers victoriously while Maxi just slumps back into her seat with the biggest smile on her face.

Okay, now I feel like I know what we're working with, and I'm low-key terrified.

'Now we're warmed up,' Geri practically cackles. 'Next. The boy whose birthday comes first in the year should get into a sex position with the boy whose birthday comes last. And then we'll see who comes first.'

My eyes widen at Geri's joke, and the idea that two of the boys in our friendship group are going to find this within their comfort zone.

Clarky springs to his feet.

'DJ, quick,' he commands.

DJ stands up with less enthusiasm than he did for Maxi.

'Mate, I'm not sure...' DJ starts, but Clarky clearly wants to win, so he wastes no time in jumping up into DJ's arms, locking his legs around his waist.

'Is this actually happening?' Mike asks no one in particular.

'This is actually happening,' I confirm.

'Okay, great, now have your shot,' Tom tells them.

Clarky hops down and grabs his drink, thrusting another one into DJ's hand. DJ throws it back like he needs it. I don't think he ever expected he would get so up close and personal with Clarky in his lifetime.

'I feel dirty,' DJ says as he sits back down.

'Because he's a boy?' Maxi says, raising an eyebrow.

'No, because he's Clarky,' DJ jokes. 'And I'm not even sure of the physics of that position.'

'Oh, trust you to find a way to make this nerdy,' Clarky complains. Then he turns to Tom. 'That counts, right?'

'Yeah, I'm happy to sign off on that,' Tom jokes. 'Get ready for the next one.'

'The tallest girl...' Geri starts, which I know is me. Please let it be Cam, please let it be Cam. '...should kiss the shortest boy.'

No! Not Clarky, again.

'Come on, let's get this over with,' he half jokes.

'Someone get him a chair to stand on,' DJ teases.

We don't meet with the same enthusiasm as Maxi and DJ, that's for sure, but Clarky goes for it, wrapping his lips around mine, trying to jab at mine with his tongue but I keep them tightly closed, like a barrier, and bring my hands up to his face to hide the fact that I'm not really giving back what I'm getting.

'Okay, shot,' Tom commands once he's happy we've done our job.

I wipe my wet lips with the back of my hand, trying not to pull a grossed-out face until I've knocked back my super-strong shot, so at least I can blame it on that. Come on, it's Clarky, he's like a (older, confusingly) little brother to me.

'You're an unusual kisser,' he tells me as we sit down, clearly oblivious to what I was going for by keeping my mouth closed.

'Thanks,' I reply with a laugh.

'Good work, my short kings,' Geri says. 'Who put you up to doing that, ey?'

All of Geri's jokes are met with laughter but that one definitely sounded like far more girls were laughing than boys.

'Next,' Geri says. 'Now this one should be interesting. The shortest girl should snog the person she fancies the most. This will be a fun one to watch.'

Once again, Maxi and DJ snap together, locking lips like there's no one else here.

'Old habits die hard, eh?' Clarky jokes quietly – actually, it's probably not that quiet, but Maxi and DJ are too oblivious to hear them.

As they knock back their shots, I wonder about what's going to come next. When the competition calls for a girl, it's always going to be me or Maxi, and I don't know what I'll do, if I get a question like that. I'd probably have to kiss Maxi, just to avoid the mess that would come from me choosing one of the boys, because while there very much may be one obvious choice, I don't know how well it would go down if I made it.

'The girl whose name comes first alphabetically should kiss

the boy whose name comes last alphabetically,' Geri commands next.

Oh God, that's me. Me and…

Mike stands up.

No. No, no, no. It would be less awkward to kiss Clarky again.

I can feel Cam's eyes on me as I stand up. I'm trying to keep my brain from darting back to the past but it's all I can think about. I didn't even kiss Mike when we were together – in fact, it was a whole thing, he went around telling people I had some sort of problem, and then there's the fact that Cam told me how jealous he was, when me and Mike were together, and while I'm sure he doesn't care now, in the context of this game – does he care? Is it bad that I want him to?

Mike gives me a friendly smile before moving his face close to mine, but as our lips touch, I don't know, something about it just freaks me out. It reminds me of when I was younger, of feeling like I was stuck with something I didn't want, and I know this is just a game, but I can't do it.

I can only describe my next move as unsubtly recoiling in horror. I pull away quickly, and I can tell by the look on Mike's face what he must be thinking – that I *still* don't want to kiss him, not even in a game – and so I stumble back into the table, knocking over some of the shots, which knock over other shots like dominoes. I snatch up my camera, which was sitting on the table, just as one of the drinks hits it.

'I'm sorry, I, erm, I'm not feeling very well,' I babble. 'I think I just, yeah, I need to lie down. You guys stay here, have fun, I'm fine.'

'Are you sure?' Maxi asks.

I think she realises that I need to get out of this situation, and that I'm not ill at all. That or she just really wants to keep playing this game that gives her a free pass to get off with her ex-boyfriend.

'Yeah, honestly,' I insist. 'Bye.'

I weave through the tables, heading back towards the hotel, desperately seeking the solitude of the swingers' suite.

I turn on my camera to make sure it's okay. Thankfully, it springs to life, but it's a bit wet on the outside, and very sticky.

I use some of the material from my dress to give it a wipe, inadvertently clicking through the photos I've taken on the trip so far as I clean the buttons, like a really fast slideshow.

I just about feel like I've cleaned it up when something catches my eye. I flick forward a couple of photos again and I can't believe what I'm looking at. It's the photo I took, back when we thought we were shipwrecked, when I got up in the night to try to see what was going on in the dark, to try to scare away whatever terrifying creature was lurking in the bushes. The photo I took when I flashed my camera for the light wasn't a creature at all, although it is still terrifying. Clear as day, with no room for interpretation, the photo shows Maxi and DJ, at it against a tree. She has her legs locked around his waist, he's kissing her neck – they're both clearly into it. I quickly avert my eyes, feeling like a pervert for making a Kodak moment of it, before turning my camera off.

I can't believe it's been fifteen years and yet, throw us all back together, and we start acting like we did when we were kids again. Maxi is married – happily married, as far as I know, why is she risking it all for a holiday fling with DJ?

Oh, Maxi, what are you doing?

21

THEN – 27 JUNE 2008

It's hard to believe that today is the last proper day of sixth form. I know, we're doing our A levels, but there has been something almost comforting about doing them here, instead of going to college. It still feels like we're at school – because we're still in the school, obviously – so it feels like we've been able to avoid growing up for just a little longer.

It's lunchtime and Maxi, DJ, Mikey, Cam and I are in the library, where we always love to hang out at lunch. I can't believe this is the last time we're going to hang out here.

I think Jemima, the cool school librarian, a woman in her early forties who has always let us call her by her first name, is going to miss us – or at least that's how she's making us feel, which is the sign of a good person in education. I swear, some of my teachers probably couldn't pick me out of a police line-up, but that's just where being shy and well behaved gets you.

One of the main reasons I think Jemima is so cool is the fact that she doesn't just sit at the desk, scanning books in and out, she likes to engage with the students, and set us these fun little challenges.

Today, for our final challenge, she has set us the quest of each finding a book with what we believe to be the oldest check-out stamp in it, and whoever finds the oldest one wins. The school has been around for decades – my dad actually went here – so there are plenty of old books on the shelves.

So we all run off to different sections, all hoping to find the oldest book we can. I remember last year sometime picking up a book on etiquette for ladies, that was originally published in the 1940s or 1950s, and having a laugh at all the stuff in it, like the fact ladies had to wear gloves, and men had to stand up whenever a lady entered the room. A book that old must have some old stamps in it, so that's the one I'm looking for. I finally lay my hands on it, the smelly old book with the browning pages that for some reason I find so charming.

'Time's up,' Jemima calls out. 'I'll give a bonus prize to the first person to get a book back to me with a stamp before the 1980s.'

I'm on my way back when I notice Mikey and DJ both rushing towards the librarian's desk, trying to be the first to present their book for the challenge. They crash into each other, and while DJ manages to stay on his feet, Mikey hits the ground with a thud.

'What the hell are you playing at?' Mikey snaps at DJ, his face burning red with a level of anger that is unnecessary given that this was just a silly accident.

'I'm sorry, buddy, it was an accident,' DJ says, offering Mikey a hand to help him up from the floor.

Mikey slaps DJ's hand away, still furious, and pulls himself to his feet.

'You're such a careless idiot,' Mikey snaps as we all gather around, rushing to the scene to try to defuse things.

'Hey, Mikey, calm down,' I say softly, taking his arm, but he shrugs me off.

'Don't talk to me like I'm a kid, I won't calm down,' Mikey

insists. 'DJ is trying to play the clown again, trying to make me look stupid.'

'You're making yourself look like a clown,' Maxi chimes in, rushing to her boyfriend's defence, standing between them.

'Piss off, Maxi,' Mikey snaps.

I feel my eyebrows shoot up.

'Right, okay, that's enough,' Jemima says, stepping in. 'Mikey, I think you need to take a break. Go outside, get some fresh air, cool off and then come back in and apologise.'

Mikey storms out.

'What's his problem lately?' Maxi says, her voice wobbling from the confrontation.

'Babe, it's okay, sit down for a minute,' DJ says, wrapping an arm around her reassuringly as he ushers her to the quiet reading area.

Now it's just me and Cam.

'Shall we go to the computers?' he asks. 'Have one last go on that daft learning game?'

I give him all the smile I can muster.

'Sure,' I reply.

We take a seat at one of the PCs and Cam fires up the game. He aimlessly clicks around for a bit but I can't really focus.

'Are you okay?' he asks me. 'Mikey is just being an idiot. He'll come back and apologise and it will be like it never happened. You know what DJ is like, he won't hold it against him. He'll be happy when it's forgotten about.'

'It's not that,' I reply. 'It's Mikey. He's so different these days, always in a bad mood, not the fun leader of the gang like he used to be.'

'Self-appointed leader,' Cam jokes. 'But I know what you mean. Is he being okay with you?'

'It feels like we hardly speak,' I reply. 'He never texts me, he's so moody. Honestly, it feels like such a mistake, the two of us going out, I think we would both be happier if I ended things – I know I need to break up with him for my own happiness, for sure – but I'm so scared of breaking up our group. I've made such a mistake.'

Cam gives me a kind, reassuring smile.

'Jas, you need to do what's right for you,' he insists. 'Don't be worrying about everyone else. The group will be fine – we'll be friends forever, whether we want to or not. You need to think about yourself, and make sure that you're happy. That's what matters the most.'

'I know,' I reply. 'Deep down, I know that, but it's such a mess. We've all been friends for so long, and now there's going to be this awkwardness, and...'

I run out of steam and let out a sigh.

'I know it's hard,' Cam says reassuringly. 'But you need to be true to yourself and stop worrying about everyone else. You know me, Maxi and DJ will support you no matter what you decide, and we'll still be friends – and Mikey will come around too. He knows you were friends, before you were a couple, and I think he knows it's not working too, that might be why he's being so moody.'

I shoot Cam a glance.

'Don't tell me he's been feeding you all the crap about me being frigid too?' I say.

'He's just confused, I think,' Cam explains. Then he smiles. 'Imagine having the kind of ego where you're baffled because someone doesn't want to kiss you.'

I hate the idea of Cam thinking there is something wrong with me, that I have a problem with kissing, or whatever negative picture it is that Mikey is trying to paint of me.

'It's just him I don't want to kiss,' I blurt. 'I know this isn't a very cool thing to say but, I don't know, it just doesn't feel right, and I don't want to waste...'

My voice trails off. Why am I telling the boy I've had a crush on for years that I've never even had a proper kiss before?

'It's okay,' Cam says. 'You know I won't judge you.'

'I just want my first kiss to mean something,' I confess. 'Even if that's sad.'

As Cam smiles, his kind eyes sparkle at me.

'I don't think that's sad,' he tells me. 'I feel the same.'

'I don't want any trouble, Mikey,' Jemima calls out.

I glance over and see Mikey walking towards us. When he reaches us, he exhales deeply.

'I'm sorry,' he says, perhaps not sounding like he means it, but clearly wanting to move on from what happened. 'I don't know what I was thinking but I didn't mean it. Where's DJ?'

'Over on the sofas,' I reply.

'I'd better go apologise to him but, yeah, I'm sorry,' he says again, still not sounding all that convincing.

I feel a wave of relief wash over me, not just because Mikey is back and calm and trying to make amends, but because I know what I need to do. I need to end things. Neither of us is happy and it's starting to affect our friends now. I was worried that breaking up might unsettle our group but we're clearly already unsettled. I just need to do it, and the sooner the better.

'Thanks, Cam,' I tell him. 'You always know exactly what to say to make me feel better.'

'Anytime,' he replies. 'You know I'll always be here for you.'

22

NOW

There's something almost creepy about our hotel room when you're in it alone. It's a different kind of strange, when you're in here with other people, surrounded by a variety of, shall we say, intimacy items all staring at you expectantly, waiting for you to use them. But when you're in here alone it just feels uncomfortable, sitting surrounded by all the unfamiliar apparatus, feeling almost outnumbered by it – which I guess is normally what you want in a room for swingers, but you take my point. You can't quite get lost in your thoughts when you're lying on your bed, staring at a sex swing.

There's a knock on the door before it opens. It's Cam.

'Hello,' he says gently. 'Mind if I join you?'

'In this room, the more the merrier,' I joke, quickly wiping away the last tear to escape my eye.

Cam lies on top of the bed next to me.

'I've made things really awkward, haven't I?' I say.

'No, of course not,' he replies. 'That was the point of the game, and we're all in the same boat.'

'Is Mike upset?' I ask.

'Ah, I'm sure he'll be fine,' Cam says, which doesn't exactly have me convinced. 'It would knock any man's confidence, if a girl would kiss Clarky, but not him.'

I laugh.

'My gosh, that kiss with Clarky was... wow. Not good wow,' I quickly add.

'Yeah, he's baffled,' Cam replies with a laugh. 'He says he's never met anyone who liked to kiss with their mouth closed, whereas I suspect the rest of us know you just didn't want to let him in.'

'I can live with that,' I admit. 'I can't believe that wasn't the most awkward part.'

'Anyone would feel strange, kissing their ex,' Cam reasons. Then he thinks for a moment. 'Well, except Maxi and DJ. You'd never know they'd broken up.'

'No, you really wouldn't,' I say with a heavy sigh.

I really can't believe Maxi would cheat on her husband with her school boyfriend. Don't get me wrong, I know old feelings can come flooding back, because I still look at Cam like he's that cool boy on the bus I wish I was brave enough to ask out, but I'm not a happily married woman.

I open my mouth to say something to Cam but it would feel like an act of disloyalty to tell him about Maxi and DJ, about the photo I accidentally took of the two of them. So I don't say anything.

'How difficult do you think it is to get in that swing?' he asks me curiously.

I smile. He knows me so well. He knows I don't want to talk, that I want to change the subject, and the sex swing is a great distraction.

'Do you know how they work?' he asks me.

'Do *I* know how they work?' I reply through a snort. 'Oh, actually, I think I do.'

Cam widens his eyes at me.

'Only from an episode of *Sex and the City*,' I quickly add. 'And even then, I'm not sure how confident I am about it.'

'Well, let's see how strong it is,' he says with a cheeky laugh, hopping to his feet. 'Let's see if it can hold me – are they always so high?'

'It looks like it's adjustable,' I point out, sitting up, ready to spectate. 'But I'm not about to start trying to yank it up and down.'

As Cam playfully narrows his eyes at me, I realise exactly what I just said.

'You know what I mean,' I insist.

All in the name of cheering me up, Cam steps from the windowsill into the swing, his feet in each of the... oh, like I know what to call what part, the leg holes, I guess? He's balancing on them like a gymnast as he slips his arms through two holes that look like they're for arms? Gosh, we're both such sexually sophisticated adults, aren't we?

It all happens in an instant, Cam loses his footing and both his legs slip through the leg holes, as he does the weight of his arms tightens the wrist straps, essentially leaving him in the exact position you're supposed to be in when you're dangling in it, his legs secured spread wide by the leg straps, and his wrists held tightly in place above his head.

For a second, we're silent. Then we both erupt with laughter.

'Well, I think I'm in,' he says as he catches his breath. 'But how do I get out?'

I run over to the complicated pulley system, to see if I can lower him to the ground so I can untie him.

'Okay, I can't make heads nor tails of this,' I say, only making the two of us laugh harder as I realise my choice of words *again*.

'I could get out if my wrists weren't tied together high above my head,' he points out. 'Are you feeling energetic?'

'Rarely,' I reply. 'But I'll give it a go, since you so clearly need rescuing.'

'Jasmine Bartlett, you're my hero,' he teases.

I approach the man of my dreams as he dangles from the sex swing, legs akimbo, and think about how I'm going to get up there to untie his hands.

'If you step onto the windowsill, like I did, and then stand on my thighs, you'll be able to untie my wrists,' he suggests. 'Then I can help lower you down, and climb out myself.'

'Oh, Cam, you credit me with so much you shouldn't,' I point out. 'I don't have the poise, the core strength – the anything to do this.'

He laughs. 'Come on, I believe in you,' he tells me.

'On your legs be it,' I warn him as I pull myself up onto the windowsill.

I do as he suggested, stepping from the sill onto his thighs, one foot on each, hoisting myself up to reach the wrist straps that are holding his hands in place.

'This is quite the predicament you've found yourself in here, Cameron,' I tell him with a faux seriousness. 'I could do anything I wanted to you right now and there's nothing you could do to stop me.'

'I, er, I'm not really sure I would try to stop you,' he says flirtatiously.

'I'm the one in control,' I say, as we edge further away from joking, and closer to something more flirtatious. Of course, I am me, so this burst of sexiness is short-lived. I lose my footing, just like Cam did, and both my feet slip off Cam's legs. My legs slip through above the leg straps on both sides, as I quickly wrap my arms around Cam's neck.

And now I'm stuck in the sex swing too, sitting on top of Cam, my body pressed up against his, our faces just centimetres apart.

'Well, we've figured out how to use it,' he says.

We both fall about laughing again, and it's that rare, powerful laugh when tears fill your eyes, you feel like you can't breathe, you feel like you'll never quite be able to stop laughing.

But then we do stop. We fall silent, all at once, and stare into each other's eyes.

'Any more bright ideas?' I ask him.

'Just the one,' he says.

I can feel a heartbeat between our bodies. I don't know if it's mine or his, but it feels like one big, powerful shared heartbeat.

All of my senses feel heightened – I can feel everything, from Cam's muscles moving around under his shirt to his breath lightly tickling my lips.

My hands feel clammy as I separate them from behind Cam's head. I hold on to the back of his neck with one while I carefully bring the other one to place lightly on Cam's face. I bet it would feel so good if I kissed him right now. I wonder if I could...

The hotel room door opens and Clarky has no sooner stepped through it when he falls about laughing.

'Oh my God,' he blurts. 'What the fuck are you two doing in there? As though I even need to ask.'

'We were just messing around,' I quickly insist as I realise everyone is here. Clarky, Maxi, DJ *and* Mike. Brilliant.

'Yeah, that's what it looks like,' Clarky teases. 'Shall we come back later? You couldn't have left a sock on the door handle or something.'

'Not messing around like that,' I insist.

'I was joking around, seeing if it could take my weight,' Cam says, cringing slightly at how ridiculous that sounds. 'And I got stuck, and Jas was trying to help me down, then she got stuck.'

'And you didn't think to just lower it?' Maxi says through narrow eyes and a suspicious, knowing smile.

'We didn't know how,' I reply.

She clicks her tongue and rolls her eyes.

'Honestly, it's like you guys have never been on a yacht,' she jokes. 'Let me.'

Maxi lowers us to the ground where DJ helps us out of the straps.

'Honestly, this is just the best holiday ever,' Clarky says, creased with laughter at the whole situation. 'There's a place here that does tattoos – we should get commemorative tattoos. What do you say?'

His enthusiasm is kind of cute, but there is no way I'm doing group holiday tattoos.

'Oh my God, would you just give it a rest for a minute?' Mike snaps at him. 'No one wants to get a tattoo with you. When are you going to grow up?'

My breath catches in my throat. I've seen Mike take his frustration out on Clarky before. I didn't like it then and I don't like it now.

'All right,' Clarky says sheepishly, almost cowering, like a dog when you accidentally step on its paw. 'You could've just said no thanks.'

'Maybe we'll get T-shirts or something less painful,' Cam says kindly. 'I'm too old for a holiday tattoo.'

'But never too old to get in a sex swing, eh?' Mike adds.

'Hopefully none of us will ever be too old for antics like that,' Maxi chimes in jokily, trying to defuse the situation. 'Anyway, it's late, I think we've all had far too much to drink. Perhaps it's time we went to bed?'

Everyone takes Maxi's hint that perhaps we've all had enough of each other for today, which would be fine, if we could all go off to our separate rooms, but our beds are all right here, barely metres apart.

I never thought I'd be jealous of Clarky sleeping in the bathroom but right now a bit of space from the others sounds like just what I need.

Except Cam, of course, because now all I can think about is how I can get close to him again.

23

It's our second day waking up on the island but our first day waking up in an actual bed – or a sofa, in Clarky's case. I must say, I definitely prefer it.

Maxi is easy to share a bed with. She hasn't changed much from when we were younger and we would share beds at sleepovers. She sleeps flat on her back, perfectly still, like Sleeping Beauty. I'm not so graceful through the night. I cycle my sleeping positions – any but flat on my back – and only seem to be at my most comfortable when my body is making the shape of a letter or a number. It's a big bed, though, so we kept out of one another's way.

We're all heading down for breakfast now. I know it sounds off but this whole scenario very much has the feel of a school trip. Not just because they're my old school friends, and we're on a trip together, but because it's like staying in a dorm, taking turns in the bathroom, doing everything together like going for breakfast – bloody hell, we're even walking in pairs.

Cam and I are at the back, chatting as we walk. As we near the breakfast room, he hangs back a little.

I look at him expectantly as he seems like he's thinking of something to say to me.

'Do you want to do something later?' he asks me. 'Something with me, I mean, something specific.'

'That sounds... interesting,' I reply with a smile.

'I have something in mind, but I thought I'd keep it a surprise,' he tells me. 'I know you love surprises, and I think you'll love this. What do you say?'

'I cannot resist a word you just said,' I say. 'Count me in.'

'Perfect,' he replies, smiling with what looks like relief. 'Lunchtime-ish. I'll get it booked and confirm a time with you.'

'Booked?' I repeat back to him. 'Now that is intriguing.'

Cam just smiles.

My heart flutters as we catch up to the others. What on earth could Cam be planning?

'Come on, we thought we'd lost you,' Maxi insists.

Clarky pushes past Maxi and DJ like it's Christmas morning. I can't help but smile, he is clearly having the time of his life on this holiday now that we're doing things the way he wants to do them.

A waiter guides us to our seats before taking our drink orders, but breakfast is a self-service buffet, so God help us all. Clarky has already shared his strategy for packing as much food as possible onto his plate, and while I don't have a system, I have been known to devour a plate of pastries in my time.

Maxi and DJ are sitting across from me, and I can't help but notice their flirting. I think they think they're being subtle, but it couldn't be more obvious to me – then again, after the photo I saw of them (that I so, so wish I could unsee) perhaps I'm a little more in tune to their, shall we say, clearly unresolved history together.

'Right, I'm off to fill my plate,' Clarky announces. 'Sooner we start eating, the more we can fit in.'

Because that's the aim of the game here, obviously.

'I'm going to get them to cook me some fresh eggs, even if it isn't hotel policy,' Maxi says. 'I can't eat eggs that have sat out for God knows how long.'

'Oh yeah, and how are you doing to do that?' DJ asks – somehow sounding flirtatious.

'Perhaps I'll flirt with the waiter,' Maxi threatens, chewing her lip lightly.

'You think your flirting skills are up to that?' he asks.

'Don't you?' she replies.

I glance at Cam, to see if he's picking up on this. He raises his eyebrows subtly – actually subtly, not subtle like Maxi and DJ think they are being.

'I think you must've had a good teacher at some point,' DJ reasons as they both stand up to go and get their breakfast. 'Perhaps you need a little more practice, though...'

'Sensible shoes today, by the way,' Cam says to me quietly.

'Is a flatform heel a sensible shoe?' I reply.

'Is a flatform a shoe?' he jokes back. 'My advice is wear flats.'

'Hey, Jas, I was thinking we could go for lunch today?'

Cam's whispers are suddenly drowned out by Mike's booming voice.

I pause for a moment, not wanting to offend him but also knowing I just made plans with Cam.

'Ah, sorry,' I say. 'I've already made plans with Cam this afternoon.'

Mike's face sinks, and I can see a hint of anger in his eyes.

'Of course you have,' I just about hear him mumble to himself before he heads off to join the buffet line.

I feel a twinge of guilt, but I really have just made plans with Cam, and I can't abandon him because Mike asks me to. I can meet Mike for lunch another day; I'll suggest it to him later, and hopefully he'll come around. It seems like a strange thing for him to be so bothered by. Mike from school was moody, had a temper, would strop if he didn't get his own way. And Clarky would be overexcited about the silliest things, just constantly trying to have a good time – or what he thought was a good time, at least – and Maxi and DJ would be flirting. And then there was me, pining after Cam, and Cam always feeling just out of my reach.

This really does feel like a school trip because everyone is slowly slipping back into old habits. And I'm just as bad as the rest of them.

24

THEN – 12 JULY 2008

I love our park – the one we always hang out in – especially this beautiful green space, with tall trees surrounding the wide-open lawn in the centre. It's not very busy so, sometimes, when it's just our gang here, it feels like there's no one else in the world.

The sun is shining high in the sky, and the July weather is just perfect today, warm but with a gentle breeze that carries the scent of freshly cut grass. The birds are chirping happily, and you can just about make out the kids playing on the swings on the other side of the trees, but here it's just us, eating crisps, drinking pop, and enjoying the summer as results day looms.

Oh, and Clarky is here too, home from uni, and on top Clarky form.

'Seriously, guys, it's insane,' Clarky brags, his voice laced with excitement. 'I've got so many girls trying to shag me, it's hard to keep track.'

'Trying to shag you?' Cam repeats back to him. 'Are you having some sort of problem?'

We all laugh at Cam's joke – apart from Clarky, who gives Cam the finger, and Mikey, who seems distracted. He's like this all the time at the moment, we're barely speaking, and I definitely don't feel like I can talk to him, which is making breaking up with him really hard.

'What about your lectures?' DJ asks.

Clarky's eyes light up.

'Actually, there is this one lecturer who's been really cool. I think she might be into me,' he replies.

I can't help but roll my eyes.

'Clarky, she's your lecturer. You can't be serious,' I reply.

'Why the hell not?' he asks, offended I think he might not have sexual prowess (he doesn't). 'I'm just saying, I've got my suspicions.'

I shake my head, trying not to laugh. 'Sure,' I say, not wanting to get into it.

'And it's not just the girls,' he continues, his grin widening.

'Really?' Maxi replies, practically singing the word.

'Nah, not like that,' Clarky corrects her. 'I mean the parties are insane. And the booze? Let's just say I've been doing a fair bit of drinking. I had almost a whole bottle of vodka to myself the other week.'

'Sounds like you're having a good time,' DJ says, his tone a little sarcastic, but Clarky is oblivious and keeps talking.

'And I've got some cool housemates lined up for next year. We're going to be partying every night.'

'What are your grades like, though?' Maxi asks him.

Clarky scoffs. 'You guys are so boring,' he replies. 'Uni is about partying! I'm glad you're all going to a different one now. I bet you have such a dull time. York sounds rubbish.'

'You say that,' DJ chimes in. 'But I'm sure I heard that York has more pubs per square metre, or versus its population, than most places in England – something like that. My point is, there are lots of places to drink.'

'Really?' Clarky replies thoughtfully. 'Perhaps I'll join you all in York then, I could do my PhD there.'

'Ha,' Mikey chimes in – his first contribution to the conversation since we got here. We all turn to him. 'You're not doing a PhD, Clarky, come off it, you're too thick.'

For a few seconds, we're all stunned into silence. Sure, we all make fun of Clarky, but it's good-natured fun, and he makes fun of us too. But that, there, that was just plain mean.

'Steady on, mate,' Cam warns him gently.

'And you can piss off,' Mikey snaps at him. 'Honestly, you lot are pathetic.'

Mikey gets up and storms off, his feet thumping the ground as though he means harm to every blade of grass he steps on.

'Well, that was vile,' Maxi says softly.

'Should one of us go after him?' DJ asks.

'Don't you dare,' Maxi replies. 'I don't know why he's being horrible at the moment.'

'I'll go after him,' I say.

'Jas, no,' Maxi says, concerned.

'It's okay,' I reassure her. 'We need to talk.'

Maxi knows what that means – she knows I've been trying to find the right time to break up with him, and I can't think of a better time than now, after he's been so horrible. He can't expect me to want to stay with him, if this is how he's going to act.

'Mikey, wait a sec,' I call out, trying to catch my breath as I run after him.

He turns around, looking at me with a mixture of anger and surprise, and stops. He couldn't look less approachable if he tried, but I couldn't be more certain that I'm doing the right thing by ending things with him, I just need to do it at the right time, and to figure out what's going on with him first.

'What do you want?' he asks, crossing his arms in front of his chest.

'Charming,' I reply, finding my confidence a little. 'What's wrong with you? You've been so distant and so mean lately. I don't get it.'

Mikey scoffs.

'You don't get it? Of course you don't,' he replies. 'You don't care.'

'What do you mean I don't care?' I reply. 'Of course I care. That's why I'm here, trying to talk to you.'

'You won't even kiss me,' he replies. 'So either something is wrong with me or something is wrong with you.'

That remark stops me in my tracks. Wow, he really is being mean.

'Mikey, things clearly aren't working out between us,' I say softly. 'And with sixth form coming to an end, and the summer ahead of us, perhaps we need to spend some time apart.'

I'm proud of myself. I had no idea what I was going to say but I think that was the best way it could've come out. It feels kind, gentle – there's no need for me to kick off at him for the things he's saying, perhaps this way we can keep our friendship intact, and by the time we go to uni we might all just be friends again.

'You've just been waiting for an excuse to break up with me,' he says accusingly. 'Well done, you finally did it. This is what this is, isn't it? You breaking up with me.'

I nod, feeling bad, but unable to ignore the sense of relief washing over me at the same time.

'I think we both need a clean break to figure out who we are and what we want,' I tell him.

Mikey's face flushes.

'Fine,' he says through gritted teeth. 'If that's what you want.'

'It is,' I say, not wanting to leave any room for interpretation.

Mikey pauses for a second, as though he's considering his next words carefully.

'Is there someone else?' he asks me. 'Have you been cheating on me?'

'How can you even ask me that?' I reply.

'That's not a denial,' he points out.

I take a step back, not wanting to be near him if he's going to be like this.

'I'm not doing this,' I say. 'Go home, cool off, give me some space.'

With that, Mikey storms off and I head back towards my friends. I feel so silly but I want to cry. I know I'm doing the right thing, but that was horrible.

'Are you okay?' Maxi asks me as I sit back down on the picnic blanket.

'I'm fine,' I reply, smiling, trying to hide the wobble in my voice.

One tear manages to escape so I quickly flick it away, pretending to push my hair behind my ear instead, looking down at my knees until the feeling passes.

I feel a hand on mine – well, just a little finger, linking itself with mine. I glance up to see Cam give me a reassuring smile. I smile back.

Not all boys are bad.

25

NOW

As I walk down the corridor towards our room, I can hear faint music and what sounds like giggling coming from behind our door.

Clarky has gone off to find the girls he was talking to yesterday – I swear, he's forgotten Drea exists, but she appears to have forgotten him too so it's probably for the best – Cam is finalising plans for whatever we're about to do, and that just leaves Maxi, DJ and Mike, who I think are all in here.

I've just popped up to change my shoes, but as my hand hovers over the door handle, I can't quite shake the feeling that something's not right.

Rather than using my key card and walking straight in, my instinct tells me to knock and wait for someone to answer.

The music cuts out. Maxi eventually opens the door.

'Oh, Jas, hello,' she says, looking and sounding a little flustered. 'Do you not have your key card?'

'I think I left it up here,' I lie.

For a few seconds, neither of us says a word or moves a muscle.

'Well, come in, come in,' she eventually insists.

When I walk in, I see DJ sitting in the centre of his bed, messing around on his phone. He glances up for a moment, giving me a nod.

Pretty sus, if you ask me.

'How's it going?' I say casually as I look for my shoes, in an attempt to seem like I'm not picking up on the awkwardness. There is a definite tension in the air, though, and you could smash through it with a spanking paddle.

Maxi and DJ exchange a glance – one they think I don't notice – before Maxi answers my question.

'Going good,' she says. 'Just chilling, waiting for Mike to get back so we can see about what to do today – while you're on your mystery date with Cam.'

Oh, Maxi, don't think making this about me is going to take the heat off you.

'Where is Mike?' I ask.

'He had a phone call,' she replies. 'He seemed like he wanted privacy, so he left.'

'Oh, okay,' I say. 'Well, I'm just going to swap my shoes.'

I pause for a second as I wonder whether I should mind my own business or say something. I feel like Maxi always has my best interests at heart. I should say something, for her sake.

'Can I have a quick word?' I ask.

DJ's head snaps up.

'I'm going for a shower,' he tells us.

I can't help but notice him tighten up the string on the waist of his shorts as he heads for the bathroom. Tell me I'm being paranoid!

As soon as DJ is in the bathroom and the water is running, I cut to the chase.

'Is something going on between you two?' I ask her.

'Jas, I'm a married woman,' she replies, squeaking with offence.

'Sit down with me for a moment,' I say softly.

I grab my camera from my bag on the coffee table/cage and sit down on our bed. Maxi sits next to me.

'I only spotted this yesterday,' I tell her. 'When we were sleeping on the beach, I was struggling to sleep, I was freaked out, it was dark, and I thought I could hear some sort of animal or something.'

I cringe. Telling the story exactly as it happened is all well and good but now that I know what the noises were, my description makes me wince at my own choice of words.

'Anyway, I was feeling brave so I went to see what it was,' I continue. 'But I wasn't feeling *that* brave so rather than look into the trees, I used this camera, to flash a light, to hopefully spook whatever... it was.'

I'm careful not to compare the sound of Maxi having sex to a wild animal again.

Maxi's face falls.

'I heard your voice, after the flash, so I figured you were having a wee,' I explain. 'I didn't want to embarrass you, so I just went back to where I was sleeping, and didn't think of it again. Until yesterday, when I saw the photo.'

'What did you see?' she asks me quietly, although I suspect she knows the answer.

'You,' I tell her. 'And DJ.'

'Oh, God, Jas, listen to me, it's not what it looks like,' she insists.

I can't help but pull a face.

'Maxi, there was no way that photo wasn't what it looked like,' I reply.

'Well, that was obviously what it looks like,' she corrects

herself. 'But I was scared, I thought I was going to die, I was freezing. You see these things in the movies, don't you? People are in a situation, they think they're going to die, their primal instinct kicks in.'

'I managed to sleep next to Mike without sleeping with him,' I point out.

'Well, you've always found that easy,' she replies, a little nastiness coming out. 'Perhaps if it was Cameron next to you, even you might have struggled.'

Maxi stops, takes a short, sharp breath and then places a hand on my leg.

'I'm sorry,' she says, softening. 'That was uncalled for.'

I get it, she's in a corner and she's trying to attack her way out.

'I know it was a tough night,' I explain. 'I was there too. I love DJ, he's one of my oldest friends, but come on, Maxi, you're married, and we all know how much you love Rupert. Are you going to throw it all away on Darren Junior from school?'

I have nothing against DJ, or Maxi and DJ as a couple – everyone always thought they would get married – but I have to look at Maxi in isolation, as my friend, my happily married friend.

'It was just old feelings surging back,' she tells me. 'A one-off – it won't happen again. Promise me no one will ever see that photo, Jas.'

'I deleted it right away,' I tell her.

Maxi exhales deeply. 'It was just a silly mistake,' she says. 'I suppose I've been kind of lonely recently. I don't see much of Rupert, he's always so busy, and being with you guys just feels so great. Like the good old days.'

I do get that. It is nice, to be around everyone again, to feel like that strong support network is back. I couldn't have got through my teens without my friends around me.

'Was it really just a one-off?' I ask her.

'Jas, you know I would never lie to you,' she insists. 'It's just old feelings. Come on, you're clearly having them with Cam.'

'Yeah, but I'm single,' I reply. 'And he's, well, going to be officially single soon. I know he hasn't told me but it's none of my business, is it? I'm just trying to be a grown-up, trying not to let it bother me, seeing how things go...'

Maxi looks so, so guilty. I don't really feel like she's listening to me.

Then she bursts into tears.

We're interrupted by the door opening. Mike stops in his tracks when he notices the two of us, Maxi sobbing.

I jump to my feet and meet him at the door, ushering him outside.

'We should probably give her a minute,' I tell him. 'She's just feeling a bit emotional today, she's okay, though.'

'Oh, right, okay,' he replies. 'Women stuff?'

'Yes,' I say quickly, unsure how I feel about that, but happy to take any excuse. 'Anyway, are you okay? Maxi said you were on the phone.'

'Work stuff,' he replies. 'Are you off to meet Cam now?'

'Erm, yeah,' I say, trying not to sound as awkward as I feel.

'What's going on with you and Cam?' he asks.

'I'm not actually sure,' I reply. 'He's arranged for us to do something, but not told me what. So that will be interesting.'

'No, that's not what I mean,' he says – I knew what he meant. 'Is something going on between the two of you?'

I think for a moment. I'm not actually sure how much of Mike's business this is. I know, he's my ex, but a brief one from a lifetime ago – we didn't even do anything.

As I shake my head, I feel my cheeks flush.

'Nothing is going on between us,' I say casually. 'We're just catching up, hanging out.'

The truth is that I wish something was going on between us – of course, that's not something I should mention now.

'That's good,' he says, nodding with relief. 'I was just concerned about you getting hurt.'

I raise my brow. Why is Mike asking? Why does he care? Oh, God, he doesn't want to get back together, does he? I need to nip this in the bud ASAP.

'There's nothing to worry about, I'm not going to get hurt,' I insist. 'To be honest, I'm not looking for a relationship at the moment.'

'Oh, okay,' Mike replies. 'Well, I'll let you go.'

I feel bad, lying to him like that, but I really can't have him getting the wrong idea. But while it may be a lie, that I'm not looking for a relationship right now, it is technically true that nothing is going on between me and Cam.

But, more and more every day now, I really, really wish there was.

26

THEN – 27 JULY 2008

'Are you two married?' a small boy with brown hair and a jazzy SpongeBob SquarePants wetsuit asks us as he roots around in his nose with what looks like the best part of his index finger.

'You think just because she's dressed as a mummy shark and I'm dressed as a daddy shark that we're married?' Cam jokes. 'No, we're not married, we're just friends.'

Even hearing him say this to a five-year-old makes me a little bit sad somewhere in the back of my brain, which is just so silly.

The kid runs off, leaving the two of us to our stint as lifeguards, while our two colleagues dressed as fish lead a water dance class. They're more like professional... somethings, whereas Cam and I are more like clowns, but I swear the kids have more fun with us chasing them around the water, screaming with a mixture of fear and delight, than they do dancing to corny kids' music.

Cam and I have been working here together all summer. It's not exactly theatre, wearing a shark fin while you essentially babysit kids, but we're enjoying it.

The indoor kids' pool is a brightly lit, lagoon-shaped pool with a tropical theme. The walls are lined with large windows that let in natural light, making the space feel airy and open. All of the trees are fake, of course, but it still gives the place a sort of summer holiday vibe. The pool has a large slide and so many inflatables it can sometimes be hard to spot the kids between them, but we do a good job taking care of them, and we haven't had any accidents yet, even if we do have a regular six-year-old called Daniel who always forgets he can't swim and keeps jumping in the deep end, only for us to have to help him out, time after time. I'm not even sure that Daniel can't swim, I think he can, but somewhere between feeling brave enough to charge towards the edge of the pool and jump in, and splashing around in the water calling out for help, he just loses his nerve. You can't fault his initial confidence and bravery, though.

'You seem really happy,' Cam tells me with a smile. 'It's nice to see.'

'I feel happy,' I confess. 'Which is funny, given how nervous I am about my exam results.'

'Have you heard DJ is throwing a results day party at his house?' Cam says. 'While his parents are away.'

'I have,' I reply. 'That's a cool house, for parties.'

DJ lives on the outskirts of the village, in a house surrounded by woodland. Well, I say in a house, he lives in a sort of granny flat, in a separate building, above the garage and his dad's workshop. You would think this would make it easy for him to sneak Maxi in but his dad works all sorts of hours, sculpting things out of wood, and he's the naturally suspicious type so he keeps a close eye on his only son. DJ's parents are really religious, and really strict, so even though he's eighteen, he still has to pretend he doesn't drink and stuff like that, he says it's not worth the lecture. However, now that DJ is going off to uni, they've decided to invest in one of those caravans at a holiday park. It's not too far from here, but I suppose it's a nice change of scenery for them, something to distract them from their soon-to-be-empty nest. Anyway, apparently they're spending their first night there on results day, going later in the day after taking DJ out for a celebratory lunch, so DJ is shooting his shot, and throwing a house party. He says it's to celebrate all of us getting our results but Maxi has pretty much told me this whole thing is just so the two of them have an opportunity to sleep together – but I suppose isn't that why every teenage boy throws a party?

'Do you think Mikey will be there?' I ask him. 'I haven't spoken to him since...'

'I'm sure he will,' Cam says. 'Don't take it personally, that you haven't heard much from him, no one has. He's working for his dad over the summer, it sounds like it's keeping him pretty busy.'

I nod. 'I know I did the right thing, breaking up with him, I just wish we could go back to being friends,' I reply.

'The party will be a good place to start,' he reassures me. 'I think his pride is hurt but he'll get over it.'

'I really hope so,' I say. 'I know we're all busy working summer jobs, but I hate that we don't all hang out like we used to. We're not seeing each other as often, or people will be missing – it's strange.'

'It is, but I guess this is what growing up is like,' he replies. 'Leaving school, leaving all your friends behind. We're lucky we're all going to the same uni.'

'Yeah, I love that we're refusing to grow up properly,' I add with a laugh. 'But it will be weird, all being on different courses. Apart from us, obviously.'

'Yeah, although I'm kind of looking forward to spending more time, just the two of us,' Cam says, keeping his eyes on the pool.

I glance at him, trying to read his mind. We've been getting on so well this summer, having a laugh – flirting, even. I don't know why neither of us can just come out with it.

Daniel goes charging past us, making his way to the pool before belly-flopping into the water. He goes under before quickly popping back up. We wait to see if today is the day he's going to swim and for a second it seems like he might, but then he starts flapping his arms, calling out for help.

'I'll get this one,' Cam says, jumping into the water to help Daniel out.

I sigh, but then I smile. With determination and bravery like that, he'll get it one day. Perhaps that's what I need, I need to be more like Daniel. I need to be confident, determined, and brave if I'm going to get what I want. I can't spend my life in the shallow end hoping things will change, just because I want them to.

After returning Daniel to his mum – who is always far too engrossed in a novel to realise what is going on – a soaking wet Cam sits down next to me again. He runs a hand through his hair, to get rid of the excess moisture, and then grabs a towel to dry his face.

Come on, Jasmine, be more like Daniel. You can do this.

'Taking the plunge is actually the hardest part,' Cam says as he dries off.

'What?' I blurt quickly. How does he know what I'm thinking? God, tell me he can't read my mind. I know he can't, of course I do, but I still blush at the idea.

'Daniel,' he says, so I know what he's talking about. 'Running up and jumping in is the hardest part.'

I know just how he feels. But I need to do this.

'Jas?' Cam says, half-concerned, half-amused. 'Are you okay? You look like you're trying to sneeze but you can't get it out.'

'I like you,' I blurt.

I quickly place my hand over my mouth, as though I can't quite believe that just came out.

Cam smiles.

'I like you too,' he replies.

'No, I, like, like-like you,' I tell him in an attempt to clarify what I mean, even though that sounds incredibly confusing.

'I like-like you too,' he says with a laugh.

'Really?' I squeak in disbelief, because I've always wanted to hear him say those words, but never really believed it would happen.

'Of course,' he says, smiling widely, as though he's as relieved as I am to finally get it out there.

'Oi, no heavy petting,' June, one of the water dance teachers, says as she passes us. 'And it's your turn to get back in the pool.'

I puff air from my cheeks.

'Come on then, let's go,' Cam says. 'Oh, but before I forget, have you heard about that crazy golf place that's opening?'

'No,' I say with a laugh, amazed he's bringing it up now.

'It looks awesome,' he replies. 'It's opening in about a month. Do you fancy going with me?'

'Just me, or me and the gang?' I can't help but ask, still worried I'm getting my wires crossed.

'Just you,' he says. 'Just me and you. Like a date.'

Just when I thought I couldn't smile any wider.

'I'd love that,' I tell him as I grab our shark fins from next to us, ready for us to get back in the water.

I've taken the plunge. Now all I have to do is swim.

27

NOW

As tragic as it sounds, I feel butterflies in my stomach when I spot Cam in the hotel lobby, waiting for me.

His smile is beaming from ear to ear.

'Hello,' he says.

'Hi,' I reply, trying to sound a lot cooler than I feel.

'Are you ready for... this?' he asks cryptically.

'Let's do it,' I say, allowing myself to show a little bit of excitement – I say allowing myself, I can't stop it from spilling out of me.

'Okay but, first of all, let's grab a bite to eat,' he suggests. 'They have a street food area and the scent is pulling me in, like a cartoon character smelling a pie.'

I laugh. 'I suppose you can keep me in suspense just a little longer, if there is going to be food,' I say with a smile.

Never mind the food – although obviously I'm really into the eating segment of... whatever this is – but the thought of making it last longer floods every inch of my body with excitement. Forget the journey, forget the baggage – hell, forget the destination. For this part of the holiday, none of it matters. We're in international waters (jokes aside, we could actually be), the rules are out of the window, I'm focusing on the here and now, even if it's only for a day.

Cam leads me outside and down a pathway I haven't been down before until eventually we reach the street food market.

My senses are overwhelmed by the sights, sounds and smells that surround me as we walk through the busy market. The scent of freshly baked bread, sizzling meat, and simmering sauces fills the air, and I can hear vendors calling out to passers-by, enticing them with their wares. I don't think I'm going to take much persuading.

Cam walks beside me, his eyes wide with wonder as he takes in the scene, his head tilted up slightly, which makes me smile – he really is like a cartoon character following the whiff of a pie. I can feel my stomach grumbling with hunger, and my mouth watering at the delicious smells. I don't even know where to begin, I just know that I want *everything*.

As we walk, we come across a vendor selling arancini, and Cam orders a few for us to share.

'Don't worry, we can charge it all to the room. I told Maxi I'll sort it out later,' he reassures me. 'But she says this whole trip is on her, even the detour. We'll see.'

Oh, they're going to taste even better, if they're free.

The crispy golden rice balls are stuffed with a warm, savoury tomato sauce and melted cheese. I take a bite, savouring the flavour.

We continue our way through the market, sampling various bites from various vendors. Cam orders another slice of pizza, while I choose a bowl of pasta for my next snack.

'The pesto in this is incredible,' I say as I take another bite. 'I'm not sure I've ever had anything like it.'

Cam agrees with a nod, his mouth full of pizza.

'It's a thousand times better than what we're used to back home. I'm not sure I can go back to the pizza at home after this.'

'And to think, we've not even started on the desserts yet,' I point out. 'I've already scoped out a few flavours of gelato, and a sweet arancini filled with rice pudding and chocolate.'

'Well, that should probably wait,' he replies, wiping his hands with a serviette, before putting our rubbish into one of the nearby bins. 'I'm sure we'll regret eating too much before we do the thing we're about to do.'

'Well, that's terrifying,' I point out through a laugh. 'But so very exciting at the same time. Come on, let's go.'

'Follow me,' Cam says with a nod of his head, his face giving nothing away.

Cam leads me to another part of the resort that I haven't visited yet – honestly, this place is massive, I'm surprised we didn't hear it sooner – but as we arrive at our destination, it all becomes clear.

I laugh.

'Is this a minigolf course?' I ask. It so very clearly is, but I can't quite believe it.

'Well, we always said we would play minigolf together,' he reminds me – as though I needed the reminder. It hit me like a ton of bricks the second I realised where we were. 'So when I realised they had a course here, I knew we had to give it a go. Although it's certainly not like the "under the sea" one we were going to go to when we were kids.'

As I look around, my mouth drops open. I've never seen a minigolf course like this one. It has a sort of romantic, if not outright sexy, theme. Some of the obstacles look nothing short of hilarious. I can't wait to play.

'I can't believe you've done this,' I say through a smile.

Cam shrugs causally.

'A million years ago, I promised you minigolf,' he says. 'And you promised me it would be our first date.'

I'm holding my breath. I need to breathe.

I'm amazed that he remembered, that he's kept it – me – in his thoughts all these years. Of course, I've done the same.

'I remember,' I tell him. 'Does that make this a date then?'

'I upheld my end of the bargain,' he says with a cheeky smile. 'You tell me.'

'Let's give it a go,' I reply. 'See if it's any good. I'll decide if it's a date if I enjoy it.'

'No pressure then,' Cam laughs.

We step up to the first hole where a giant heart-shaped structure stands tall in the middle of the green. Cam lines up his shot, takes a swing, and then we both watch as the ball ricochets off the side of the heart and rolls right back towards us, gently hitting my foot.

'I always have been hopeless in love,' he jokes.

'Let's see if I'm any better,' I reply.

I line up my shot, hit the ball, and send it exactly where it needs to go. My ball goes straight through the heart. We walk round to look to see that it's gone straight in.

'Unbelievable,' Cam says with a laugh. 'A shot straight through the heart.'

I curtsy playfully.

As we play on, I am pleasantly surprised to discover that I'm actually quite good at minigolf – well, it feels more like luck than skill, but I'll take it. Cam's not bad, he seems like he has actual skill behind him, but I keep getting lucky, doing just a little bit better than him on each hole.

At the heart of the course, hiding away from the view around it, is a hole with an interesting obstacle – a gigantic plastic couple having sex, and the aim of the game is to get the ball in her open mouth. Subtle. So subtle.

I can't help but laugh at how ridiculous it all is.

'The eye contact is putting me off,' I joke.

'Good,' Cam replies. 'Perhaps I'll beat you on this one. I actually learned to play golf a bit, loads of people I meet through work play, it's one of the few ways serious businessmen know how to relate to one another. I like to think I'd thrash you if we were playing eighteen holes, but you're clearly the better minigolf player.'

I laugh because I know he doesn't really care.

'I think you're right,' I reply. 'I can throw the club further than I can hit the ball. Luckily I'm not a serious businessman – although you don't seem much like one either.'

'I'm not,' he insists. 'I had a word with Maxi earlier, about my creative hub, she wants to invest in it. I think it might actually be happening.'

'Oh, Cam, that's amazing,' I reply – grabbing him and hugging him without really thinking about it.

'Thanks,' he replies. 'Well, if you ever get tired of your job, or fancy a new challenge, you know there's a place for you.'

I don't know how much he means it but I'm not going to let this opportunity pass me by.

'If you're serious then I would love to join you,' I tell him, but then I backtrack slightly. 'But if you're just being polite, never mind.'

'I'm definitely serious,' he says. 'But don't quit a good, stable job that you love for my silly venture that might not work out.'

I think for a second. Screw it, it's about time we started being honest, and if I am about my less-than-ideal situation then maybe he will be too.

'I'm not working there any more, actually,' I confess. 'I finished there, just before this holiday. I was too embarrassed to admit it because everyone else seems to be doing so well but, yep, that's me, unemployed. But I don't just want this job because it's a job, I want to be involved, I want to make a difference.'

'Oh, Jas, I'm sorry,' he replies. We're still holding each other. 'You should never be embarrassed about something like that, especially with your friends.'

I take a step back, stepping on the golf club I dropped to the floor when I went to hug him. I lose my footing and stumble towards the water trap that surrounds this hole.

Cam extends his arm like a flash and grabs me, stopping me in my tracks, before pulling me back.

'Whew, that was lucky,' he says. 'You're having a run of good luck today. A new job, crushing it at minigolf. What do you say we make this more interesting?'

'Go on,' I reply, allowing a little flirtation to creep into my voice.

'How about if you make this shot, we call this a date,' he suggests. 'And if you miss, well... no hard feelings.'

'Sounds like a plan,' I reply.

I smile to myself, filled with confidence. I take a deep breath, line up my shot, and swing.

The ball rolls effortlessly over the loved-up couple and lands in the woman's mouth with a satisfying clatter. I let out a triumphant cheer, as if I'd just won the Masters, around the same time my ball triggers some kind of mechanism in the woman's mouth that plays the sound of a screaming orgasm.

'Well, that sounds like the perfect end to a perfect date,' Cam replies.

'It doesn't have to be the end,' I tell him. 'It's the end of the world tonight.'

'The end of the world?' Cam replies.

'That's what the club night is called,' I tell him.

'Oh, well...'

We're interrupted by a man clearing his throat. We've clearly spent too much time on this hole, there's a couple waiting to take their turn.

'I'd invite you back to my room, but it's full of our oldest friends,' Cam jokes.

I laugh. 'We should head back there anyway, get ready for tonight,' I tell him. 'But I'm looking forward to seeing what happens, at the end of the world.'

'Me too,' he replies.

I wonder, if we hadn't ended up here on this island, if Cam and I would be flirting like we are now. Perhaps if we had stayed at the villa, things would still be platonic, civilised.

Maybe Clarky was on to something, leading us here. Either way, suddenly I can't wait for the end of the world...

28

THEN – 14 AUGUST 2008

I am officially going to York St John University in September because I absolutely smashed my A levels – I can't quite believe it. You do all your coursework and you revise until you feel like you can't possibly squash any more information into your tiny little brain but you never think you're going to do very well, and yet here we are, your girl is going to York.

My mum and dad were over the moon, taking me out for a celebratory lunch afterwards, because they knew I have the party tonight. Well, they know I'm seeing my friends tonight to celebrate with them, they don't know we're having a house party.

Cam and I went to collect our results together and, while I might feel like I smashed it because I got the grades I needed, Cam has absolutely knocked it out of the park with As across the board. Honestly, when his mum and dad picked him up, I thought they were going to cry, they were so proud of him, and so they should be.

I haven't heard from anyone else yet. I did text Maxi, to ask her how she did, but she said she would see me here at the party and we could chat. Obviously, DJ will be here, Clarky is coming, and even Mikey is going to show his face for the first time all summer. Cam is the one I'm looking forward to seeing the most, though. We've seriously upped our flirting game, since we both admitted that we like-like each other, but we're taking things slowly, and we're finally going to have our first date together next week, when the crazy golf place opens. I can't wait. But right now, things between us are top secret – I haven't even told Maxi. We want to make sure things are right, that we know what we want before the others find out.

DJ's parents' house – a massive old stone building – is in the middle of nowhere, making it the perfect location for a sneaky party. Not only are we surrounded by trees but with no neighbours anywhere near, there's no one to hear the loud music.

Next to the main house is a large double garage, with DJ's dad's workshop joined on next door. Upstairs there is a lounge, a small kitchen, a bathroom, and DJ's bedroom. It's like he has his own house, perfect for parties – but with strict parents like his, we've never actually been able to use it until today.

Behind the building is a large decked area with fancy patio furniture which is already packed with partygoers. It sounds like there are lots of people inside too, because chatter and the sound of people having a good time drifts out of the open windows with along with the loud music. The party was late starting, because DJ's parents didn't leave until late, so it's getting dark out, but the patio is well-lit and the building behind me is beaming light out of every window. It's impossible for it to be creepy here, with so many people, so much noise, so much light.

Eventually I spot DJ and Clarky, over to one side on the decking, but it looks like they're arguing.

'Hi,' I say cautiously, trying to work out what I'm interrupting.

'Hey, Jas,' DJ replies. 'Have a word with him, will you? He's brought drugs to the party.'

'Clarky, what the hell?' I blurt.

'What? I brought a bag of skag, thought I'd liven things up a bit,' he explains, his tone suggesting he finds me just as ungrateful as he's finding DJ.

'Who brings heroin to a house party?' I ask him in a disbelieving, angry whisper.

'Heroin?' he repeats back to me. 'Skag is weed, you loser.'

'It's definitely heroin,' I say confidently.

Clarky pulls a clear plastic bag full of ground-up green stuff from his pocket.

'What makes you the authority on drugs?' he asks me.

DJ snatches it from him and examines it.

'I don't know, because I've watched *The Bill*?' I quip, but that might actually be true. 'Skag is not weed.'

'Neither is this,' DJ says, laughing so hard his eyes start to water.

'What do you mean?' Clarky asks. 'Of course it is. I bought it off some lads at uni.'

'Then you've been done,' DJ informs him. 'Jas, smell this.'

Curious, I sniff the contents of the bag.

'It smells like pizza,' I say, confused.

'Mate, that's a bag of oregano,' DJ informs him.

'Bollocks,' Clarky replies. 'Screw you two. I'm taking my weed and I'm going to join in the FIFA tournament, and I'm going to see if anyone fancies a smoke with me.'

Clarky snatches the bag and storms off.

'I'd say don't smoke it inside but I often cook with it in the kitchen,' DJ calls after him mockingly. He turns to me, once it's just the two of us. 'That boy is a clown. Can you even imagine him at uni?'

'I bet he drives everyone mad,' I reply with a sigh. 'I wonder if they put up with him like we do.'

'Does selling him herbs and pretending they're drugs sound like putting up with him?' he says through a laugh.

'Good point,' I reply. 'Anyway, come on, are you happy with your results?'

'I am indeed,' he says proudly. 'Are you?'

'I am too,' I reply. 'And Maxi? Where is she?'

'She's up in my bedroom, she just wanted a few minutes on her own,' he says, lowering his voice, his expression suddenly much more serious. 'To be honest, I don't think she's doing so good. I'm sure she'll tell you all about it herself.'

'Right, okay,' I reply, springing to action. 'Can I go up there now?'

'Yeah, of course, but, Jas, before you go.'

DJ places a hand on my shoulder, which makes me think something bad must be coming.

'Mikey is here,' he tells me.

'Thanks for the heads-up,' I reply. 'I guess I'll have to face him sooner or later. Tonight is as good a night as any.'

'That's the thing, I don't think it is,' DJ says, and something about the look on his face worries me sick. 'He messed up his exams, he's not going to uni.'

'Oh, God, that's awful,' I say honestly. 'How is he taking it?'

'Bad,' DJ replies, his eyes widening for emphasis. 'He turned up drunk, for one thing, but he was looking for you, saying he needed to talk to you. I felt like he was going to try to get you back but, I don't know, you might want to avoid him. He wasn't in a fit state for a sensible conversation.'

'Thanks for the heads-up,' I reply. 'I guess I'll go hide in your bedroom with Maxi.'

'Tell her I'll be up soon, I'm just making sure everything is okay out here.'

I nod before heading inside. Wow, the place really is packed

– I don't even recognise some of these people but I suppose that's what it's like with house parties, word spreads, people bring their friends, and you end up with a house full of randoms. I would never throw a party at my parents' house, even if they were away for the night – no, especially if they were away for the night – because anything could happen. What if something gets broken or something bad happens? I know, that's not exactly in the party spirit, I guess I'm in worrying mode now. I just can't shake the feeling something bad is going to happen tonight.

I knock on DJ's bedroom door.

'Maxi? Max, it's Jas, can I come in?' I call out.

'Jas, oh my God, am I glad to see you,' Maxi says as she lets me in.

She sits down on the bed, so I sit next to her.

'Wow, so this is DJ's room?' I say. 'It's... kind of what I expected?'

'Yeah, me too, I guess,' she replies, laughing quietly, but I can tell she's upset about something. 'I knew he was a nerd but this... yeah.'

In some ways, DJ's room is exactly as you would expect a teenage boy's bedroom to look – the colours, the way things have so blatantly been sort-of tidied by being kicked under various items of furniture, the smell of cheap deodorant like the boys' changing rooms at school (but only in that small window after PE when they're all blasting the various flavours of Lynx at the same time). His personality shines through, though, in all the retro games consoles, and the bits of random tech on his desk – gadgets I don't recognise, things he's been dismantling, random wires and plugs and all sorts.

'The flowers are nice,' I say, nodding towards the vase on the desk.

They're a brightly coloured mixed bunch, the kind you get from the supermarket. 'A bit out of place, though.'

'They're for me,' she says with a slight smile. 'Tonight is supposed to be *the* night.'

I think everyone and their mate somehow knows that this whole party is in honour of Maxi and DJ having sex for the first time, which is probably weird, but here we are.

'I guess it's sweet of him, to put flowers out, and that random candle over there,' she continues.

Sure enough, on the chest of drawers by the window, there is a long, skinny white candle with a gold cross on it. I suppose it's the thought that counts.

'You know, it's totally okay to change your mind,' I reassure her. 'DJ is a good guy, he'll understand. He just wants to make you happy.'

'I know,' she replies. 'Believe me, I know. I didn't get into York.'

'What? Really?' I reply in disbelief. 'Oh, Maxi, I'm so sorry.'

'I didn't get the English grade I needed,' she says with a shrug, her eyes filling with tears. 'It's fine, I have my other options, but they're all just so far away, and I was so looking forward to us all going to York. I don't want the gang to break up. DJ is being amazing, though. We coordinated some of our backup unis, so he says wherever I go, he'll go. But he's so smart, he has such a bright future ahead of him, I don't want to hold him back.'

'DJ is smart,' I agree. 'And he'll do what's right for him, don't worry about that. We just need to worry about you, and what's right for you. But please, please don't worry about us not all being in the same place – we survived when Clarky left.'

Maxi snorts.

'But seriously,' I continue. 'We're all going to be fine, no matter where we go to uni, we'll be friends forever.'

'Do you think?' she sobs.

'Of course,' I insist. 'I love you, Max. I'd miss you, if we went to different unis, but we would talk all the time and see each other in the holidays.'

Maxi wipes her eyes.

'You're right,' she says. 'As always. Thank you.'

'Just don't be so hard on yourself,' I insist as I give her a squeeze. 'Mikey didn't get the grades to get in anywhere, apparently, and he's taking it way worse than you.'

'Wow, really?' she replies. 'But, wait, you know what that means, don't you?'

I look at her, waiting for the answer.

'That means it's just you and Cam going to York,' she points out.

My heart stops for a second.

'Ah, yeah, you're right,' I reply casually.

'Come on, you can't tell me you're not excited at the thought,' she says. 'It's actually pretty perfect for you, if it's just the two of you. You might be able to finally get together without worrying about what anyone else thinks. If I know you – and I do – I'll bet you've been flirting up a storm with him all summer, but you'll be worrying too much about Mikey's feelings to do anything about it. Just promise me, if it is just the two of you, you'll give it a real go. Swear it to me, because then at least all of this was for something.'

'You're such a sweetheart,' I tell her, kissing her on the cheek. 'Wherever you do go, I know you're going to do something amazing.'

'And you're going to do Cam,' she jokes. 'Promise me.'

Before I get a chance to say anything, DJ joins us.

'Is everything okay?' he asks.

'Yes,' Maxi tells him. 'Jas has really cheered me up.'

'I'll give you two some space,' I suggest. 'I'm going to try to find Cam.'

'Remember what I said about Mikey,' DJ warns me again. 'He's really not in a good place.'

I leave Maxi and DJ to do whatever they're going to do and make my way back through the hallway to head downstairs. As I pass the lounge doorway, I notice Mikey in there, watching the FIFA tournament, but boy does he look in a bad way. Not just drunk, but tired, deflated, unhappy. It crosses my mind, for a second, that me breaking up with him could have been the reason he did so terribly in his exams. I know, that makes me sound like an egomaniac, I just mean that my timing wasn't ideal, but if we're being honest he clearly had something going on already, which is *why* I broke up with him. He turns his head so I dart out of the way and hurry back downstairs, and hover outside while I text Cam to find out where he is. He replies saying he won't be long and sure enough he turns up shortly after. I'm so happy to see him when I spot him walking up the driveway. I feel weirdly relieved too.

'Hey,' I say brightly.

'Hi,' he replies with a smile. 'How's the party?'

'Clarky bought a bag of herbs thinking they were weed,' I say excitedly.

'Of course he did,' Cam says, laughing as he shakes his head.

'And Maxi and DJ are up in his room.'

'Tonight's the night,' Cam jokes.

'That's what everyone is saying,' I reply with a roll of my eyes. 'I could do with talking to you, actually.'

'Yeah, it would be good to chat,' he replies. 'Is there a quiet spot in there?'

'It's a house party, what do you think?' I joke. 'Actually, I know where we can talk.'

I take Cam by the hand without really thinking about it, but the second my hand touches his, it's almost as though my skin starts to tingle, like I'm having a reaction to him – a good one, though.

I lead him around the back of the building, past DJ's dad's workshop, to a small shed I noticed attached to the building. I try the door and it's unlocked so we step inside. There's an ancient-looking light on the wall so I turn it on, we don't get much light from it, but it shows us where we are – in some kind of wood store, full of logs, cobwebs and various creepy-crawlies, but this place is so old with missing wooden panels that I'm not surprised it has its own ecosystem.

'Interesting place for a chat,' Cam jokes.

'I didn't know it was a knackered shed full of logs and bugs when I picked it out,' I reply with a smile. 'But it's the only place we're going to get any privacy.'

'Then I guess I'll take it,' Cam replies. 'Are you okay? You look a little... blah!'

Cam makes a sort of wild, excitable, stressed kind of sound which, yeah, to be honest, that's pretty spot on.

'Things are just... I don't know,' I reply, confusingly. 'Mikey is here, drunk and looking for me to talk, but he didn't get into uni.'

'At all?' Cam replies.

I shake my head.

'And Maxi didn't get into York,' I continue. 'And DJ doesn't want to go if Maxi isn't.'

'Wow,' Cam blurts, clearly speechless.

'So, it's looking like it's going to be just me and you, and I'm gutted for everyone else, but...'

'Jas.'

'Wait a minute, let me finish, because if I don't say this now, I'll probably bottle it like I have every day since I met you,' I tell him with a laugh, stalling for time as my confidence grows slowly.

I take a deep breath.

'Cam, I like you, I've always liked you,' I tell him. 'I think you're amazing. Just the smartest, funniest, cutest boy I've ever met. And I've felt that way pretty much since the day we met and if you don't feel the same way as me, well, I'm still glad I told you. But if you do feel the same way, and it's just the two of us going to York, then perhaps we can give things a proper go, start from scratch, get to know each other properly without our friends around and see where this goes.'

Wow, putting yourself out there is scary, and it feels like it's taking him *so* long to reply. My confidence is slipping again, with every second it takes him to speak.

'Of course I feel the same way,' Cam replies. 'And I've always felt that way too. You're so witty, so intelligent – and so, so beautiful, but it's almost as though you haven't realised it yet, which only makes you seem even cuter. I've wanted to say this to you forever, and I'd finally talked myself into it when Mikey got there first. I didn't know what to do, other than help him ask you – I just really hoped you'd say no.'

'And I thought you weren't interested in me, which is why I said yes to him, to try to get over you,' I blurt. 'But the whole time I was with him, I couldn't get you out of my head. I couldn't even kiss him, but all I wanted to do was kiss you.'

'The jealousy was eating me alive,' he admits. 'I was almost relieved, when I heard the two of you hadn't even kissed.'

'Because I want my first kiss to matter,' I reply. 'And I only want it to be with you.'

Wow, when the time is right, something somewhere in your brain just switches on, and everything becomes clear. Chances are, if you're wondering if the time is right, then it probably isn't, because now that it is I can safely say I have never been more sure about anything, and with absolutely zero regard for the consequences, all I can think about doing is jumping in.

I practically throw myself at him. I've never leaned in for a kiss before but my lips are on his in a split second. Whatever I felt in my hand when I touched his – this is like that times a thousand. The most intense pins and needles I've ever felt, starting in my lips, surging to every inch of my body. I wrap my arms around his neck as Cam locks his around my waist. I have no idea what I'm doing so I just do what comes naturally. I run a hand up the back of his head, into his hair. Cam squeezes my hips. I'd always heard first kisses were supposed to be rubbish but perhaps when they're with the right person, at the right time, they're just right.

The screams of joy from the party seem to suddenly intensify, jolting us apart for a second.

I'm smiling so widely my face aches. Cam doesn't look quite so happy, though.

'Jas, there's something I need to tell you,' Cam says seriously.

'What?' I blurt quietly.

'I'm not going to York either,' he says, cutting to the chase.

'What?' I say again, a little louder this time, more panicked than worried. 'What do you mean?'

'You know how my results were much better than anyone thought?' he says. I nod my head. 'Well, you know what my parents are like, they started talking about if I might be able to get in somewhere better. Mum started going on about when my cousin got her results and they were higher than her predicted grades, so they started calling other unis, got her in somewhere better, she graduated with a first and now she's doing a master's at Cambridge. I guess on results day lots of people don't get the grades they need, so a bunch of places open up on different cour- ses, and universities try to fill them. I didn't get to catch my breath before they were ringing around, seeing where else they could get me in, and they found me a place. They barely even asked me before they accepted on my behalf.'

I can't say I'm surprised. Cam did so well, and of course his parents would want the absolute best for him.

'Where?' I ask.

'Edinburgh,' he replies. I stare at him for a second and he nods his head.

'You're going to Edinburgh,' I say, pointlessly, because he obviously knows that.

I can't believe it, just as it starts to seem like we might have good timing for once, that we might finally be able to get to be together, it's not going to happen.

'It's such a good opportunity to... smoke,' Cam says.

I frown at him.

'What?'

'Smoke,' he says again, pointing to a hole in the wooden wall behind me. 'Quick, we need to get out of here.'

The wooden door sticks for a few seconds and I swear my short, boring life starts to flash before my eyes. Eventually, it opens and we run around to the front of the building. That's when I realise the screams aren't people enjoying the party, they're screams of panic. And then I notice the faint sound of sirens in the distance, growing louder by the second.

I had a feeling something bad was going to happen tonight. I just didn't realise it was going to be this bad.

29

NOW

I make my way through the club, already feeling the beat of the music. Even in an outdoor club, the thumping bass vibrates the ground beneath my feet, travelling through my body, pounding like my heartbeat. I imagine that's why people come to a resort like this, for the club nights. It never would have been my first choice, or even my second, but now that I'm here, I have to admit, it's thrilling. I push my way through the crowd, the music getting louder and more intense with each step.

It was funny, all of us getting ready in the one room, sharing the bathroom (apart from when we showered, obviously) – it reminded me of *Love Island*, when the islanders change out of their bikinis and get dolled up for the night. Presumably, tonight will be nothing like an episode of *Love Island*, though, given that I'm the only single girl, and I can't see the boys coupling up. I imagine it will be less dramatic too, with no arguing and nobody getting dumped from the island, although you know what they say, the night is young. Well, it isn't actually young, we're in the early hours of the morning now, but there's always time for drama with our lot.

The club is stuffed to the brim with partygoers. Everyone is dancing, laughing and having a great time. The air smells strongly of sweat and alcohol, but no one seems to mind. Everyone is here for the same reason, to have fun. The warm weather isn't going to get in their way, in fact, it's almost as though the heat charges everyone up, it makes them want to party harder.

The lights are flashing, casting a rainbow of colours across the dance floor. It's like being in an alternate universe, one where anything goes. The energy in the room is electric, and I can feel it coursing through my veins.

I walk over to the bar and order a drink. The bartender hands me a cocktail the colour of the bright blue ocean. I take a sip, the sweet and sour flavours dancing on my tongue. It certainly hits the spot on a warm night like tonight, although I must admit, I've had quite a bit to drink already – I think we all have.

As I walk back to find my friends, I move in time with the music, letting it take control of my body. It's hot and humid outside, but I can't help but smile. The DJ is mixing like a pro, dropping beats in all the right places. Every now and then, the DJ changes but the music stays on point. I was sceptical about this place, when we arrived, but I'm actually starting to love it here. It encapsulates everything a good holiday is all about: letting go, forgetting your worries, and having a good time. I close my eyes and allow the music to wash over me. I've never felt so alive and without a care in the world.

Running along the edge of the club area there is a neat little row of beach huts, each one looking like a small, brightly coloured shed – but a fancy shed, of course. I've noticed people popping in and out of them all night, laughing and chatting joyfully as they go. As soon as Maxi saw them, she became curious, she wanted one, she had to have one. It looks like she may have got her wish when I spot her standing there, grinning wildly.

'I got the keys,' Maxi sings, waving them at me excitedly.

She looks great, in a purple crop top and matching miniskirt. She says it's the first time in years she's worn an outfit that cost less than fifty pounds. It's giving her this fun sort of energy, the kind non-rich people have when they're in fancy dress.

My own resort-bought dress is a tight, short, strapless red thing. Not the sort of thing I usually wear but options were limited and I figured nothing about any of this is me, so why not try wearing something a little out of my comfort zone. Any awkwardness I felt in the dress to begin with has faded to nothing with each brightly coloured cocktail I've slurped down.

'Honestly, you're going to love it,' she tells me. 'They're so much more than we thought.'

Each hut is painted a different colour – from bright pink to lime green to sky blue. Maxi unlocks the door on the pink one and leads me inside.

It's small but cosy, with a little sofa, a mini fridge stocked with bottles of water, and a second small room with a toilet and sink in it.

'Wow, this is incredible!' I blurt. 'No more waiting in line for the loo or struggling to find somewhere to sit for a minute.'

'And the best part is you can lock it,' she adds, handing me the key. 'You can stash your valuables in here or leave your drink in here if you want to dance without worrying about someone spiking it.'

'What a time to be alive,' I joke with a sigh.

Something is really wrong with a society where you have to lock your drink in a room to prevent people from spiking it, but here we are.

I go to hand her the key back.

'Hang on to it,' she tells me. 'It has a cute little band, to wear it on your wrist. I've just been to the loo, so you'll probably need it before I do. Come on, let's find the boys.'

Back outside, in the midst of the club, we find the boys where we left them, at a table surrounded by drinks.

Clarky and Mike are throwing back shots. DJ gets excited when he sees Maxi and runs over to her. The two of them start dancing and it's as though there is no one else on the island. If nothing is going on between them then Maxi is playing with fire, because she's flirting up a storm with him.

And then there's Cam. He's wearing a pair of chinos and white shirt. He's got a couple of the buttons undone, flashing the very top of his chest, showing me just enough to plant the idea of wanting to see more in my head.

After having such an amazing time with Cam at minigolf, and the tone turning to something much flirtier, with Cam actually throwing the word 'date' around, unprompted, and then offering me my dream job, no questions asked, I feel like I'm falling. I fell for him once when I was a teenager – but what do you really know, when you're a teenager? – and now it's happening all over again, only now I'm an adult, who makes smart adult decisions. I trip over absolutely nothing and spill the last of my drink. Cam gets up, to see if I'm okay.

'Can I get you another?' he asks me.

I don't want a drink, I want him.

There was a night, when we were younger, when it finally felt like we could be together and – for one reason or another – we blew it. I don't want to waste the opportunity again, I want to strike while the iron is hot.

'Can we go for a chat?' I ask him. I show him the key. 'Maxi got us a hut, we could pop in there, talk for a minute.'

'Erm, yeah,' he replies, pleasantly surprised.

As I let us into the beach hut, I cast my mind back to the last time the two of us were alone together, in a situation like this, considering whether or not we had a future together. It didn't work out that day, but I feel like we've wasted fifteen years – fifteen years when we could've been together. I'm not going to make that mistake again.

I lock the door behind me.

'Is everything—'

I don't give Cam a chance to finish, or the generous level of alcohol in my system a chance to wear off, before I launch myself in his direction. I'm on him in a flash, hesitating for just a second, as my lips are about to meet his, to let him show me that he wants me too. He kisses me, to show me that he does. Our lips pull together like magnets. As we kiss it feels frantic, desperate almost, like we're finally acting on more than a decade's worth of foreplay. I suppose we are.

I reach down to unbutton Cam's shirt as we kiss. My dress has basically worked its way both up and down as we've been kissing, turning it into a sort of pointless belt.

Cam naturally falls back onto the sofa, so I whip off my dress and sit down on top of him. The problem we had, all those years ago, was that we hit the brakes too soon, we stopped to talk things through, we killed the moment. If we'd just gone with our feelings, acting on them, instead of skirting around them like we always did, then the genie would've been out of the bottle, with no way to walk it back. But we stopped, we overthought it, we let life get in the way. Not this time.

I finally break our kiss, Cam's lips trying to chase mine as I pull them away. I walk across the sofa on my knees, as gracefully as I can, and try to remember one of the dodgy limericks from yesterday, because playing Assume the Position with Cam felt like a 'try before you buy' type situation, and I want to buy it all.

'There once was a man named Kyle...' I say as seductively as I can. I would've thought it was impossible for a limerick to be sexy but this one supercharges Cam as he grabs me by the hips.

I need to set my stall out, to show Cam that I'm a catch, and to capitalise on this.... whatever this is that I've become. Island Jasmine is wild, she wears what she wants, drinks what she wants, goes for what she wants. We're leaving this island tomorrow, back to the civilisation of the villa, I'm making the most of this while I can.

Perhaps it should occur to me that sleeping with Cam in a drunken holiday frenzy might not be the best way to kick things off but for two people like us, who have always found any possible reason not to be together, I can't think of a better way to break the cycle.

Eventually, I lie down on top of Cam, resting my face on his chest. His heart is beating fast, I can hear it loud in my ear. I stroke his chest, to relax him. Cam wraps a strong arm around me and gives me a squeeze.

'Well, that was—'

Cam doesn't get to finish his sentence before there's a loud bang on the door.

I jump to my feet, hurrying into my dress, running my hands through my hair to make sure it doesn't look like we were doing what we were doing. Cam has his clothes back on in a flash, although his buttons take more concentration to fasten than they did for me to unfasten. Oh, wow, it looks like I might have just ripped one off.

'Just a sec,' I call out, buying us some time.

With Cam decent, I open the door and Mike comes storming in. He has a face like thunder, red with rage.

'Mate, come on, calm down,' DJ begs him as he follows him in.

'Look, this is ridiculous, they're just chatting, see,' Maxi reasons.

'Nah, look, her dress is on backwards,' Clarky points out as he enters the hut too.

And the gang's all here.

I quickly glance down at my dress to check it.

'No, it isn't,' I tell him.

'You checked, though, didn't you?' he reasons with a smile. 'That says it all.'

'I don't need DC Clark Clarkson to help me figure out what is plain to see,' Mike says, unable to resist a dig at Clarky as he paces back and forth, pounding the wooden floor of the beach hut.

'Mike, why don't just the—'

'I know what's going on,' Mike snaps. 'The two of you, my best friend and my girlfriend, carrying on behind my back for years.'

'I'm not your girlfriend,' I say, stating the obvious.

'But you were back then,' he replies. 'And I saw the two of you. That night, at DJ's party, I followed you, watched you sneak off together like you did tonight, I saw the two of you kissing.'

It's on the tip of my silly drunk tongue to ask him if he's talking about back then or tonight.

'It was only weeks after we'd broken up,' Mike says, confirming that he's referring to back then, but as I glance over at Cam, I can see the telltale remains of my red lipstick on his face. He's done his best to wipe it away but there's no hiding that red glow around the lips.

'But we had broken up,' I point out. 'And that's the point.'

'What the hell?' DJ says. We all look to him, to see him staring down at his phone.

'What's wrong?' Maxi asks him, suddenly even more worried.

'A photo,' he replies, widening his eyes at her, as if to tell her that he knows something.

'Ah,' Maxi replies. 'Look, it's not a big deal.'

'Not a big deal?' he replies.

'Yeah,' she insists. 'It was just, you know, a mistake. She didn't even mean to take it, and she's deleted it.'

'What the hell are you talking about?' DJ asks her.

'The photo Jas took,' she replies. 'What are you talking about?'

'I get news alerts,' he tells us, turning his phone around for us all to see.

Under the headline 'Beaumont gets a new babe ahead of divorce' is a photo of Maxi's husband, Rupert Beaumont, on a sunny beach somewhere, frolicking with a young, slim brunette.

Oh my gosh, no, poor Maxi! Suddenly, so much makes sense.

'Oh,' Maxi says softly. 'Well, what's the problem?'

'I thought we were having an affair,' DJ replies – surprisingly angrily, given that an affair is not usually what you want to be having. If Maxi is single, surely that's good news?

'Well, there you go, now we can be together,' she tells him.

'You've been lying to me,' he tells her. 'I've been feeling so guilty, shagging you, you telling me you were going to leave your husband for me – except you're not, he's already left you. It's the dishonesty.'

'That's a pretty strange moral high ground for a man who thought he was shagging someone else's wife to take,' I can't help but point out, jumping to my friend's defence – I don't think I'll ever quite lose that reflex, no matter how many years we go without seeing one another.

'What's your part in all this?' he asks me accusingly. 'What's this photo you took?'

'Leave her alone,' Maxi insists. 'It's no big deal, Jas accidentally took a photo of the two of us, *you know*. But she deleted it, it's fine.'

'Come on, you can't really be mad at Jas over the photo,' Cam says, springing to my defence.

'I suppose you've seen it then? Were you there when she took it? What are the two of you doing, sneaking around, watching us at it?' DJ asks accusingly.

'They can't help themselves,' Mike adds, jumping on it. 'They're liars, the both of them.'

'Jas isn't a liar and neither am I,' Cam says. He turns to me. 'Right?'

I hesitate for a second. I don't mean to, but when something is on your mind, it stays there even when you're not actively thinking about it.

'Jas?'

'Nothing, nothing,' I insist. 'Of course you're not a liar.'

Cam is unconvinced.

'What am I lying about?' he asks, unable to move on until he knows.

'Just, you know, your unfinished relationship business,' I say, perhaps too cryptically.

'What do you mean?' he asks.

'I know about your wife,' I practically whisper. 'It's not a big deal.'

'You have a wife?' Mike asks – his anger intensifying, which I didn't think was possible.

'I'm single,' Cam tells me.

'Yeah, I know you are, look, it's not a big deal, we can talk about it later,' I reassure him. 'You didn't lie, you just didn't tell the whole truth. You're not a liar.'

'I'm just not a truth teller?' he checks.

I don't say anything.

'Unbelievable,' Cam says as he heads for the door.

'Cam, wait,' I call after him.

I grab my shoes and start hurrying them on, to follow him and straighten all of this out, but he's out of here like a shot.

'This is all rich coming from you, Mike,' Maxi scoffs. 'Getting jealous, blatantly trying to get Jas back, all the while having a young bird back home, one who you're FaceTiming any chance you get, telling her you love her.'

Maxi's accusation stops me in my tracks.

'What?' I blurt.

'I don't have a girlfriend,' Mike insists, his tone shifting to something more gentle. He looks like a rabbit caught in the headlights right now.

'I saw her,' Maxi tells him. 'On your phone. And I distinctly heard you telling her you loved her, DJ did too, didn't you?'

My jaw drops again.

'Oh, when I walked in on the two of you about to shag?' Mike adds. 'Having your twisted affair-not-affair.'

'You're dodging the subject,' Maxi says. 'You have a girlfriend, just admit it. I didn't say anything because *I* mind my own business, but if you're going to be like this...'

I don't know how I'm looking at Mike right now but he must not like it because he cracks instantly.

'She isn't my girlfriend, she's my daughter,' he blurts.

'Bullshit,' Maxi replies. 'That wasn't a kid.'

'I'm telling you, that's my daughter,' he insists. 'She's fourteen – fifteen next year. Her mum lets her wear make-up, she looks too grown-up for her age.'

I'm taken aback by the idea of Mike with a daughter. He should have told us, it's nothing to be ashamed of.

'If you have a daughter then when's her birthday?' DJ asks.

'It's the tenth of February,' he replies. 'Honestly, she's my daughter.'

Clarky starts making clicking noises with his mouth as he holds out his fingers one at a time. He's counting.

'The answer is 2009,' DJ tells him.

Mike runs a hand through his hair and puffs air from his cheeks.

I'm too caught up in worrying about Cam to understand what I'm hearing.

'Meaning she was conceived sometime around May 2008,' DJ adds.

Suddenly it clicks into place. My jaw falls open. Did... did Mike cheat on me while we were together? Did he have a baby? Did he know, when we were together, that this girl was pregnant? Oh my God, is that why he was so horrible right before I finished with him?

I look at him for an explanation, as though anything he might say could make this better.

'Look, Jas, we were having a tough time,' he explains. 'You didn't want to sleep with me – you didn't even want to kiss me. It was messing with my self-confidence, and then I went on holiday with my parents, and there was this girl there, and she did want me...'

'So you cheated on me because I wouldn't sleep with you?' I say. 'Just to confirm.'

'You didn't have to jump straight into Cam's arms,' Mike says, getting defensive again. 'Are you telling me there was no overlap? I doubt it. You weren't ready to kiss me, but you kissed him without a problem.'

'We're supposed to be friends,' DJ points out. 'But you're all liars. Don't think I've forgotten one of you started the fire at my parents'—'

'Oh, for fuck's sake, shut up, shut up, shut up,' Clarky yells. 'Listen to you all, lying, cheating, whining, banging on about shit from fifteen years ago that no one cares about. You think you've got problems? I think I'm dying. Grow up.'

Clarky is the next one to storm out. Let me tell you, there is something seriously sobering about the most immature person in your group telling you to grow up, but his revelation that he might be ill is the thing that really knocks some sense into us all. Is he just being dramatic, or is he telling the truth? Either way, he's right, what does any of this matter?

'Maxi, come on, we need to go after him,' I tell her.

'I'm coming,' she says.

Clarky disappears into the crowd pretty quickly. We head after him, in the direction we think he's gone.

Oh, poor Clarky. Suddenly, his erratic behaviour makes sense. This is why he's been trying so hard to have a good time.

We just need to find him, to talk to him, to be there for him. He's our friend, after all, and right now nothing else matters.

30

THEN – 14 AUGUST 2008

'I said can you step back, please,' a firewoman demands, her cheeks bright red through a combination of having to scream her instructions at us *again* and the intense heat coming from the burning building in front of us.

A fireman runs back out from where the door used to be. He's wearing breathing apparatus, so he gestures to one of the other firefighters out here.

'No sign of him,' the second man shouts, confirming our worst fears.

I cough to clear my lungs as the smoke burns the back of my throat.

'DJ, are you okay?' Maxi asks him. Until now we've been standing here in silence, watching as the building blazes out of control. If there is one thing to be thankful for it's that the party was in the building next to the house, so the main house is fine – although I'm sure that's not giving DJ much comfort, seeing as though his bedroom is being destroyed, not to mention the trouble he's going to be in with his parents.

Right now, though, all we can think about is Clarky. Most of the partygoers have scarpered, not wating to get in trouble, others have stuck around to watch. No one seems to be missing any of their friends – no one but us. We can't find Clarky and, by the looks of things, neither can the fire brigade.

'Where is he?' DJ asks no one in particular.

'I think it's a good sign, that no one has found him,' Maxi insists, tightening her grip on the armful of folders she's holding.

I glance to my right, to exchange worried yet reassuringly motivated smiles with Cam. Then I look left and look at Mikey.

'You okay?' I mouth at him, because he looks even worse than he did earlier.

He nods as he squeezes his mouth in one of his hands.

'I see someone,' the firewoman calls out. We all look to the building but when no one emerges we follow her gaze to the woods.

'Clarky,' DJ calls out.

Sure enough, running out from the trees is Clarky. At first, he seems like a superhero, running in slow motion, but I think he's just not very fast and his arms are stuck out because he's holding what I can now tell is a black cat at arm's length.

He joins us, standing in a line, staring at the house, watching it burn, each of us holding something.

'You've got a cat,' DJ blurts, as though today just keeps getting stranger and stranger.

Clarky nods towards Maxi.

'She's got your coursework,' he points out.

'DJ said grab something important,' Maxi replies. 'His work is important – it's his portfolio.'

I'm holding DJ's laptop, Cam has a small shoebox that DJ had tucked under his arm when he ran out, Mikey has his Xbox, and DJ himself is holding some sort of wooden sculpture he ran into his dad's workshop for. The six of us must look so strange standing here, watching the fire burn, holding such a random selection of supposedly must-save items – and the fact Clarky is holding a cat (one that clearly doesn't want to be held and is clawing at him every now and then) only makes us look sillier.

'Why do you have a cat?' DJ asks him.

'It's your cat,' Clarky replies. 'The fire scared it, so it darted off into the woods. I ran after it.'

'That's just a random cat,' Maxi points out.

'So I just kidnapped a cat?' Clarky confirms. 'Not saved one?'

We all nod.

Clarky and the cat hold hostile eye contact one last time before he puts it down on the floor, quickly whipping his arms away so it can't scratch him again.

'My God, I'm in so much trouble,' DJ says.

'I think we all are,' Cam adds. 'You didn't throw this party alone.'

'I know, but the fire is my fault,' DJ admits.

'What?' a loud, angry male voice bellows.

We all turn to see DJ's parents furiously marching towards us, their car abandoned halfway down the driveway. If only they'd picked a caravan park further away, we could've figured this out before they got here – or tried, at least. Got our story straight, pretended it wasn't a party, *anything* to make this seem less bad.

'Darren, what the hell have you done?' his dad asks as his mum just sobs. I'm not surprised they're angry and upset, part of their home is burning down, but obviously none of us meant for this to happen. I don't even know what did happen.

'I had some friends over, it was an accident,' DJ begins to explain.

'Is anyone hurt?' his dad asks, looking us all up and down.

'No, no one at the party was injured as far as we can tell,' a fireman interrupts.

'A party?' DJ's dad repeats, his anger building again. 'And was there drinking at this party? Drugs?'

Oh, definitely not drugs, given that it was only Clarky and all he brought was a pizza topping, but our guilty silence confirms that we were drinking.

'Do you know what started the fire?' the fireman asks.

'It was me,' DJ admits. 'I lit a candle, in my bedroom, then knocked it over and it burned the bedroom curtains a bit. I thought I had put it out but then I heard a commotion in the lounge so I went to sort that out. Next thing we knew, the place was on fire – it must have restarted or something.'

'Why were you lighting a candle in your bedroom if you were having a party?' his dad asks.

DJ can't help but glance at Maxi, then back at his dad, which pretty much tells his dad everything he needs to know.

'No,' his dad replies. 'No, no, no. Not my son throwing a party with alcohol and sex and God knows what. And I suppose you used your mum's expensive candles?'

'No, I just used that old white one in my bedroom cupboard,' he says quickly, keen to try to win some favour back by having not used his mum's candles.

Still, his mum's jaw drops.

'Darren, are you telling me that you used your baptism candle to deflower this poor girl and then set our home on fire?' his mum replies in disbelief.

Oh... my... God! Just when you think there is no way for this to get any worse.

'I didn't deflower her,' DJ insists. 'And the candle would've been destroyed in the fire anyway so...'

'That's not the point,' his dad snaps. 'Right, that's it, Darren, you're grounded. The rest of you, I'm calling your parents, and they can deal with you as they see fit.'

I don't think any of us knows what to say. Today was supposed to be a good day, results day, one that shaped the rest of our lives.

But if we're starting as we mean to go on then there's no hope for us.

31

NOW

It was never going to be as simple as we would walk into our room and find Clarky just sitting there.

We've been looking for him for God knows how long – I've been keeping an eye out for Cam too – with no luck.

Our room is still nice and tidy, from when housekeeping came in to make the beds earlier, so you can tell that no one has been here.

Maxi plonks herself down on the bed.

'I've messaged DJ, told him and Mike to sleep in the beach hut tonight,' she tells me. 'I think we need a bit of space.'

'I can't believe Mike cheated on me,' I say softly. 'I mean, I wasn't happy with him anyway, and we didn't stay together much longer, but getting someone pregnant when you're a teenager, behind your girlfriend's back – that's huge.'

'Do you think that's why he didn't go to uni?' Maxi wonders. 'Why he ended up working for his dad, because he had a child to support?'

'Probably,' I say with a sigh. 'God, what a mess. To be honest, I don't even know how mad I am, it was a long time ago – I just feel sorry for him, for feeling like he couldn't tell us. I feel the same way about Clarky, keeping his health problems from us, and you, not wanting to tell us about Rupert.'

'I've been trying not to think about it,' Maxi replies. 'To be honest, that's what this holiday is all about. A sort of last hurrah with Rupert's credit card before he takes it off me and leaves me with a modest settlement. That's why I'm so keen to invest in Cam's venture, to have something for myself. DJ has been pestering me, to introduce him to Rupert, and I know that what he is working on would be right up Rupert's alley, but connecting them would mean DJ finding out exactly what was going on and...'

Maxi stops for a moment, lowering her gaze to her hands as she composes herself.

'I wanted him to want me for me, not for my money, or my connections,' she explains. 'Everyone always wants something from me, and all I want is to be loved. DJ wanting me, even though he thought I was married, showed me that it was me he wanted. And then, well, it just felt easier to tell him that I would leave Rupert for him, rather than admitting that Rupert was already leaving me.'

I take her arm in mine.

'I can't believe I'm getting divorced,' she blurts with a sob. 'It feels so strange, to finally say it, it makes it feel so real. Who am I, without Rupert?'

'You are you,' I remind her. 'Brilliant, funny, talented you. And I'll tell you what I told you all those years ago, after you and DJ broke up: you don't need a boy – or a man – to define you. You are you, you are amazing, and you will always land on your feet because *you* make things happen. Rupert will miss you more than you miss him.'

'And yet I'm the one who got dumped,' she says with a heavy

sigh. 'And I've stuffed things up with DJ. Maybe I'm destined to be alone.'

'I'm here for you,' I remind her. 'And I understand more than you think – and I think DJ will understand too.'

'Do you really think so?' she replies hopefully.

'I'm sure of it,' I tell her. 'It's like, with Cam, when I found out he was getting divorced, I was annoyed he hadn't told me about it, and every time he could have told me since, he hasn't mentioned it, but I've been overthinking it. I just feel bad now, that I brought it up in front of everyone, making it seem like I thought he was a dishonest person when, in reality, I don't care if he's been married before or if he's divorcing now, just like no one will care if you are. The past is the past. I just want to start over with him – we've missed so many chances to be together. God, I hope I haven't blown it.'

Maxi wipes tears away from her cheeks.

'Jas, listen, I need to tell you something,' she says, twisting her body so that she can look me in the eye. 'Cam isn't getting divorced.'

'What?' I reply. 'What are you talking about?'

My brain races ahead of me, trying to make sense of it. I fight it to try to give Maxi the benefit of the doubt, but it's not looking good.

'I found those divorce papers in your room,' I remind her. 'You read them, you told me they were his.'

I feel a wave of anger and hurt wash over me.

'Look, I know, I know,' Maxi says as she raises her hands defensively. 'I lied and said they belonged to Cam, because I was too embarrassed to admit they belonged to me. I wasn't ready to tell anyone yet.'

'You could've told me,' I insist. 'Or you could've said they were anyone else's – Clarky's, the person who owned the house, a member of staff, a total stranger, just not the one man you know I'm interested in.'

I'm so hurt that Maxi would lie to me about something like this, and about Cam especially. Getting to know Cam this week, I've been forming an inaccurate image of him in my head, thinking he would be perfect if he was more honest, or had less baggage, and it's just not true. And the worst thing of all is that I'd just decided I didn't care, that I wanted to give things a go anyway.

'Maxi, you lied to me,' I say, my voice quivering with emotion. 'I can't believe you would do something like that. In fact, you've been lying to me this whole time. When I asked you if you were having an affair with DJ, you said you would never lie to me.'

'Technically I said you know I would never lie to you,' she reasons, wincing at her own bullshit. 'You knew that. It was just this one thing. And, anyway, you're the one who is always saying you're not interested in Cam, so it felt like a harmless white lie.'

'Are you joking me?' I ask, jumping to my feet. 'That's your reasoning, that I would never admit my feelings, so it's fine to lie? Maxi, you are so selfish sometimes.'

'I know, I'm a cow,' she says, backtracking slightly. 'I'm sorry.'

'You know what, Clarky was right,' I start as I go to grab my bag – aside from a few items of clothing I bought here, all of my things are in there. 'We're supposed to be friends, but we're all just a bunch of liars.'

'Jas, wait,' she calls after me, but I ignore her, heading for the door, letting it close slowly behind me as I run for the lift, before Maxi has a chance to catch up to me. I don't need to hear any more of her bullshit tonight – I say tonight, it's nearly morning.

I wander around the resort with no idea where I'm going or what I'm going to do. I'm hurt, angry, confused. I feel so many things and yet I don't know what I'm feeling. But suddenly it all feels so high school, when all that really matters is whether or not Clarky is okay.

I take my phone from my bag but my battery is flat, so I can't even call him. Wherever he is, I hope he's okay. Cam too. God, he must think I'm such a crazy bitch. But knowing Cam, and what a sweetheart he is, he probably doesn't feel that at all, he probably just feels hurt.

Somehow that's so, so much worse.

32

La Fine del Mondo is more like a sort of purgatory than the end of the world. It's like someone took everything I hated about high school (apart from PE) and created my own personal hell with it. All the worst traits in my friends, and if I'm being honest, in myself, have all come out now that we're all back together. I can't help but wonder whether or not this is all just unfinished business, causing the past to seep into the future, or if this is just whom we really are – or whom we are when we're together, at least. Is it possible that the strongest friendships when you are a kid just cannot survive into adulthood, not without being toxic, from all your silly teenage baggage?

One thing you can say about La Fine del Mondo is that, given how large, varied and stuffed full of people it is, you're not forced to bump into anyone you know. It reminds me of school, in that sense, and the way Clarky would only hang out with us in certain spots, away from the gaze of the kids he was trying to get in with.

After sleeping in, on one of the sofas in the twenty-four-hour café (you've got to love that they'll let you do that here) – which actually was quite a nice, quiet, chilled-out place to snooze – I woke up to the sound of the coffee machine hissing – thankfully without anyone stealing my bag or drawing a moustache on my face – feeling like someone was hitting me repeatedly, right between my eyes, with a hammer. Thankfully, my sunglasses were in my bag and putting them on helped to take the edge off the light, just a little.

I strolled over to the counter, casual as you like, trying to style my hangover out as best I could.

The barista gave me a sympathetic look.

'Long night?' she inquired.

I just nodded before ordering an extra-strong coffee and a very large muffin. That helped.

Next, I wandered out to the pool area, hoping some fresh air might do me some good, so I sat on a sunlounger in the shade for a while, the events of last night bouncing around in my brain, only adding to my headache.

I still can't get over Maxi lying to me like that. I know she had her reasons but why drag me and Cam into her mess? She's really in a mess. If there's one thing I'm sure of it's that I need not have worried, when I arrived, about being the only person who didn't have their life together. I think we're all in a bad spot. Poor Clarky is having health problems, Maxi is getting divorced, DJ seems to have a lot of unresolved emotional baggage, Mike has been hiding a child from us! Even Cam, as wonderful as he is, seems like he's been looking for a new direction in life. Suddenly, me not having a job seems like no big deal.

After taking a breather, trying to clear my head, I made my way to the pool showers to freshen up – because I really, really couldn't face going back to our hotel room, seeing Maxi, the chance of it being just the two of us and us having to talk, when I had no idea what I was going to say.

I hoped the pool showers wouldn't be too busy and luckily

they weren't. There was only one girl in there, who very kindly lent me some of her products, noticing that I didn't have any of my own. That's one of the things I love about girls, they're always willing to help out another girl in need. It's only once you become friends with them that they betray you, apparently.

The water felt so nice and cool against my skin, a welcome relief from the scorching sun. The sound of other guests outside, all having a great time in the pool, echoed into the shower; hearing everyone so happy was comforting. It made me believe that if my lot and I can just figure things out, we can get back on track.

I caught a glimpse of myself in the mirror as I stepped out of the shower. There wasn't much I could do about my soaking wet hair, other than roughly towel-dry it before letting the sun take care of the rest. I scrunched it lightly with my hands, hoping beachy waves would form as it dried. It's worked out okay, although it's going to take a lot of conditioner to get the knots out – but that's a problem for later, when I'm back in civilisation.

Finally, before leaving the confines of the changing rooms, I put on some of the make-up I bought at the hotel shop when we arrived here. I felt a bit like a warrior putting on warpaint. Well, today might well shape up to be a battle of sorts. I'm not sure what is going to happen, but I want to be prepared for anything – even all-out war.

After that, feeling a little more human again, I found another sunlounger and took a seat, stretching my legs out into the sun, and that's where I am now. I'm currently draining the last of my cocktail – the final cocktail I'll drink here. Let's call it Dutch courage, before I make my way back through the forest, to the supposedly deserted beach, where the boat should be waiting to take me back to reality.

'Hello,' I hear a familiar voice greet me.

I open my eyes to see Cam standing in front of me, and as cliché as it sounds, my heart skips a beat. More than the fact that he's talking to me at all, a huge wave of relief washes over me as I realise that he doesn't look like he's angry at me.

'I come in peace,' he says, smiling widely, waving a finger like a white flag. 'Can we talk?'

'Yes,' I say without a moment of hesitation. 'I owe you the apology of all apologies.'

'I spent the night with Clarky,' he tells me, pausing to laugh, as he hears his own choice of words out loud. 'He found me at the bar, told me everyone was falling out, that he'd had enough. You know me, I hate the drama, especially the kind that seems to go hand in hand with that lot. So, when he told me his new friends would let us sleep on the floor in their room, I thought best to give you all some space, while I figured out what was going on.'

'Is Clarky okay?' I ask.

'Yes,' he replies. 'Why?'

Cam sounds concerned suddenly. Clarky must not have told him.

'The last thing he said, before he stormed off, was that he thought he was dying,' I fill Cam in.

'Shit,' he replies. 'No, he never mentioned it. Do you think he was exaggerating, or just trying to stop everyone arguing? He did tell me about everything else, about Maxi, DJ, Mike... I'm sorry about that, I'm sure it goes without saying, but you didn't deserve that.'

'Thanks,' I reply. 'But, to be honest, I don't care. I care about you, and what I said...'

'What you said was completely understandable,' he replies. 'I'm guessing Maxi told you I was married, to hide her own divorce?'

I nod. I feel so stupid now, for just believing her, or for not bringing it up with Cam sooner.

'I guessed as much, eventually,' he replies. 'She's your childhood best friend, why wouldn't you believe her? I probably would have believed Mike, if he had told me the same about you. Well, not now, obviously, now that I know he's had a child this whole time – a child that is now a teenager.'

'I can't believe it,' I say. 'Keeping it a secret, all this time.'

'If you're after a silver lining, because why not, right?' Cam starts with a cheeky smile that instantly makes me feel more relaxed about everything. 'If Mike had told you the truth at the time, it definitely would have destroyed your friendship. It might have broken the group right down the middle, we might not be here now... It's a stretch, but always better to focus on a positive.'

I can't help but smile.

'That's a great way to look at it,' I reply. 'Thanks.'

'Jas, last night was amazing, until it wasn't, obviously, but the bit when it was just me and you, it felt like everything finally clicked into place,' he says, again, not realising his own words until he hears them out loud, and sees me giggling back at him. 'Oi, stop it, I'm being serious. I really like you – I've always liked you. And last night, I'm hoping, was just old habits dying hard, the group imploding, but this time I'm hopeful that the dawn after the storm will be different. Me and you, living in the same place, working together again. It feels like everything we want is in touching distance, if we want it. If you want me.'

'I do,' I admit. 'I really do. It's always been you – not even fifteen years apart has changed my mind about that. I know, we probably don't know each other all that well in the present, but we did in the past, and I'd love to give it a go, see what happens.'

'Me too,' he replies.

Cam leans forward and takes my face gently in his hand. We

kiss. It isn't like last night's wild kiss, it's something more controlled, something more sustainable. Something I hope I get to do again and again and again.

'Are you ready to hike back through the forest?' he eventually asks me. 'We wouldn't want to miss the boat.'

'That wouldn't be like us at all,' I reply through a grin. 'But I suppose we'd better. I'd suggest we stay here but I'd rather take my chances with the awkwardness back at the villa, than rebook that swingers' suite for just the two of us.'

'Yeah, that would be a lot of pressure, from all the kit in there,' he jokes.

'Okay then, let's go get this boat, and face the music,' I say with a sigh.

Walking back through the forest is a different vibe. Not just because on the way here we were desperate for civilisation but because I'm walking back with even more hope, holding hands with Cam, excited about my future.

After a lovely stroll, we eventually arrive back at the beach. Cam and I approach the boat, relieved to see that it has arrived to transport us back to civilisation. I let go of Cam's hand, and he smiles to let me know that he understands.

The captain greets us, to show us on board.

'Wow,' he exclaims. 'Usually people don't come back looking better than when they arrived.'

'What can I say? We're survivalists,' I tell him.

On board, we find Maxi, DJ and Mike sitting awkwardly spaced apart in uncomfortable silence. It's as if they're all trying to avoid each other's gaze, Maxi looking down at her phone, DJ looking out to sea. Mike looks at me, briefly, as he gives me a slight smile, but then it's almost as though he takes it back, staring down at his feet.

I sit down on one of the sofas. Cam sits down next to me.

'Is everyone here?' the captain asks. 'Shouldn't there be two more?'

'Just one,' Clarky replies, huffing and puffing as he slumps down into one of the chairs, relaxing. 'Drea is staying on the island a bit longer.'

I wonder if he's seen her. You would assume so, if he's saying that.

I give Clarky a slight wave. He gives me a nod. I want to grab him and squeeze him and ask him if he's okay, but his body language doesn't make me feel like he wants me to, so I hang back.

'Okay then,' the captain says. 'Let's go.'

The boat starts moving but still, no one says a word, or moves a muscle, and I'm scared to even talk to Cam given the atmosphere with everyone else – it seems almost insensitive, to be fine in front of them.

As we get on our way, the boat hits a wave, and we all lurch forward. Maxi slides along her seat, into DJ. He grabs her to steady her, his hand lingering on her arm for a moment, but then he quickly snatches it back.

Oh, this is going to be a long trip, if it's going to be like this the whole way.

A strange noise coming from inside the boat grabs all of our attention. I cock my head, listening closely to see if it happens again, but I don't hear it. What I do notice is that we're slowing down, then stopping. Oh, this can't be good.

Eventually the captain appears.

'Just a small technical problem,' he tells us. 'It happens, from time to time, but we can fix it, and be back on our way in no time, just talk among yourselves, and enjoy the sunshine for a little bit longer.'

Wow, okay, this really is going to be a long trip.

The captain vanishes as fast as he appeared, leaving us all alone again, back to our stony silence. We can't go on like this.

'Clarky, are you okay?' I ask him.

He shrugs.

'What you said, before...'

'Forget I said anything,' he insists. 'I'm handling it on my own.'

Wow, something really must be going on.

'Well, you shouldn't be,' Cam insists.

'Yeah, we're your friends,' Maxi eventually joins in.

'We can support you,' DJ adds.

Clarky looks to Mike.

'What?' he says with a laugh. 'They've said it all. But you know I feel the same, mate.'

'Ta,' Clarky replies. 'Basically, I had a lump removed, and they did a biopsy, to see if it was anything bad.'

'And?' Maxi prompts him.

'And it's bad,' he replies. 'I got a letter, just before our trip.'

'Whatever is going on, whenever you want to tell us, we're here for you when you're ready,' I tell him. 'You don't have to do this on your own.'

Clarky itches the stubble he's grown while we've been here – it actually quite suits him.

'This is why I've been so keen on having one final blowout of a holiday, while I still can,' he explains. 'When I got my results letter, saying it was benign, that there was no further treatment, I knew my number was up. I'm sorry I've been trying so hard to have fun, but I hope you understand why.'

My heart sinks, I feel so sad for him, but... hang on...

'Clarky, wait a minute,' I interrupt. 'Did you say "benign"?'

'Yeah,' he replies. 'Benign, no further treatment. It must be bad, if there's nothing they can do for me.'

I know it's awful, but I can't help but laugh.

'Clarky, benign means harmless,' I point out. 'And they're telling you that you don't need any further treatment, not that there's nothing they can do for you.'

'Oh, you daft bastard,' Mike blurts.

'Wh-what?' Clarky replies as a huge grin takes over his face.

He jumps up from his seat and lunges towards me, hugging me tightly, gratefully, as though I'm the one who has cured him.

'This is the Clarky-est thing to ever happen,' DJ points out, laughing – everyone is laughing, although it seems more like it's with relief than at Clarky's expense. 'I thought the desert island stunt was the Clarky-est thing, but this has surpassed even that.'

'I feel like I've been given a second chance,' Clarky says as he takes his seat again.

He pushes every drop of air from his lungs and lies back in his chair, letting the sun beam down on him, then he smiles. He closes his eyes and takes a few contented breaths.

'It's been a shit twelve months,' Clarky tells us. 'From the divorce, to all this stuff... this holiday came at just the right time. Sorry if I've been a bit intense.'

'It may have got a bit weird, towards the end, and started a bit weird if we're being honest, but I've had such a good time on the island,' I tell him honestly.

'Me too,' Cam adds.

'Drea is having a better time than any of us,' Clarky says, sitting up again. 'I saw her this morning, kissing a guy, then a girl, then a different guy.'

He seems surprisingly fine with this, so they can't have been that serious.

'I'm sorry,' Maxi tells him with a shrug. 'If it helps, I never liked her. You can do so much better.'

'Well, if I'm being honest with you,' Clarky starts, 'Drea isn't my girlfriend, we're just friends. I'm pretty sure she only came with me for the free holiday.'

'But you were sharing a room at the villa,' Maxi points out.

'I slept on the sofa,' he replies.

'But we... heard you,' Mike says tactfully. 'That night at the villa, after dinner.'

'Drea was in the shower,' Clarky confesses. 'That was just me.'

My eyes widen with horror.

'No, not like that, you dirty cow,' he ticks me off.

'Right, yeah, sorry, so silly of me to get the wrong idea,' I reply with a roll of my eyes.

'That was just me, making noises, trying to sound like it was the two of us,' he admits.

'That's sad, mate,' Mike points out – not even making fun of him, just stating the obvious.

'Yeah, well, I've just been, I don't know, trying to make the most of life,' Clarky replies. 'And then here's you lot, ruining my holiday, making it all about you.'

I laugh.

'Sorry,' I say.

'You're the last person who has anything to say sorry for,' Maxi insists. 'I owe you an apology, I owe Cam an apology and, DJ, I owe you the biggest apology of all. I should have told you that I was getting divorced but, it's like I told Jas last night, no one is ever interested in me for me, just what I can do for them, and when you thought I was married, I knew it must be me you wanted – just to be with me, even if you couldn't have me.'

'I wanted you before,' DJ reminds her. 'Back when we were at school, when neither of us had anything.'

'And now you're both rich,' Clarky points out. 'Who do you think is richer?'

'It's not a competition,' I tell him.

'Me,' Maxi mouths at Clarky. 'But maybe not, after the divorce. But I am getting some money, and that money is going to Cam, to get his project up and running.'

'And Jas is on board to help,' Cam tells her. 'I really think we can make a success of it.'

I glance over at Mike. He's uncharacteristically quiet.

'It's okay,' I tell him. 'It doesn't matter.'

'It's not okay,' he replies. 'What I did was unforgivable. Our relationship wasn't right, but I was too immature to understand, so I just slept with the first person who was interested. I found out she was pregnant when her parents told mine. My dad was furious, said I'd thrown my life away, that I couldn't go to uni, that I was going to lose you, that I had to start working in one of his showrooms, but that there was no way I was going to inherit the business. I was on a downward spiral, I pushed you away, I messed up some of my exams, missed out on uni. I think being back around you all made me want to go back to that time, to how things were, when I was cool, with my whole life ahead of me.'

He stops for a moment and smiles to himself.

'I'm sorry about the way I went about things, but I wouldn't change a thing, because I had Jenny to show for it,' he says. 'It wasn't easy, being a young dad, but she's amazing. I'd really like you all to meet her.'

'I'd like that,' I tell him.

'Anyway, sorry,' he says.

'Perhaps when we get back to the villa we can start again,' Maxi says, 'treat it like a new beginning, not just to the holiday, but to everything. To our renewed friendship, in adult life.'

'That sounds great to me,' I reply. 'Now that everything is out in the open, hopefully we can all move on.'

'And all see each other a lot more,' Cam adds.

'Erm, wait a minute,' DJ interrupts. 'It's not all out in the open

– we still don't know who wrote that message in the sand, who started the fire.'

We all groan.

'Mate, it was fifteen years ago, your life is amazing, don't rock the boat,' Clarky begs. 'Unless it gets it started again.'

'Listen, that night, the night of the party, I wasn't in a good place,' Mike begins. 'I was depressed, thinking that my life was over, and then I saw Jas and Cam slinking off together, going into that storage shed on the side of the house, so I snuck after them, watching them from a gap in the wood. They started kissing and I saw red. Clarky had given me one of his joints. I lit it, determined to self-destruct, but it definitely wasn't weed, so I dropped it on the floor. I couldn't stand seeing anything else so I stormed off. I thought I'd put it out – I was sure I had – but it wasn't long before the fire started. I think it was my fault, I'm sorry, mate.'

I'm briefly freaked out, at the idea of Mike watching me and Cam kissing, when we thought we were alone, but this is a new beginning. What does it matter now?

'It wasn't your fault, pal,' Clarky reassures him. 'I started the fire. I was in the kitchen, making beans...'

'Who makes beans at a house party?' DJ interrupts.

'Someone with the munchies,' Clarky replies.

'Except you didn't have the munchies,' Mike reminds him. 'That weed was pure oregano. That joint you gave me smelt of pizza.'

'Do you want to hear this or not?' Clarky snaps. 'So I poured the beans into a bowl, and I put it in the microwave, and I did what you're supposed to do, stirring it halfway through, and then Dom called me back to the FIFA tournament to see James's epic slide tackle, then they started fighting – DJ, you had to come and break them up, and then I did wonder, where I left the spoon, if it was still in the bowl, in the microwave... by the time we realised the house was on fire, I knew it was me who caused it, by microwaving that spoon...'

That's such a Clarky story.

'So, which one of you wrote the message?' DJ asks them.

Mike and Clarky look at one another but neither of them says a word. It doesn't seem like either of them wrote it.

'Right, okay, confession time,' Maxi says. 'Again. I started the fire.'

My eyebrows shoot up in surprise. We've got a real Spartacus situation here.

'You?' DJ replies.

'Yeah,' she says. 'We were in your room, you lit that candle to set the mood, and then it fell over, and I panicked and said it was a sign we shouldn't be having sex.'

'Right,' DJ replies. 'I put it out and then ran downstairs after you, to make sure you were okay.'

'Well, I felt bad,' Maxi continues. 'I drank a shot, to give myself some courage, and then I went back to your room and I lit the candle and I waited for you to come back, so we could do it. Then I heard raised voices and smashing so I hurried downstairs, where the boys were fighting over the Xbox. You were there, breaking them up, before they caused any more damage to the house and then, yeah, next thing we were all running for our lives. But I left the candle lit, in your room, and it was me who wrote that message in the sand. I felt guilty, and I thought I was going to die, so I wanted to confess, I suppose.'

DJ wraps his arms around Maxi and gives her a squeeze.

'Listen, we'll probably never know whose fault it was,' he reassures her. 'But you're all right, it's in the past now. Let's just focus on the future.'

The boat fires up again, and slowly starts to move. We all cheer.

'Finally,' Maxi says. 'The last thing we want is a genuine ship-wreck experience.'

'I don't know,' Clarky says. 'The last one worked out quite well.'

'Yes, well, when we all go on holiday next year, I'll make all the arrangements,' Maxi tells him.

'Next year?' I say.

'Yes,' she replies with a smile. 'Let's make this an annual thing.'

'Sounds good to me,' I reply.

I'm sure we're safe to do this again next year because, at the very least, we'll only have a year to create new issues. After airing out our dirty laundry from pushing twenty years ago on this trip, there can't be much left for next time. Then again, with this lot, you never know.

33

We're back at the villa now, sitting on the outdoor dining terrace, surrounded by festooned lights, the moonlight twinkling on the pool's flat, still water. The smell of freshly made pizzas from the villa's wood-fired oven fills the air – it really is a perfect night.

I take a bite of my pizza and exhale a contented sigh.

'This is incredible,' I announce between mouthfuls.

Maxi agrees with a nod.

'The best pizza I've ever had,' she adds. 'That oven is a game changer. I'm going to get one for my garden, although I suspect half the flavour comes from eating them on holiday.'

'Speaking of game changers,' DJ chimes in. 'What are we all planning to do for the rest of our holiday?'

'I heard there's a great, chilled-out hiking trail nearby,' Clarky suggests – the very thing Maxi wanted us to do, before we wound up shipwrecked because a hike didn't sound adventurous enough for him.

'I was thinking skydiving,' Maxi jokes.

'I thought we could climb a volcano,' DJ adds.

'I hear scuba diving is nice this time of year,' Mike says, keeping the joke going.

'I know of a beach where they'll leave you to starve to death,' Cam suggests.

'Oh, and if none of that takes your fancy, I know a resort not too far from here with a seriously top-notch room for swingers.'

'All right, all right, very funny,' Clarky says. 'But now that I know I've got a while to live, I'm a bit more keen to make sure I don't kill myself. Let's stick with the walk.'

'Music to my ears,' Maxi says. 'We can do that tomorrow but, for tonight, how about we go down on to the beach, sit around the firepit?'

'Sounds amazing,' I tell her.

'We need to relax,' she says. 'It sounds like things are going to be pretty full on, when we all get home.'

'Well, home for me is living with my mum and dad,' I point out.

'Me too,' Cam adds. 'Well, *my* mum and dad. My gran isn't well, I said I'd move in for a bit, help out.'

'And I'll be around,' Maxi says. 'I'm thinking of finding somewhere to rent, close by, if Cam and I are going into business together.'

'And, just saying, I can work from anywhere,' DJ adds. 'If you want some company, that is.'

'I'd love that,' Maxi says with a smile.

'And I'm only in Leeds,' Clarky adds. 'So not too far away.'

'Far enough, though,' Mike says with a laugh. 'I'm still living in the village too. It's going to be strange, having everyone back again.'

'I'll alert the fire brigade,' DJ jokes, finally – and thankfully – seeming like he's over it now.

It occurs to me, looking around the table at my oldest friends, that this isn't the end of our story, it's the beginning. It's a new chapter, at the very least. Now that we've put to bed our old drama, it's time to start a new one, a new series – a sort of reunion show – only now we're all older, and wiser... well, hopefully we are, at least.

But we're still the same characters, though, all still bringing the same traits (for better or worse) to the table.

This is going to be a new beginning for all of us, a chance to get to know each other again, to see where our relationships go. And as for what happens to us now, well, I suppose we'll see where we all are this time next year, won't we?

34

THEN – 1 SEPTEMBER 2008

I'm standing at the entrance of the annual fair – the one our village hosts every year without fail to celebrate the end of summer. The delicious September sun is beaming down on me, music is playing, people sound like they're having a great time, and the only thing I can smell is fresh doughnuts. I should be in my element right now, but instead I'm moping around, because Maxi, Cam, DJ, Mikey, Clarky and I would always come here together every year – it was the last day of pure, unadulterated summer fun we would enjoy before the next school term started. This was going to be our last one, before we all moved away, and not only are we spending it apart but I'm having to attend with my parents, which is not a good look.

'Cheer up, moody,' my dad teases.

'It's bad enough being here with my parents, instead of my friends, but did you have to wear that?' I can't help but ask.

Dad looks down at his T-shirt and smiles. Large lettering that says 'this is not a drill' surrounds a cartoon image of a saw. It's the most dad T-shirt I've ever seen.

'You know this is the last one before I go to uni alone, right?' I point out, even though I know that they know that.

'I know, darling,' Mum says, putting an arm around me, giving me a squeeze but then quickly backing off in case she's ruining my street cred too. 'But we'll make sure to have a good time.'

'Listen, DJ's dad told me I had to punish you as severely as I could within the confines of the Good Book and the law,' Dad says with a snigger. 'Except you did tell us where you were going that night, you didn't do anything wrong while you were there, and you're eighteen years old – you can make your own decisions. But just in case we do run into DJ's dad, it will be obvious that I'm punishing you by wearing this T-shirt.'

I allow myself a little laugh. Dad is just trying to lighten the mood but he's not wrong about DJ's dad. He went crazy, threatening to call all of our universities and tell them the kind of kids they were accepting, if we didn't promise to keep ourselves all apart for the rest of the summer. He said we were all bad for each other, that we were trouble together, and that this was the only way to ensure we didn't mess up our futures. I'm not sure all of our parents agreed with such a nuclear reaction, but no one wanted any trouble so in the end they all decided it would be best if we didn't hang out any more, at least until we had completed our studies, which seems absolutely ridiculous to me.

The community fair always has such a warm and welcoming atmosphere – I swear, everyone in the village attends, no matter what their age. There are stalls where you can buy things like handmade crafts, and jewellery, food stands with all sorts of delicious offerings, a variety of live entertainment all day and – of course – a strong selection of fairground rides.

My phone chimes with a message so I take it from my pocket to see who it is. It's Maxi.

Sending to the gang. Anyone who is at the fair, meet me at the tallest ride in 5 mins. Make it sound scary so your folks don't join you and don't forget to delete this message! X

I look up from my phone to see my mum and dad looking at me expectantly, both grinning, their eyebrows higher on their foreheads than usual.

'It's just a thing about ringtones,' I lie.

'I see,' Mum says, clearly not fooled.

'You know, you're right, I need to enjoy myself a bit more,' I say brightly. 'I think I want to go on that thing.'

I turn around and point up at the tallest ride here. I've no idea how tall it actually is, but it towers above the fair. It's sort of like the hearts and diamonds ride you'll often find at fairgrounds, except it's much smaller, for just a handful of people, and instead of tipping on its side and spinning really fast, it slowly lifts up high into the sky and slowly turns around so that you can take in the view. Despite being very high up it could sound quite pleasant, except instead of being strapped inside the ride, the people on it are strapped to the outside, so that they can enjoy the view.

'You want to go on that?' my dad says in disbelief. 'The girl who cried until they let her off the big wheel?'

'That was ages ago,' I insist.

'You were fourteen,' my dad replies with a laugh.

'Then I guess I want to face my fears,' I say.

'Okay, darling,' Mum chimes in. 'Your dad and I will go grab a bite to eat. But be good.'

'Always,' I tell them with a smile.

There's no way they don't know that I'm slinking off to find my friends but, like I said, my parents aren't all that mad at me for what happened. We will need to be careful, though. If DJ's dad sees us together, he'll go mad.

I kill time for a few minutes, eventually approaching the meeting point, but when I get there I can see that my friends are all strapped into the ride already. As I step up to the towering fairground attraction, I feel a mix of excitement and nerves churn in my stomach. Looking up at the massive metal structure, and then back down at the bit where you get on, I note that it's a hexagonal shape, with one of my friends strapped into each of the spaces – and there's one space left for me, between Maxi and Cam.

'This is her,' Maxi tells the guy running the ride. 'Thanks for saving the space for her.'

I widen my eyes at her.

'It's the only way we'll get to talk,' she insists. 'It was this or the house of mirrors, and can you imagine how much damage Clarky would do to himself in there?'

'I heard that,' I hear his voice call out from the other side of the ride.

'I'm not a big fan of rides,' I say.

'This isn't a ride really,' the guy running it reassures me. 'It's a viewing platform.'

'And you'll be okay next to me,' Cam says.

Now that I'm walking up to my space on the not-ride I get to see him properly, only for a few seconds, but it feels so good to look into his eyes again.

But then I'm placing my back to the wall, standing on a small ledge, with a small cage that closes in front of the lower two thirds of my body, and two thick metal bars that cross over in front of my arms and chest, presumably all keeping me strapped in safely. Now that I'm in my place, I can't see any of my friends.

'Here we go,' Clarky says excitedly.

At least I can still hear them.

'Okay, going up,' the man tells us. 'Hold on.'

The operator pulls the lever and we begin to ascend, slowly at first, but then it feels like the speed picks up a little.

'Oh, I don't like this, I don't like this at all,' I blurt.

I feel a hand tapping against my body, coming from Cam's direction. I look down and see his hand searching for mine, so I grab it. As I do, my lungs fill with oxygen in a way they haven't done for weeks.

The ground beneath me begins to shrink, and I can see the fairground sprawling out beneath me, looking more and more like a miniature model of one the further we climb. The sound of the crowd fades away, replaced by the rushing wind and the creaking of the metal. Finally, as we reach the top, the ride grinds to a halt, and then it slowly starts to rotate, and I mean slowly, you can barely feel it, just like you can't feel the earth turning when you're on it.

'Well, now we've got some privacy,' I hear Maxi say. 'Hello, how has everyone been?'

'Is that a joke?' DJ asks, vaguely annoyed.

'Obviously it's a joke,' she says.

'I've been pretty frigging terrible,' DJ says, stating the obvious. 'My dad checks my phone multiple times a day, I'm grounded until I go to uni – a uni they've chosen for me, some kind of Catholic uni in a town outside Leeds with a chapel and everything, as though that's going to straighten me out.'

'That's rough,' I tell him. 'I'm sorry. If it makes you feel any better, I hate the idea of going to York without you guys. I'm actually kind of dreading it now.'

'Well, I'm only going to be in Manchester,' Maxi reassures me. 'I won't be far away.'

'And I'm going to be here, working for my dad, so at least you all know I'll always be around if you ever visit home,' Mikey chimes in.

'Of course we'll visit home,' Maxi replies. 'Won't we, gang?'

'I'm not even going that far from home,' I point out.

'And I'm not sure where I'll do my PhD yet,' Clarky says, the sarcasm in his voice building. 'Oh, no, wait, I'm too thick.'

'I'm really sorry about that, mate,' I hear Mikey reply. 'It's been a difficult time, I shouldn't have taken it out on you.'

'I'm not arsed really,' Clarky replies. 'We're all thick, really, compared to Lord Cameron.'

'I don't think they make you a lord, just for going to Edinburgh,' Cam says with a laugh. 'But it's a great opportunity and I'm going to do my best to make the most of it.'

'That's exactly what you should do,' I say, because as much as it pains me, there's no way he can turn down the opportunity to go to such a great uni, just because there's a chance he and I might be happy together. 'But I'll miss you – I'll miss all of you.'

'Bloody hell, you're all talking like you'll never see each other again,' Clarky says with a scoff. 'I went to uni and you see me all the time.'

'I'm pretty sure that's because we're the only people who will be friends with you,' DJ jokes.

I sigh with relief because it's nice to hear him joking again.

'Yeah, well, you'll be sorry, when I move in with my new housemates and they become my old friends instead of you,' he snaps back.

I'm pretty sure I know what he means, but it's hard to imagine anyone putting up with him apart from us.

'I can't believe this is it,' Maxi says, the emotion building in her voice. 'The last time we're going to see each other, for God knows how long, and we can't actually see each other.'

'We should be having a blast here today,' Mikey points out. 'Our big, final blowout before uni. It's not fair.'

'There's always next summer,' I say with a sigh. 'At least we know the fair is here every year.'

'Unless DJ's parents are still on the rampage,' Clarky jokes.

'Not funny,' DJ replies. 'They might well be.'

'Okay, okay, well, why don't we all go somewhere else next summer?' Maxi suggests. 'We could all go on holiday together – what can our parents do, if we're in another country?'

I laugh.

'That's a great idea,' I say.

'We'll have a lot of making up to do, though,' DJ adds. 'Clarky, bring the drugs.'

'Yeah, very funny,' he replies. 'But I'd definitely be up for a wild summer holiday.'

'Me too,' Mikey says. 'Just give me plenty of warning so I can book the time off work.'

'Oh, and it begins, the chickening out,' Clarky moans.

'No one is chickening out,' Maxi ticks him off. 'We'll do it, next summer, no matter what. We'll all go on holiday together.'

The slow turning of the ride stops and we slowly start descending back towards the fair, back to reality.

'I can't believe this is it for now,' says Maxi. 'That we're all going off in our own directions, starting our lives on our own. How are we going to do it without each other?'

'Because we'll always have each other, no matter where we are,' I reassure her. 'Even if we go off on our separate ways, it's hard to imagine us not coming back together at some point.'

Cam switches from holding my hand to intertwining his fingers with mine, locking our hands together tightly. I don't want to let go either, but it's the right thing to do – for now, at least.

'They can't stop us hanging out when we're grown-ups,' Clarky says, sounding very much like a child, and we all laugh.

Yeah, *if* we ever grow up, which, for some reason, I can't quite see us ever really doing. And I wouldn't want it any other way.

ACKNOWLEDGEMENTS

Thank you to my editor, Nia, and to the brilliant team at Boldwood HQ for all their hard work on our fourteenth book together.

Massive thanks to everyone who takes the time to read and review my books. Your lovely messages mean so much to me.

Thank you to my family and friends for all their support. Thanks to Kim for everything she does for me (and for the best publication day presents ever), to Pino, and to the amazing Aud who might just be my biggest fan. Huge thanks to Joey for always having time for me and answers to my questions, to James for all his (most often tech) support, and to Darcy for being my wingwoman.

Finally, as always, thanks to my husband, Joe, for holding my hand through such a challenging time. I couldn't do this without you.

ABOUT THE AUTHOR

Portia MacIntosh is a million-copy bestselling romantic comedy author of novels including *Your Place or Mine?* and *Trouble in Paradise*. Previously a music journalist, Portia writes hilarious stories, drawing on her real life experiences.

Sign up to Portia MacIntosh's mailing list for news, competitions and updates on future books.

Visit Portia's website: www.portiamacintosh.com

Follow Portia MacIntosh on social media here:

facebook.com/portia.macintosh.3
x.com/PortiaMacIntosh
instagram.com/portiamacintoshauthor
bookbub.com/authors/portia-macintosh

Just Date and See

Your Place or Mine?

Better Off Wed

Long Time No Sea

Fake It Or Leave It

Trouble in Paradise

Ex in the City

The Suite Life

It's All Sun and Games

LOVE NOTES

LOVE IN EVERY CHAPTER

WHERE ALL YOUR ROMANCE
DREAMS COME TRUE!

THE HOME OF BESTSELLING
ROMANCE AND WOMEN'S
FICTION

WARNING:
MAY CONTAIN SPICE

SIGN UP TO OUR
NEWSLETTER

https://bit.ly/Lovenotesnews

Boldwood

Boldwood Books is an award-winning fiction publishing company seeking out the best stories from around the world.

Find out more at www.boldwoodbooks.com

Join our reader community for brilliant books, competitions and offers!

Follow us

@BoldwoodBooks

@TheBoldBookClub

Sign up to our weekly
deals newsletter

https://bit.ly/BoldwoodBNewsletter